D1421625

MURDER IN THE MANSION

A gripping crime mystery full of twists

FAITH MARTIN

Published in a revised edition
2018 by Joffe Books, London.

www.joffebooks.com

First published by Robert Hale in 2008 as "Down a
Narrow Path."

© Faith Martin

This book is a work of fiction. Names, characters,
businesses, organizations, places and events are either the
product of the author's imagination or are used fictitiously.
Any resemblance to actual persons, living or dead, events
or locales is entirely coincidental. The spelling is British
English. The right of Faith Martin to be identified as
author of this work has been asserted by her in accordance
with the Copyright, Designs and Patents Act 1988.

All rights reserved. No part of this publication may be
reproduced, stored in retrieval system, copied in any form
or by any means, electronic, mechanical, photocopying,
recording or otherwise transmitted without written
permission from the publisher. You must not circulate this
book in any format.

ISBN- 978-1-912106-29-5

In memory of Dot Lumley.

CHAPTER ONE

For the second week of August, Detective Constable Keith Barrington had expected better. To be fair, this was probably due more to his mood than the weather, which, though cloudy, produced some bright patches of sunshine now and then, and an obligingly warm breeze.

Driving too fast along the motorway and leaving the capital behind him did little to make him feel better either. A London boy, born and bred, he'd enjoyed his long weekend back in the Smoke, and although Oxford was beginning to grow on him, it wasn't able to provide much by way of compensation, especially when he was also leaving behind his lover. His very unhappy lover, whose father was soon to stand trial for smuggling.

The reality of Keith's chosen profession was proving a strain on an already shaky relationship. Although Gavin seemed a lot happier since Keith's flying visit, the young constable was not about to pin his hopes on a happy-ever-after ending. Making up was one thing. Staying together was an altogether different proposition.

He tuned the radio to Fox FM when he saw his first sign for Oxford, and groaned at the lead story on the

1

news. Once again, the sniper killer was the top story, although his last victim had been killed over two weeks ago — a lifetime in the world of the media. But in this case, the story was too good not to keep it at the top of the pile. For almost two months now, some maniac with a rifle had been targeting police stations, lying on an overlooking roof or vantage point, and taking out a single individual, with one accurate shot to the head. It had all started in Durham, with a uniformed WPC. At first, it was thought to be a random incident, but when, two weeks later, an out-of-uniform DI, a male this time, had been shot and killed in Norwich, alarm bells had rung. Since then, a uniformed sergeant had been killed in Diss, and the latest, just two weeks ago, another sergeant, this time a female and out of uniform, killed in Bedford.

There was no doubt about it, the killings were getting remorselessly closer and closer — geographically at any rate — to Thames Valley Police Headquarters in Kidlington, Oxfordshire, where Keith had been working for nearly a year. Paranoia had been rife at the station when he'd left for his brief holiday, and he doubted it would have got any better now that the sniper was due to strike any time soon.

But would Kidlington really be next?

The news ended, and a tuneless pop song took its place, and Keith, with a sigh, turned it off. He glanced at the car clock and saw that it was nearly eight already. If he hit bad rush-hour traffic, he'd be late into the office. Not that he thought his immediate boss, DI Hillary Greene, would read him the riot act. He'd been due his leave, and had more than pulled his weight at his new posting; and needed to, after his rather undignified exit from his old London nick.

As he took the turn-off from the motorway and headed towards the fabled dreaming spires, his thoughts became grim. The sniper killer had to be ex-army. Nobody else could be that accurate, that consistently, with a rifle.

Unlike what the world of cinema or television drama would have the public believe, ordinary citizens just didn't get their hands on guns, train themselves to be a sharpshooter, and hire themselves out as assassins at a million pounds a hit. No, this killer was bound to be some disaffected sod with a grudge against coppers, or some nutter, perhaps suffering from his time spent in a war zone, who just felt like carrying on killing. And cops weren't soldiers exactly, or the enemy, but they weren't exactly civilians either. He could see how that might appeal to someone's twisted sort of logic.

None of which made him feel any happier as he approached HQ. He couldn't help but wonder if, somewhere, maybe from a bedroom window of one of the houses in the small, unassuming town of Kidlington, a man with a gun was affixing a sight to his rifle.

Getting ready.

* * *

Detective Inspector Hillary Greene blew across the top of her coffee mug and watched Mike Regis, a DI from Vice out of St Aldates nick, rifle through a small cupboard in search of cornflakes.

'I'm all out,' she said flatly.

Regis grunted and straightened up, shaking his head. 'I'm not surprised. You can't store a day's worth of food in these Mickey Mouse contraptions.' So saying, he flicked shut the narrow cupboard door and turned around, bumping his elbow on the tap in the sink as he did so. He winced and rubbed his arm, and Hillary sighed.

'Once you've lived on a boat for a while, you get used to moving about in a narrow space. It becomes second nature — you don't even realise you're doing it.' But even as she spoke, she knew he was hardly feeling mollified.

She had moved on to the *Mollern*, a narrowboat moored in Thrupp, just outside Kidlington, after her corrupt and useless prat of a husband had finally gone one step too far. The fact that he'd died shortly thereafter in a car accident hadn't meant her return to more conventional living quarters, and now, after nearly four years on the boat, she couldn't imagine living anywhere else.

A fact that her lover, Mike Regis, was only just beginning to seriously take on board. He watched her now, his cat-green eyes wavering between bewilderment and resentment. He wasn't a big man, but he felt, as he always did whenever staying overnight with Hillary, like a very large bull in a very small china shop.

'You got bread at least? Some toast too much to hope for?'

Hillary grinned and, taking pity on him, reached into a minuscule fridge, recessed under the fold-down eating counter, and pulled out a half-loaf of sliced wholemeal. 'Think you can get it into the toaster without dislocating something?' she asked, forcing a reluctant smile out of him. She watched him for a while, very much aware of a strange, restless feeling creeping over her.

After her disastrous marriage to a womanizing bent copper, Hillary had lived the first few years of her widowhood a happier, wiser, and celibate woman. The advent of Mike Regis in her life had coincided with her first murder case as acting senior investigating officer. At first, she'd resisted the mutual attraction between them, not least because Regis had still technically been married. But with his divorce last year, they'd finally taken the plunge and embarked on a discreet and mutually satisfying affair. Naturally, news of it had slowly leaked at HQ, but since they were both free, and over twenty-one, and not even working out of the same station house, they hadn't even been a nine days' wonder — maybe two and a half days at the most.

But things weren't working out. Hillary knew it, and she suspected Mike knew it, but wasn't about to be the first to admit it. Part of the problem was, without doubt, the *Mollern*. Hillary had no intention of moving into Mike's spacious and thoroughly nice flat in Botley, and Mike wouldn't live on the *Mollern* if he was paid to. But more than that, Hillary had no intention of ever marrying again — once was more than enough for any woman of intelligence, in her opinion, but she rather suspected that Mike Regis was thinking in terms of acquiring a second wife. He had children by his first wife, and didn't seem to want any more, so that issue at least was one they had managed to avoid. At forty-five, Hillary had no plans for motherhood either.

So where did all that leave them exactly?

'It's burning,' Hillary said quietly. Mike swore and quickly rescued his smoking bread from the toaster. He'd been investigating the shoe box that passed for a fridge for signs of margarine, but hadn't found any. However, in the back of the tiny cupboard he found a nearly empty jar of Oxford marmalade, and knifed on the last of it. Hillary continued to drink her coffee and watch him eat, still with that same restless dissatisfaction.

She knew what it was all in aid of, of course, and was in no mood to put it off any longer. 'Mike,' she said softly, and sighed as he looked up at her over his blackened breakfast.

'Mike,' she tried again, a bit more firmly. 'We've been together nearly nine months now . . .' she began, and then abruptly faltered. What the hell did that have to do with anything? Just get on with it and spit it out, she thought, angry at herself all of a sudden. Perhaps because she was already beginning to feel guilty. Mike swallowed, and reached for his mug of tea. He looked suddenly wary, and Hillary wondered how much he knew, or guessed, of what she was about to say.

'It's been good, hasn't it?' she tried next, and her anger ratcheted up yet another notch at the banality of it. Hell, now she sounded like an article from a woman's magazine. One of those naff 'How to break up without breaking anybody's heart' articles. They were both middle-aged, tough-as-nails career coppers for crying out loud. Surely they didn't need to tiptoe around? 'I mean, we get on, we're good mates and all that.' She stopped, took a mouthful of too-hot coffee and swallowed it with an eye-watering wince. 'But . . .'

'I knew there was going to be a but.'

'But,' she ploughed on, before he could get started, 'let's face it, it's not really going anywhere, is it?' Great. Now she sounded like a traffic report. What exactly was 'it' and where was it supposed to go? She made them sound like a number 7A bus stuck in a traffic jam.

From the look on Regis's face, she knew he wasn't thinking good thoughts either.

She took another breath, and tried again. 'I mean, we seem to want different things. When we look ahead, you see one thing, and I see another. Oh hell, Mike, you know what I'm trying to say.'

Mike Regis did. He didn't get to be a DI in Vice without knowing a thing or two. 'You want me to sling my hook,' he said flatly, anger cracking his voice.

Hillary sighed. 'That's not how I'd have put it,' she said, equally flatly. She was not in the mood to take any flack today. And she was through putting up with shit — any kind of shit — from men. Not that Mike Regis was another Ronnie Greene; of course he wasn't. Far from it. He was a decent copper for one thing — not in the job to line his own pockets, but to put away the scum who needed putting away. And, as far as she knew, he'd never cheated on his wife whilst their marriage was still working, nor had he cheated on Hillary.

Still.

It didn't mean she appreciated being made the bad guy in all of this. Regis had to know they were on the rocks as well as she did. 'Look, Mike, there's no one else,' she said flatly, and truthfully. 'And I like you, I always have done. But . . .'

'Spare me the buts,' Mike Regis said heavily, tossing his piece of toast down on to the counter top. 'I don't need a diagram drawn for me.' He turned towards the narrow opening that led down the length of the narrowboat and banged his shin against the side of the cupboard as he went. Then he laughed. 'Well, at least I don't have to put up with this bloody pencil box any more.'

He couldn't even give the door a satisfying slam on the way out, seeing as he had to climb a steep set of stairs first, and then manoeuvre his body on to the stern. But, out of the open window, Hillary heard him swearing, as he stalked off down the towpath.

She sighed and sipped her coffee. So that was that. She was man-free again. And at least the restlessness was now gone. She just felt vaguely depressed, instead.

* * *

Puff the Tragic Wagon, her ancient Volkswagen Golf, started first time, and Hillary turned on the radio as she headed down the narrow lane out of the tiny hamlet of Thrupp. Kidlington was on her back doorstep, making her commute on a good day less than five minutes. In rush hour, it was more like twenty. Stalled in traffic at the first set of lights she came to, she tuned her radio to a sixties oldie channel, and hummed along to 'Last Train to Clarksville' in an attempt to lift her mood. The clouds were breaking up, promising another warm day, and she rolled down the window and watched, vaguely, as the man in the car pulled up alongside her used a cordless shaver on his chin.

She grinned, wondering what he'd do if she flashed him her badge and told him to put it away. But she couldn't be bothered. She'd just split up with her lover, somewhere out there a man with a rifle might be planning on killing her, or any of her colleagues, and she hadn't had a decent case in months. Just another mundane

Wednesday. The lights changed to green and she pulled away, and soon was indicating the left turn into HQ.

The car park was deserted as she parked Puff in a space at the back. Every space near the large main doors into the building was already taken. Normally, there'd be the usual little cliques of smokers out and about, forced outdoors by the universal smoking ban in public places. Then there'd be the patrol car teams, parked up and chattering before setting off. Cops who liked to come in on bikes, 'green' badges to the fore, or even those who walked. Normally, the car park would be buzzing.

But now it was empty. Utterly deserted. As she parked, she noticed a uniformed DS further along, getting out of her car and locking up double-fast, before sprint-walking to the door. Hillary felt the skin on the back of her own neck begin to crawl as she also got out of the car. But she was damned if she was going to hurry. As she'd been telling anyone and everyone who'd listen to her, ever since the sniper killer had first struck, your individual chances of being the next victim had to be one in a million. Or however many working coppers there were in the country currently. She locked Puff, wondering vaguely why she bothered. They were in the police station car park after all, and besides, no self-respecting car thief would be caught dead trying to pinch her ride. Then she stuffed her keys into her handbag and sauntered across the car park, weaving at her usual pace through the parked cars. Her spine felt as if spiders were crawling all over it, but her face, when she finally pushed through the big swing doors, was bland.

Inside the large foyer were all the usual familiar and half-familiar faces. The desk sergeant, always the one to go to if you wanted to know the latest gossip; the woman sergeant who'd come in before her; and several groups of uniforms, hanging about and looking unhappy. At this time in the morning, it was hard to tell if they were the night shift, gathering up the courage to leave, or the day shift, in no hurry to get started.

'Hill,' the desk sergeant said admiringly, who'd watched her progress from the get-go. 'I thought you were gonna stop and smell the roses.' The car park did, in fact, have a few green spots scattered throughout, which the Cherwell District Council, in their wisdom, had used to plant bushes of various species. Most of which wilted and died from lack of watering.

Hillary smiled grimly. 'I keep telling you lot. You've got more chance of being hit by lightning, etcetera, etcetera.' She waved a hand vaguely around and headed for the stairs.

She was aware of many eyes watching her as she went, and out of the corner of her eye, saw the desk sergeant grin. Well, if you couldn't lead the troops by example, she thought, grimly entertained, you could always try the old 'Don't do as I do, do as I say' ploy. But in her experience, nobody paid you any heed whatever you did.

The desk sergeant grunted. 'Good copper that,' he said, which at least made the day shift contingent blush a little, and got them out the doors. Most of them all but ran to their patrol cars, however.

* * *

Detective Superintendent Philip 'Mellow' Mallow leaned forward and pressed the button on his intercom when it buzzed. 'Yes, Sue?'

'DI Greene, sir. Says she had a message on her desk that you wanted to see her when she got in?'

'Oh yes, send her right in.'

Hillary pushed open the door to his office and looked around, smiling to see that the office was empty of people apart from him. When she'd got to her desk and seen the summons to her old friend's office, she half expected some sort of meeting to be going on. The boring kind that never seemed to have anything to do with crime, or the solving thereof.

'Hey,' she said, shutting the door behind her, and making herself comfortable in the large padded chair facing his desk, without being asked. She had no need to stand on ceremony with Mel, who was one of her oldest friends. 'How's Janine?' A few months ago, he'd married DS Janine Tyler, who'd been working on Hillary's team for three years. Now, with the marriage, Janine had moved to Witney nick, and Hillary had a new DS.

And if Hillary wasn't exactly missing her feisty, rather sensitive-skinned DS, she wasn't about to say so. Janine had made no secret of the fact that she didn't like working with a woman as her boss, and her ambitions to make DI had often led her into doing something reckless. Not that her replacement, DS Gemma Fordham, was exactly a bowl of cherries to work with either. If for vastly different reasons.

'Janine's fine,' Mel said, then frowned and shook his head. 'Well, maybe not, but that's neither here nor there.'

Hillary raised an eyebrow and grinned. 'Well, that's clear as mud.'

Mel grinned and ran a harassed hand through his hair. He was nearing his fiftieth birthday, but didn't look it. His dark hair was well cut as usual, and showed not a sign of grey. His suit, impeccable as always, covered a lean body that showed little signs of middle-aged sag. 'Mellow' Mallow had earned his nickname by seeming so laid-back and mellow as to be almost somnolent. But it was a very deceptive nickname, as villains very quickly realised.

'It's the Myers case,' Mel said now, walking to his window and glancing outside. As a superintendent he was entitled to an office with his own window — albeit a small one. 'I just want to vent a little, as the Yanks would say.'

'I shouldn't stand there if I were you,' Hillary said drily. 'Haven't you noticed how deserted it is out there?'

Mel turned and looked at her blankly, then she saw the comprehension reach his eyes. 'Oh right. The sniper.'

He moved away from the window, but she could see he wasn't really thinking about the cop killer. Unlike her own bravado, which had been mostly forced, Mel Mallow seemed genuinely uncaring.

'Is it as bad as all that?' she asked sympathetically.

She knew the basics about the Myers case of course — most of the nick did. One of the DIs under Mel's remit had handled it, but had somehow botched it. Evelyn Myers, a fifteen-year-old schoolgirl, had been attacked and raped by a gang of youths following an impromptu disco at a village hall. She'd returned, tearful, to her mother, who'd promptly called the police. A rape crisis counsellor had been called in, and the girl had been taken to the local hospital, where all the necessary testing had been done. The result was more DNA than you could shake a stick at. Also, youthful witnesses at the disco helped the DI assigned to the case, Pete Gregg, to quickly round up, interview, and subsequently charge three teenage boys, aged fourteen, fifteen and sixteen respectively.

The case had gone to trial only two weeks ago, with everyone confident of a guilty verdict, when disaster struck. A clever little cove on the defence team of the oldest boy, the sixteen-year-old, had noticed a one-word mistake on the warrant that had allowed DI Gregg to search the boy's house and take away the clothes he'd worn that night. Clothes with enough forensic evidence on them to convict the boy, practically without the need of a jury.

The defence barrister had pointed this out last Friday afternoon, making a motion to have all subsequent evidence gained by the questionable warrant thrown out of court. If that motion was granted, the CPS had warned them, the case against the eldest boy would crumble. They'd literally have to proceed without any of the valuable blood and semen evidence that rape-trial juries found so necessary. And since the sixteen-year-old had been the chief perpetrator, the case against the two younger lads would almost certainly fade away as well.

'Has the judge come back with a decision yet?' Hillary asked, watching her friend pace up and down.

Mel shook his head. 'Not yet. He was due to come in with it yesterday, but there was a postponement. Gregg's down at the courthouse now, biting his nails. But I've got a bad feeling about it.'

The warrant, of course, should have been checked not only by the judge issuing it, but by the judge's clerk, probably a secretary or two, and Gregg himself, but the buck stopped with Mel, being as he was in overall charge. And, of course, nobody over the rank of detective superintendent ever made a mistake, let alone got called to account for it.

'And you blame yourself?' Hillary asked. 'Mel, did you even see the warrant? Let alone read it?'

'No, of course not.' Such minutiae hardly ever crossed his desk. 'I know in my head it's not down to me, but that's not it. It's the Myers I feel sorry for. The girl's been admitted to a mental ward, did you know? And the mother's so depressed she can hardly speak. What's more, Clive Myers is fairly radiating rage. He used to be in the paras or something, so he has a military heart and mind. He simply can't understand administrative cock-ups like this. He doesn't have the mentality for it. It was all Gregg could do to stop him going after the lads himself and dishing out some of his own discipline. We only kept him on side by promising the judge would come down hard on the vicious little bastards. Now it looks as if he's going to have to dismiss the case. And all because some overworked legal clerk got his wording wrong.'

Hillary commiserated, but there was little she could do. They'd all had cases go to hell in a handbasket before. It was a sad and teeth-grinding fact of life.

'Oh well, perhaps the judge can wangle some way around it.' Mel sighed heavily. 'Coffee?' Hillary nodded, and he poured her a mug. 'Gregg seems to think he's well and truly on our side. The fact that two of the boys already have form was working in our favour.' Although he tried to sound upbeat, Hillary could sense the defeat already dragging him down.

'Why don't we go out for a drink lunchtime?' she said, and was rewarded with a bleak smile and a half-promise.

When she returned to her desk, however, it soon became apparent that the lunchtime drink with her troubled pal would have to wait.

DCI Paul Danvers, her immediate superior, watched Hillary Greene making her way through the large open-plan office towards her team's nest of desks and chairs, and rose from behind his own desk in his sectioned-off cubbyhole and moved to intercept her. In his hand was a piece of paper with the scant details of what was almost certainly a case of murder that had just come in.

As he walked quickly towards one of the best murder detectives in the station, it wasn't her detective skills he was admiring. With her curvaceous figure, meltingly dark eyes, and lush nut-brown hair cut in a long bell shape and highlighted with delicious tints of Titian red, Danvers had been smitten with her the moment they'd first met. Unfortunately, at the time, he'd been one of two men assigned to investigate her for corruption.

But that was long ago. Now he was her immediate superior. But not, alas, any closer to being anything else. But he was patient.

'Hillary.' He glanced across and saw the tall, blonde Gemma Fordham glance his way. Lean and martial arts trained, she watched him with curiously unreadable eyes. Beside her, sitting at his own desk, the carrot-topped Keith Barrington was busy typing at his console. Frank Ross, the other DS on Hillary's team, was slouched in his chair drinking tea. He looked, as ever, vaguely hungover, and smelt of the canteen version of bacon and eggs. He had a blob of grease on his tie and one on the lapel of his jacket. He eyed Danvers balefully, rightfully guessing that he brought with him the unwelcome prospect of work.

'Hillary. We have a murder in Bletchington. Know it?'

Hillary nodded. 'Small village about halfway between here and Bicester.'

'Uniforms have just radioed it in. It looks messy and nasty.'

Hillary nodded, silently holding out her hand for the piece of paper.

Just another mundane Wednesday all right.

CHAPTER TWO

Bletchington looked quiet and deserted as Hillary and
Barrington approached it from the quiet country lane
leading from its nearest neighbour, the village of
Kirtlington. But as she turned her car towards the village
green, she saw two patrol cars parked up outside a large
detached residence, and a small knot of people milling
around on the pavement trying to look uninterested. She
parked off-road, whilst behind her Gemma and Frank
pulled up beneath the shade of a large oak tree. They all
climbed out and Hillary took a moment to look around
her.

It was a typical Oxfordshire village, with a mixed
bunch of houses and styles, some gardens well-kept and
colourful, others mere mowed lawns with a shrub or two
for form's sake. There was, wonder of wonders, a village
shop still managing to cling to existence, and behind her
she heard the church clock strike ten. The house that was
attracting all the attention was the biggest one in sight,
built solidly of the local stone, maybe two hundred years
old, but with all mod cons installed. Double glazing,
satellite dish, burglar alarm box, and no doubt a myriad of

other gadgets that the original owners could only have boggled at. The gardens, too, were large and well-kept, either by an owner who must have had green fingers and plenty of leisure time, or, more likely, a gardening contractor.

Hillary walked towards the ten-foot-high garden wall that surrounded the property and saw the uniform on guard by the gate straighten up a little at her approach. He was holding a clipboard. Hillary showed him her warrant card and watched as he signed her in and added the time. She walked through the gate, a pristine white-painted affair with a black iron ring handle in the centre, and heard her team signing in behind her. The house in the warm fitful August sunshine looked mellow and welcoming. Hanging baskets full of frothing colour hung at either side of a wooden white-painted porch, which had a grey-tiled upside down V-shaped roof that echoed the tiling in the main roofline. The windows were sparkling clean, the white paintwork of the window frames brand new.

Whoever lived here had money, and didn't mind spending it. The gravelled drive led away to a walled back garden, maybe where someone grew vegetables for the table. She could see, over the wall, the ripening fruit of apples, plums and pears. The original kitchen garden, no doubt.

A uniformed constable came around the side and coughed discreetly. 'The body's inside the hall, ma'am, right behind the door. SOCO are on the way, as is the police surgeon.'

Hillary took the hint and turned away from the main entrance, glancing down automatically as she did so. The gravel drive went straight to the front porch step, so would probably be useless as far as footprints were concerned. Likewise, the well-manicured lawns on either side were hard and flat after a week of very little rain. She doubted SOCO would get much joy here, but nonetheless was careful where she put her feet and kept well away from the entrance.

Instead, she approached the uniform, a man in his late forties, hefty but not quite fat, with thick fair hair going that dirty white that looked in need of washing.

'PC Rodgers, ma'am.' Rodgers knew Hillary by sight, and wasn't surprised to see her here as SIO. So far, she'd solved all seven of her previous murder cases, so it made sense. He'd always wanted the chance to watch her work.

'You were first on the scene?'

'Me and my partner, ma'am, PC Cantor. We received a call at,' he checked his notebook, '8:02 a.m. from a man identifying himself as Arnold Watts, postman. He called at the house at his usual time, and was surprised to see the front door ajar. He called, and pushed it open and saw the victim, the resident of the house, a Mrs Matilda Jones. He immediately left and called us. He's sitting in the patrol car with PC Cantor now. He's a bit under the weather. It might be a good idea for the doc to see him. It's not a pretty sight in there.'

Hillary nodded. 'OK, see to it, will you? I take it you looked at the crime scene?'

'Just briefly, ma'am, when I first arrived, to make sure it wasn't a hoax or a mistake.' Standard procedure.

'No mistake?' Hillary asked, not without sympathy, as she noticed the man pale slightly and swallow hard.

'No, ma'am.'

'Describe what you saw, please.'

Rodgers took a deep breath. 'Female Caucasian, in her mid-forties, early fifties, I'd say. Lying on her side, feet nearest to the door, head pointing towards a large, semicircular staircase. She was wearing something white and brown, I think. It was hard to tell, on account of the huge amount of blood on her person. She had short dark hair, and wore no watch, rings or other items of jewellery that I could see. She looked to me as if she'd been stabbed many times. No sign of a weapon by or on her body. No sounds from inside the house — radio or television. I called, but nobody answered. I called for backup and kept an eye out, and posted a man on the back entrance as soon as I could. But I don't think anyone was inside the house. It just had that empty feeling.'

Hillary nodded and knew instantly what he meant.

So, somebody rang the doorbell, the victim answered, and no messing about, straight into the stabbing. It appeared frenzied, driven by hate or rage or maybe fear. Left the victim lying where she fell and left, not bothering to close the door. Hillary frowned, running it through her mind. It was possible, of course, that the victim had been lying there all night, but the autopsy would answer that one. The killer probably took the weapon away with them — unless it was still underneath the body, a fact that couldn't be established until the body was moved. And if the attack was as bloody as it appeared, the killer would be bound to have bloodstains on them. Did they bring a long coat to slip on afterwards? It certainly had all the makings of a premeditated crime. The killer must have bought the knife or sharpened screwdriver or whatever it was with them. Unless, of course, the killer had come calling, chatted about something, managed to grab a knife from the kitchen, and then killed the victim in the hall on the way out.

But she was getting ahead of herself.

She nodded to Rodgers and turned back to her waiting team. 'We can't do much until SOCO and Doc Partridge get here. Start canvassing,' she instructed them bluntly.

* * *

Steven Partridge parked his classic MG as far from the gaggle of cars and people as possible and climbed out, grabbing his bag as he did so. As one of Thames Valley's pathologists, there was nothing unusual in him being called out to the scene of a murder on a nice summer's day, but it tended to depress him slightly, nevertheless.

He showed his credentials to the man at the gate, aware of a vague muttering of interest behind him, as they heard the uniform repeat his professional title. For some reason, the arrival of a doctor always seemed to liven up the gawkers. He pushed open the gate and walked into a scene of organised mayhem. Men and women in white overalls and hoods crawled on the grass, inspected gravel and dusted a white-painted front door with black powder, but there was a general pulling back as he appeared, giving him room. From his bag, he pulled out and donned a similar all-over white garment and a pair of gloves, slipped white plastic covers over his shoes, and approached the house.

He pushed open the door gingerly and grimaced at the sight that met him. It was like a Rorschach inkblot in red, white and black. The hall was decorated traditionally in tiny black and white tiles set on the diagonal, which covered a large area. But, in stark contrast, the woman who lay sprawled on them was mainly red. The colour had seeped and oozed and sprayed from her, painting the surrounding white walls with splashes of scarlet and pooling around her.

He sighed, trod very carefully, and knelt even more carefully. It took him only seconds to declare her dead. There could have been no doubt, of course. Nobody lived after losing that much blood. He made a few more observations, but didn't linger. There was little point. Once outside, he was meticulously careful in climbing out of the now blood-stained protective clothing and bagging it up. Around him, the SOCO officers once more got on with their job. A police photographer began taking pictures from the doorway, his photographic strobes almost invisible in the strong sunlight now shining down. The last of the clouds seemed to be disappearing, and a cheerful blackbird sang incongruously from a nearby ash tree.

Steven saw his favourite detective standing over by a bed of perfectly pruned roses, and smiled. He walked forward, a small, dapper man in a dark blue suit that would have cost Hillary Greene more than a month's wages.

'Hillary, one of yours, then?' he greeted her amiably.

Hillary smiled at the medico and reached out to shake his hand. 'Looks like it. Haven't even taken a look yet.'

Partridge nodded. 'Multiple stab wounds, almost certainly with a clean-bladed, wide knife — probably one of those kitchen knives that are so popular nowadays. Nothing clever or technical about it — random slashing as far as I can see.'

'Man or woman?'

'Either. There needn't have been much upper body strength or arm strength needed, if the knife was sharp. And it undoubtedly was.'

Hillary sighed. 'Has she been dead all night?'

'Oh, I don't think so. It's a warm day, and the door was found ajar, right?' Hillary nodded, and he looked back over his shoulder at the open doorway. 'No rigour, body temp still way up. I'd say she was killed between seven thirty and eight thirty this morning. But I wouldn't be surprised if it was nearer seven thirty than eight.'

'Postman called it in at two minutes past eight.'

'There you go then, cuts it down for you even more. Well, I'll be off. Got an old woman to disembowel,' he informed her cheerfully and needlessly, and Hillary grimaced.

'Always a ray of sunshine, Doc,' she said drily.

* * *

Outside, standing under the shade of the oak tree, Gemma Fordham used her phone to leave a text message. She'd never met Gary Greene, Hillary Greene's stepson, but she was hoping he'd be intrigued enough by her message to respond.

She needed a few words with that young man.

Gemma Fordham had met Ronnie Greene many years ago — before she'd even joined the force. She hadn't known it then, but Ronnie had a penchant for leggy blondes, but preferred them dumb. Perhaps that's why they hadn't lasted long. At the time, Gemma had been getting her degree in criminology from Reading University, and Ronnie had been seconded from Thames Valley to help in a child abduction case.

When, nearly eight years later, he'd died in a car crash, and a subsequent investigation had proved he was as bent as a two-pound note, and must have salted away a fortune from an animal parts smuggling operation he'd masterminded, Gemma had decided to transfer from her old nick to Thames Valley. She'd been on the force for nearly five years by then, and had won several martial arts medals. She'd aced her sergeant's Boards, and when she'd requested a stint on Hillary Greene's team, nobody had questioned it. Hillary, after all, was well respected in the force, had a rep as a good detective, and there was nobody better at training up young DCs and sergeants who wanted to climb the ladder. Anybody would give their eye teeth for a chance to watch and learn from a maestro.

Of course, Gemma was far more interested in getting her hands on a fortune than achieving the rank of DI. But who said she couldn't do both?

Since coming to Kidlington, she'd managed to get on to Hillary's boat, but the search had been disappointing and inconclusive. If her immediate boss knew where her late and unlamented husband had kept his money, it didn't show. And she certainly hadn't spent any of it — it was one of the first things Gemma had checked. Her car was ancient, and her home was still a bloody narrowboat of all things.

No, she'd all but concluded that Hillary Greene, as a stepping stone to wealth and happiness, was something of a washout. Which was why Gemma was now turning her attention to Gary Greene.

Her text message sent, she closed the phone with a snap and turned her attention to the group of gawkers currently being questioned by Keith Barrington. Frank Ross, on spying the local pub, the Blacks Head, had quickly shuffled on over to it, muttering something about local knowledge. What he really meant, of course, was local beer. Or whisky. Or whatever he was able to afford today.

Gemma turned her eye towards the village shop, smiled to herself, and trotted over. If you wanted to know the gossip, it was as good a place as any to start.

* * *

Hillary Greene didn't really want or need to see the body, but she knew it was expected of her. And with the police surgeon been and gone, the body photographed and SOCO more or less happy with the preliminaries, now was as good a time as any. She walked to the door, nodding at the photographer as he stepped out of her way, and glanced inside.

It was bad. As bad as any she'd seen. It was hard to see the victim at all, under her macabre body paint of red. She looked tallish and slender. No doubt her white slacks had once been pristine and tailored, and her blouse, which looked to be raw silk, the epitome of good taste. Now they were just soiled and useless rags.

She sighed and turned away. 'Tell the mortuary people they can remove the body when SOCO's ready,' she said to Rodgers, who'd been keeping an eye on her and was waiting for orders.

'Ma'am.'

'And when they're through, I want you to take a team and inventory the house. She might be the kind who didn't like to wear jewellery, or she might have been robbed. See if there are any signs of burglary inside. There's bound to have been plenty of small silver baubles, collectibles, that kind of thing. In a house like this, there always are. Get on to her insurance company to check what she had listed.'

'Ma'am.' Hillary nodded and walked down the gravel path, pausing to admire a stand of bright orange montbretia that were attracting half a dozen or so tortoiseshell butterflies. She'd have to get on to the next of kin of course — once they were known. Breaking the bad news to grieving relatives wasn't something she often delegated.

She carried on walking, out through the gate, ignoring the small knot of people who only pretended to ignore her, and looked instead around the square. It was old and spacious, and clearly designed in a more elegant age. A slightly smaller stone house was set back a little to the left of Matilda Jones's, and Hillary decided to start there.

She heard a ripple of speculation from the crowd follow her all the way up the garden path, and Hillary could almost hear their minds buzzing. Was this particular neighbour suspected of something? What did the police know? Who, what, why?

The door of the house opened before she got there, and a tall, thin, white-haired woman watched her approach. Before Hillary could say anything, she crossed her arms over her scrawny chest and spoke. 'Trouble next door, is it?' she asked crisply. Her voice was educated, cool, and showed no signs of unease.

'Yes, madam. May I have your name please?' Hillary asked. Something about the way the woman leaned firmly against the doorjamb and met her eyes with an unimpressed, level gaze told her that she was not about to get invited in for tea and biscuits. But the woman wasn't actively hostile either, so far as Hillary could tell.

'Dorothea Grimmett. I'm a widow. Lived here for forty-six years.'

Hillary appreciated the no-nonsense approach and decided to take advantage of it with a simple question-and-answer session. The cosy chat was definitely not going to work here. 'Do you know the woman next door?'

The white head bobbed once. 'I do. Don't like her much, to tell the truth. Matilda Jones, or Mattie to her friends. Which, I suspect, are few. Married, no children, about to be divorced from her husband Barry Jones, who moved out at the beginning of the year. She drives a Mercedes Benz, currently white, but she changes it every two years, always for another Mercedes model. She seems to have a fetish for white. Clinical and cold, I always think.' The woman paused, thought a little more, and gave a small nod, as if mentally approving her next choice of words. 'Doesn't seem to work, isn't interested in charity, and likes to dine out a lot. Has a lot of money that she likes to spend. But quiet, and gives no noisy parties. I could have worse neighbours.'

Hillary blinked. 'You say the Joneses were about to divorce. Was it friendly?'

Dorothea Grimmett snorted. In some strange way, she managed to make it sound quite elegant. 'I should say not. Barry left her for a much younger woman, who I believe worked for his company. Jones & Cartwright, or J&C Construction. He used to drive a big van with it written on the side, and parked it right there, out on the green.'

She sniffed, showing exactly what she thought of that kind of behaviour. No doubt it lowered the tone of the neighbourhood considerably.

Hillary hid a smile. 'Did you hear anything untoward at the Jones residence this morning, Mrs Grimmett? Shouting, anything of that kind?'

'No. But I'm afraid I'm a little deaf, and until I put my hearing aid in first thing, I'd be unlikely to.' The admission came out levelly enough, but with just a tinge of angst. She shifted restlessly against the doorjamb, as if unwilling to contemplate the indignities foisted on her by creeping old age. And who could blame her?

'And what time did you rise this morning?' Hillary asked, using more formal language almost instinctively now. Years of experience in dealing with all sorts of witnesses had taught her that it always paid to talk to people in a way they expected to be talked to. Unless, of course, you wanted to shock them out of their complacency.

'At my usual hour — eight twenty.'

Too late, Hillary thought instantly. The victim was already dead by then.

'Did you happen to notice any vehicle pull up in front of Mrs Jones's house this morning?'

'No. But my bedroom faces the other way.' Dorothea Grimmett waved a vague hand behind her, indicating the back of the house, and Hillary sighed. Of course, it made sense. If you lived in a big house, you'd choose to sleep in the quiet rooms at the back.

Hillary nodded, sensing there was nothing more for her here. 'Thank you, Mrs Grimmett.'

The old woman nodded graciously, turned, and closed the door behind her. If she was burning with curiosity, she'd not shown it by so much as a flicker of an eyelash. But then women of her generation and ilk would rather die than do anything so vulgar as to show honest human emotion.

* * *

The arrival of the mortuary van caused its usual brief stir in the slowly enlarging crowd, and nobody paid any attention to Hillary this time as she crossed the green and walked up the path of the house directly opposite the victim's.

She had to ring the doorbell twice before it was answered, this time by a younger woman in her late twenties. She was running a little too fat, and appeared apprehensive. Like Dorothea Grimmett before her, but probably for vastly different reasons, she seemed unwilling to invite Hillary inside.

'Hello, I'm DI Greene.' Hillary held up her ID and smiled gently. 'I just need to ask you a few quick questions about your neighbour, Matilda Jones.' She kept her voice light and unthreatening, and was rewarded by seeing the younger woman's shoulders relax a little.

'I don't really know her. My husband and I only moved here last year. And Mrs Jones isn't really the sort of woman we mix with. She is a bit grand, to be honest.' The woman had bags under her eyes, and was without make-up. She looked as if she might have been ill recently.

Hillary smiled. 'And you are?'

'Oh, sorry. Jennifer Potter. My husband Mike inherited this house from his granny. You're lucky to find me in; I'm usually at work by now, but I'm having some time off. I work at Sainsbury's, by Kidlington roundabout?' Her raised voice made it a question, and Hillary nodded, instantly getting her measure. Her husband was probably some mid-level manager type, and his grandmother had probably been born in this house, with no idea that one day it would be worth a cool half-million at least. Far more than the likes of Jennifer Potter and her husband would have been able to afford on the open market. No wonder she didn't mix much with the likes of Matilda Jones, who seemed to have money to burn, and would almost certainly have considered herself a cut above the likes of a supermarket checkout girl.

'Were you up early this morning, Mrs Potter?' Hillary asked hopefully.

'Oh yes. I just had a baby three weeks ago.' Her tired face wreathed itself in a self-satisfied smile. 'Jacob. He's wonderful. So I tend to be up all hours.' She shrugged in a what-can-you-do? gesture.

Hillary nodded. 'Did you happen to hear anything from the Jones's place this morning? Anything odd at all?'

Jennifer Potter frowned and shook her head. 'No, I'm sorry. Has something bad happened?'

'Yes, I'm afraid it has,' Hillary said, and swept on before she could be asked what. 'Did you see a car pull up outside Mrs Jones's house any time this morning?'

'No, I don't think so. I saw people leaving from all over the square, of course. From around half seven onwards, you see them all go, like bees leaving the hive. Then, at five thirty or so in the evening they all start to come back.'

'But you didn't notice any car come to or from the Jones residence?'

'Oh no.'

'Do you think you would have noticed if there *had* been a car or van?'

Jennifer Potter thought a while, then shrugged. 'Maybe. It depends. My kitchen faces the square, and I was doing Jacob's bottle about sevenish. I fed him at the table, and I usually look out the window when I'm doing it, you know, just to see what's happening. There's a thrush nesting close by and I like watching him banging snails on the pavement to crack them open. But after I fed Jacob, I put him down in his cot, then got on with my chores. So . . .' She shrugged her chubby shoulders helplessly.

Hillary nodded. 'And you didn't see anybody go through Mrs Jones's gate?'

'No. Sorry. Is it . . . I mean, is she all right?'

'I'm afraid not,' Hillary said, again without elaborating. The last thing she wanted to do was scare an already timid witness into forgetting something that might later prove vital. 'Do you know anybody with a grudge against Mrs Jones?'

'Oh no. Well, not unless you count Vera. But she's a nice woman, so I'm sure she doesn't count.'

'Vera?'

'Vera Grearsley, she lives over there.' Jennifer pointed to the house directly on the right of the victim's. 'Vera makes lovely jewellery. She made this.' Jennifer held out her arm on which a silver bracelet dangled. The links were large and heart-shaped, with various stones set in the middle. 'She sells her things on the Internet and everything,' Jennifer carried on admiringly. 'She was one of the first to welcome Mike and me to the village. Came over with a cake, she did. It wasn't really a good cake,' Jennifer said with a smile. 'A Victoria sponge, a bit dry. But it's the thought that counts, isn't it?'

Hillary agreed that it was. 'Why do you think Vera and Matilda don't get on?' she asked, very careful in her phrasing of the question. The last thing she wanted was for the young and somewhat naive mother to get reticent now. 'Oh, because of Oscar,' Jennifer said blithely.

'Oscar?' Hillary asked, her antenna perking up. A man on the scene. Always a good start.

'Oscar Wilde,' Jennifer said, making Hillary, who'd taken an English literature degree, blink. Then blink again. Visions of *Lady Windermere's Fan* flashed through her head. 'Her cat. Vera's cat, that is, not Mrs Jones's,' Jennifer burbled on. 'I don't think Mrs Jones likes animals much.'

Hillary gave a final blink and got with the programme. 'Oh. A cat. OK. Er, what's wrong with Oscar Wilde exactly?' she asked.

'He's always getting into Mrs Jones's garden and scratching up her plants and, you know, doing his business on her lawns. She doesn't half make a fuss about it. But cats roam, don't they, you can't do anything about it.' Jennifer sighed philosophically. 'Anyway, Oscar got sick and almost died, oh, about six weeks ago now, and Vera swore blind Mrs Jones poisoned it. My Mike told her she ought to be careful what she said — that it was libel or slander or something, and that Mrs Jones is just the sort to take you to court over something like that. She's really clever, you know,' Jennifer added, nodding sagely. 'Mrs Jones, I mean. A friend of mine told me she used to keep the books for her husband's company, and she knows all about taxes, and the law, and stuff like that.'

Hillary nodded, almost overloading on information now. 'I understand from Mrs Grimmett that Matilda Jones and her husband were divorcing?'

Jennifer nodded, trying to look sympathetic and almost managing it. 'Oh yes, we all know about that. He left her for his secretary, or so I heard. Mrs Jones was so mad about it. She said it proved he had no imagination. She said the banality,' the young mother stumbled a little over the unfamiliar word, 'made her sick.'

Hillary smiled wryly. 'Yes. I can imagine it would.'

* * *

Vera Grearsley was a small, dark-haired, dark-eyed woman, the kind who seemed to buzz with invisible energy. When Hillary called at her house, a voice beckoned her down the garden path to what had once been a large double garage that was now decked out as a workshop. Hillary could smell solder and the tang of metal as she stepped through the large open doorway.

Vera was dressed in filthy dungarees far too big for her, and turned off a small acetylene torch as Hillary approached her, for which the policewoman was grateful. She'd regarded the wicked blue flame at once as a potential threat, and the heat of it still lingered viciously in the air.

Vera seemed to sense her unease, and pushed the protective goggles she'd been wearing on to the top of her head. 'Sorry. Want to step outside? It gets a bit ripe in here after a while.' She followed Hillary out into a messy but beautiful garden, and absently began to dead-head a rambling rose that was climbing over a disused sundial. The lawn needed mowing, and in one corner a very overgrown garden pond plopped to the sound of busy frogs.

'DI Greene.' Hillary showed her ID to the little woman, who looked to be in her early fifties.

'This is about Mattie, I expect,' Vera said glumly. 'I saw all the hullabaloo next door. She dead?' she asked bluntly.

'Yes. I'm afraid so.'

'Lot of police about,' Vera said, casting her a quick up-and-under look from beetling dark brows.

'It wasn't an accident,' Hillary said succinctly, and began to dead-head the roses too. It was a beautiful apricot-coloured thing, a floribunda type, and there were a lot of dead heads to nip off. It was a strangely soothing pastime. She followed Vera Grearsley's example of simply letting them drop on to the mossy ground beneath.

'Thought as much.' Vera heaved a sigh. She was sweating slightly, no doubt from the warmth of her workshop, and Hillary could see damp patches beneath her armpits. 'And, of course, you've come hotfooting over here to ask me about the feud?'

'Was there one?'

'Oh yes, 'fraid so,' Vera admitted glumly. 'It started with Oscar crapping on her lawn. And from there it escalated into daft threats about growing leylandii against her wall nearest my workshop, thus blotting out my light. The latest thing was that she was going to paint her far garden fence a hideous fuchsia pink, knowing I can't stand that colour, and that it would be directly in my eyeline from my main living room and dining area. Daft really, because I knew she wouldn't do it. Whatever else she had, Mattie had taste. Besides, white was her colour.' She sighed and decimated a few more browning flower heads, and shook her head woefully. 'The really sad thing is, before all this, we got along all right. She even bought several pieces of jewellery from me — a turquoise and silver set, and a jet and amber one. A very nice pair of platinum twisted earrings too. But, there you are.' She shrugged her bird-like shoulders. 'Neighbours fall out.'

'I understand she was in the middle of a divorce?'

'Yes, and pretty messy it was, too. She wanted her pound of flesh, with interest, and her poor mutt of a husband, for once, was putting up a fight. But if you're thinking Barry done her in, I reckon you're barking up the wrong tree. Hasn't got it in him, in my opinion.'

Hillary continued dead-heading roses. 'Did you see or hear anything odd this morning at her place?'

'Nope. Well, might have done. I thought I heard a cry — something or someone call out. But I was in bed. And you know how it is, in the countryside? You're half asleep and you hear something, and you wake up fully, but it could have been anything. A vixen, a magpie even.'

Hillary did know how it was in the country. She also knew that a high-pitched, panicked or agonized human voice, muffled by walls, needn't have sounded very human at all.

'What time was this?'

'About twenty past seven. Something like that.'

So, it was ten minutes outside Doc Partridge's 7:30—8:30 timeframe, but not by much. And no pathologist was going to quibble about ten minutes, which meant that she certainly wasn't either.

If the witness was to be believed.

'Can you account for your time between, say, seven and nine this morning?'

Vera grunted. 'Now there's a leading question,' she murmured, but shrugged, and thought about it for a moment.

'Well, I was in bed till about seven twenty, like I said. Woke up, shot out of bed, brushed my teeth and ran outside. Didn't even stop for coffee. Bloody alarm clock hadn't gone off,' she explained, seeing Hillary's raised brow. 'There must have been a short break in the electricity or something during the night, and I had to be in Oxford at eight, to see a physics don from St Jude's about a pendant she wanted made. She'd got this drawing of an atom, or molecule or something. I dunno. Might have been a spiral galaxy. Anyway, it had to be made to her exact specifications and size ratio and whatnot. You know what they're like. She had an undergraduate due in at eight thirty or some such unworldly hour, and only eight o'clock would do, as she was committed from now until Doomsday or whatever. In the event, I didn't get there till gone quarter past. Stuck in a bloody traffic jam, and she wasn't best pleased, I can tell you. But she still gave me the commission — that's what I've started working on now.' So saying, she waved a hand back to her workshop, then took a large, much-needed breath, and grinned. 'Not much of an alibi, is it?'

Hillary had to agree that it wasn't. She nipped off the last dead head on the rose bush, thanked her and left.

She walked back towards the village green, mentally filing and mulling over all that she had learned.

One thing was for sure. Their victim was the sort of lady who made enemies. And plenty of them, by the sound of it.

CHAPTER THREE

It was nearly noon before SOCO gave Keith Barrington permission to go into the house and the first thing he did was search for the victim's computer. He found it in a small library-cum-office on the ground floor, overlooking the back garden. The model was the latest offering from Bill Gates, and he admired it for some moments before he set about breaking the user's password. It took him a long time. Matilda Jones hadn't used her name, date of birth, telephone number, or any of the other easy-to-remember digits that many people favoured. Instead he had to run a specialist program of his own devising to break the code. It was not, strictly speaking, legal. So he made sure no one saw him do it.

At first glance, all the effort seemed to have been in vain. Matilda Jones was not the sort of woman to keep an electronic journal in which to pour out her heart or jot down any other interesting titbits — like who might want to kill her — and seemed mainly to use the PC to keep her household accounts up to date. He found several letters to the tax man and all her files for the last five financial years and dutifully printed them off. He had no doubt Hillary would want to read them later. He whistled as he ran his eye down the figures — their victim had certainly lived well, and right up to her means.

He found some vaguely interesting personal letters to what seemed to be an old university friend now living in Melbourne, but it wasn't until he found a folder labelled, intriguingly, 'GYYB' that he hit pay dirt. The initials, according to the title heading, stood for 'Got You, You Bastard,' and it was a complete, accurate, and detailed listing of all the work Matilda Jones had done for J&C Construction over the years.

It took him a while to read it all, and by the time he was finished, he couldn't help but feel reluctant admiration for the dead woman. Matilda Jones, née Cartwright, had set her husband up initially in business, after selling a house she'd inherited from an elderly relative. Neatly detailed time sheets followed, showing every last second of time Matilda had spent working the growing business's accounts, her dogged efforts at chasing contracts, and even her expenses for cooking expensive meals at home when her husband brought back councillors, city planners, and major contractors in a bid to woo them. Most wives probably did as much for the sake of their husband's business, but how many bothered to make such careful, cast-iron records? Some of which went back nearly fifteen years? Since, presumably, the Joneses' marriage had started off happily and cheerfully enough, it spoke of amazing forethought, if nothing else. It was as if the young Matilda Jones had realised right from the start that one day she might need meticulous records to show a divorce court judge that she was entitled to half the business, if not more. It was almost as if she'd been *expecting* the marriage to fail.

He printed off the entire folder and went in search of his boss.

* * *

Hillary Greene was in the victim's bedroom, staring somewhat bemusedly at a vast built-in closet. There were racks of evening gowns, trouser suits, skirts, blouses, jackets and tops, most with matching accessories. And the woman had more handbags, shoes and purses than Hillary could have stored using up the entire length of her own home. A vast array of cosmetics, face creams, curling tongs and some things that looked like instruments of torture, were crammed into the upper shelves. She reached for a particularly vicious-looking contraption and, after some thought, supposed that they must be eyelash curlers. She put it back with a shudder.

Her own dark lashes had always been allowed to go their own way. She hastily turned her back on the eyelash curlers — or at least that's what she *hoped* they were — and shut the door, jumping a little to find Barrington standing right behind her.

'What the hell were *they*?' he asked curiously.

'Not sure. But I hope they weren't a sex toy,' she added with a grin. 'If so, I'm not surprised her husband left her.' Barrington shuddered. 'And don't creep up on me,' Hillary added, glancing at the sheaf of papers in his hand.

'Sorry, guv. None of the floorboards creak in this place, have you noticed?'

Hillary hadn't, but nodded anyway. 'What you got?'

'From the victim's computer. Thought you'd want to see them.' He handed them over, but also gave a quick precis of their contents as she scanned them.

'She wasn't going to take any prisoners in court, was she?' Hillary mused, agreeing with his assessment of the victim's thinking. 'I wonder if her husband knew about this . . .' She waved the papers thoughtfully. 'If *her* brief had got around to parlaying with *his* brief, he might well have done. And, given all this, I can't see any judge not allotting our victim at least half the worth of the business, if not more. You say she initially funded the start-up of the firm?'

Keith nodded. 'Before she came along, Barry Jones was a sort of one-man labourer, who occasionally hired others. You know, if you wanted a garden shed put up, or a cheap conservatory, some walling done around the garden, that sort of thing, by the look of it. Then he married Matilda, and she used her inheritance to put it into a whole different ball game.'

Hillary nodded. 'I see the name changed from Jones Construction to Jones and Cartwright round about then too. Cartwright being her maiden name. So she obviously wanted her own name in the title. Clever psychology that.'

Barrington nodded. 'Their first big project was a barn conversion near Heathfield. Then a stable block over near Blenheim. Some enterprising incomer wanted them converted to a tea shop and souvenir place. A few years later they were doing house builds from scratch. Started off small — some homeowner with a bit of ground, selling it off to J&C, and the company then building a clone next door. No hassles with the planning officer — quick and easy. Just recently, though, the company's been growing even more, and the last few jobs have been erecting small estates out near Bicester way.'

'Big league.' Hillary whistled thoughtfully, thinking about the scandalous rise in house prices in the area. Even a small cul-de-sac of houses would net them millions. 'And this is the time he chose to up and leave her for a younger woman. Not clever, that,' she said thoughtfully. 'Not clever at all.'

'Our vic certainly doesn't seem the type to take something like that lying down,' Keith agreed.

'OK, keep looking,' Hillary said, rolling the sheaf of papers up into a loose tube and tapping it against her hand. 'Oh, and thinking ahead, find the best photograph of our vic you can and get some copies made. We might well be needing them before the case is out.'

'Right, guv.'

'And if you've finished with the computer you can carry on in here,' Hillary glanced around the bedroom vaguely. A large, modern four-poster stood against one wall, the dark, rich wood of the twisted hand-carved posts contrasting with the pure white walls. A light and wispy material in white, green and apricot was tied back, allowing access to the bed. A matching green carpet stretched from wall to wall, whilst the bed sheets were apricot. Apricot cushions lined the window seats at both large dormer windows and the colour was picked up here and there in various other soft furnishings. It was beautiful, tasteful, and made her narrow bunk on the *Mollern* seem pitiful by comparison.

But when Hillary thought of their victim, lying alone in that big bed, probably with her mind full of revenge on an erring hubby, she found herself totally incapable of envy.

'I take it you didn't find anything personal on the PC?' she asked sharply.

'Not really, guv. Just some letters to an old pal in Oz.'

'Then this is the place she probably kept the secret stuff,' Hillary mused. 'The modern computer age might be great for storing data, but when it comes to matters up close and personal, you can't beat the old-fashioned touch. So don't leave a potpourri jar unturned. Every attractive woman under seventy has *something* intimate stashed in her bedroom. And I want to know what Mattie Jones found necessary to hide.'

'Guv,' Barrington said, with a slight gulp. When his boss walked away and left him to it, he gazed around the feminine room and sighed. When in doubt, go straight for the knicker drawer. Right?

* * *

J&C Construction had offices in a small business park on the east side of Kidlington. The building was strictly modern, yellow-brick and single-storey, functional and neat enough, but hardly likely to appeal to someone who came to J&C wanting to build something innovative or beautiful. But then, that particular niche was probably not their market.

Hillary parked next to a gloriously flowering dark purple buddleia, got out and set off for the doorway, stopping to let a large red admiral butterfly have the right of way as it blundered across the path. The paving was mainly white slabs, with a few weeds already putting in an appearance in the joins. She pushed open an unlocked door, and found herself in a small waiting room, where a lone woman sat typing into a computer terminal behind a small desk positioned in one corner. She looked up with a slightly puzzled smile as Hillary walked towards her. No doubt she was aware that nobody at the company had any appointments booked for this hour.

Hillary got out her ID card as she approached. 'Hello. Detective Inspector Greene, Thames Valley. Is Mr Barry Jones in?'

'I'm not sure. He left for the Wendlebury site early this morning, but he might have come back for lunch. I'll just check.'

Hillary nodded and watched the receptionist push down the third button on the right of her panel. She was in her late thirties, with dark blonde hair and honey-coloured eyes, but something told Hillary that, attractive though she was, she wasn't the woman Barry Jones had left his wife for. Not young enough. Not glamorous enough. Her eyes were intelligent and tired, and Hillary suspected she had a husband and two or three demanding children lurking about somewhere.

'Hello, Rachel, it's me. Is Mr Jones in?'

'Just, but he's about to have lunch.' The voice sounded tinny.

'There's a lady here to see him.'

'Not a walk-in? Ask Peter to see her.'

The receptionist caught Hillary's eye and flushed a little. 'No, Rachel, she's from the police.'

There was a momentary pause, then the voice repeated, 'Police?' Even with the distortion of the apparatus, the as yet unknown Rachel sounded sceptical and not a little cautious.

'Yes. A Detective Inspector Greene,' the receptionist responded.

Another pause, then: 'Is this about the theft from the Wendlebury site? If so, Pete's dealing with it.'

Hillary was already shaking her head before the other woman could ask. 'I need to see Mr Jones right away,' she said firmly.

'No, it's something else. The lady is most insistent on seeing Mr Jones. It sounds important.'

Hillary, feeling vaguely chuffed at being referred to as 'a lady' — it had been some time since anyone had called her *that* — waited with interest to see what Rachel had to say now.

Rachel said, 'Oh.' Then: 'You'd better send her through.'

The receptionist lifted her finger off the button and nodded over Hillary's head. 'Please go on through the green door behind you. Mr Jones's office is second on the left — a yellow door.'

Hillary thanked her and moved across the room, not surprised to find, waiting for her in the narrow corridor beyond the door, a young woman. She was tall, leggy, blonde-haired and brown-eyed, wearing a tailored skirt and jacket combination in eggshell blue.

Oh yes, Hillary thought. Much more like it. This had to be the woman Barry Jones had left his wife for.

'Inspector Greene?'

'Yes. And you are . . . ?'

'Oh. Rachel Miller, Mr Jones's personal assistant.'

She was, Hillary guessed, twenty-three if she was a day. Much too young to have earned such a title, and she could almost hear thirty-something mere lowly secretaries the world over give a collective groan.

Hillary followed her into a small anteroom, where a computer displayed a swimming fish screensaver. The room was lined with neat, utilitarian grey filing cabinets, but a vase of fresh freesias sat on the desk, giving out a wonderful scent.

'Mr Jones is expecting you,' she said, and Hillary hid a wry smile. Well, he either was, or he wasn't. If he'd been out early this morning butchering his wife, a wise man might expect the constabulary to come a-calling at some point during the day. But if he hadn't, then there was no reason why he shouldn't be genuinely surprised. And Hillary would have given much to see the expression on his face when young Rachel Miller had informed him of his visitor.

She felt the young woman's eyes on her as she walked over to the only other door in the room, knocked briefly, and stepped inside.

Barry Jones's office was fairly large, with a large picture window that showed a disappointing view of parked cars. The room was predominantly beige, and none of Matilda Jones's clever colour schemes or eye for style was apparent here. Did she simply never come into the office? Had they changed location since Barry had walked out on her? Or had they just decided not to spend their cash on the workplace?

Barry Jones rose from behind a functional wooden desk. He was about Hillary's height, maybe five feet ten or so, with reddish fair hair, and eyes that turned out on closer inspection to be a sort of pale grey. He wasn't fat, but appeared solid, with large workmanlike hands and broad shoulders. But he was dressed in a good suit, and wore a gold and ebony signet ring on the little finger of his left hand. He scrubbed up well, as her grandmother would have said, and his smile, revealing large but even white teeth, was carefully comprised of welcome, puzzlement, and inquiry, in equal measure.

'DI Greene, is it?'

'Yes, sir.' Hillary showed him the ID and felt his eyes move from the official card to give her the quick once-over. He saw a woman of his wife's age, class and probable upbringing. A woman with more curves, perhaps, but eyes which never missed a thing, like Mattie's.

He didn't look particularly happy to see her.

'Please, sit down. I'm not sure what I can do for you. Rachel tells me this isn't about the problems at our build in Wendlebury? No, of course it isn't,' he answered his own question before she could respond. 'Petty theft from a building site wouldn't command the interest of an inspector.'

'When was the last time you saw your wife, Mr Jones?' Hillary asked blandly. The chair facing Barry's desk was surprisingly comfortable — generous, firm and gave plenty of back support. She settled into it, and brought out her notebook and pen.

'Mattie?' Barry Jones said, sounding genuinely surprised. Good acting, maybe. Hillary watched him closely, pen hovering over the blank page. Aware that she was waiting for him to answer, he sat back down, looking just a little ruffled.

'Good grief, I'm not actually sure,' he muttered. 'We're in the process of divorcing, you see.'

Hillary nodded.

'I left the house, well, at the end of February. I've seen her once or twice since, mostly at either my solicitor's office, or hers.'

'Not at the house?'

'Hell no.' Barry gave a rather false laugh. 'Mattie probably had the locks changed before my car had even left the garage.'

'So you haven't been back to your old Bletchington home in nearly six months?'

'That's right. Why, nothing's happened to it, has it? It hasn't burnt down or anything?'

'No. Why do you ask that, sir?' Hillary asked curiously.

Barry Jones shifted nervously on his own chair. 'Well, because you're here asking questions about it, I suppose.'

Hillary nodded. 'Nothing like that, sir, I assure you.' But it was an interesting conclusion to jump to. Had Mattie Jones threatened to burn it down in the past? Or did her husband simply suspect her of being capable of running an insurance scam? Intriguing though such thoughts were, it was time to get down to business.

'Can you tell me your movements this morning, sir? Let's begin with the time you woke up.'

'What?' he asked sharply, surprised. 'Well, I dunno. About seven thirty or so, I imagine. It's when I usually wake up. Look, what's this all about?'

'You don't have an alarm clock, sir?' She made her voice sound almost scandalized.

'No. No, I don't usually bother with one. I always wake up on my own in plenty of time to get up. I live in Kidlington, you see, only about three minutes' drive away. So it's not as if I have a commute to worry about.'

'And were you alone — when you woke up, I mean?' She kept her voice level, but even so saw a wave of colour wash over him. It was the curse of fair-skinned people everywhere, she supposed, and very telltale. So Mr Jones was not as sanguine about his new relationship with a younger woman as he probably liked to pretend.

'Yes, I was alone.' Barry Jones took a long, ostentatious breath. 'Not that it's any of your business, Inspector Greene, but after leaving my wife, I rented a one-bed flat near the Moors.'

Very nice too, no doubt, Hillary thought. 'And what time did you leave for work?'

'About eight fifteen.'

'You drove straight here?'

'Yes.'

'And you arrived when?'

'About eight thirty or thereabouts.'

'Fifteen minutes? Quite a long time to cover barely a quarter of a mile, isn't it?'

'You know what it's like. Traffic and stuff.' He shrugged. 'And I caught every red light going.'

Hillary nodded. 'And was anyone here when you arrived?'

'To vouch for me, you mean?' Jones asked, beginning to sound just a shade belligerent now. 'Yes, in fact, Rachel was here before me.'

'Is that her usual time to be in?'

'Yes. About eight thirty or so. And she leaves at six, maybe six thirty, if we have any trouble at one of our sites that needs sorting.'

'Long hours,' Hillary noted blandly.

'Rachel is very flexible,' Barry Jones said, then blushed beetroot. Hillary kept her eyes firmly on her notebook. So the lovers were alibiing each other were they? Well, up to a point anyway. But what about the earlier part of the morning — the time when the killing actually took place? Why not say they spent the night — and therefore the morning, together — as well?

'Look, Inspector, are you going to tell me what this is all about?'

No. She wasn't. 'Would you say you were close to your wife, sir?' she asked brightly.

'What? No. Well, not now. I mean, once we were, obviously, but . . . Look, this is obviously about Mattie. What's she done now? Has she been pouring some damn story into your ear? My solicitor warned me, with the divorce case about to come up, that she might try some such nonsense. But there's nothing wrong here, I can assure you. And no matter what Mattie would have you believe, J&C Construction is the success it is because I've slogged my guts out for the last fifteen years to make it so.'

'I take it the divorce is acrimonious, sir?'

Barry Jones scowled. 'That's all down to her. I was perfectly willing to be reasonable and keep it all civilized. It was Mattie who insisted on going for the jugular, so of course things are . . . well . . . unpleasant.'

'Your wife wants half the company, I take it?'

Jones flushed. 'I wish! The silly bit . . . the stupid woman thinks she can get two thirds of it. I know what she wants. She thinks if she can oust me as general manager, I'll be forced to buy her out at top-bracket rates to keep control. She must be out of her mind.'

Hillary nodded. 'If you can't afford to buy her out, and she is awarded two thirds of the company, what happens then?'

Barry Jones laughed. 'Oh, don't you worry about *that*. Mattie'll get the company over my dead body!'

Very dramatic, Hillary thought. And way too good a chance to pass up. 'Oh no, sir,' she corrected. 'It's not your dead body we're concerned with. It's your wife's.'

It took a moment or two for it to register. And she could almost see the instant the blankness left the pale eyes. His face washed with colour — not, this time, the unremittingly obvious shade of dull red, but a sickly greenish white instead.

For several long seconds he stared at her, apparently incapable of speech, his mouth opening and closing uselessly.

'What?' Barry Jones eventually said.

'Your wife, Matilda Jones, was murdered sometime this morning, sir,' Hillary said flatly. She'd had to do this before, of course, inform someone that their nearest and dearest was dead. But in this instance she had the added problem of not knowing whether she was speaking to the killer or not. If not, then this man deserved her sympathy and respect. But on the other hand, if he was responsible, then now was the moment he was at his most vulnerable, when he needed to keep his wits about him, and put on the performance of his life.

'Mattie's dead?'

'Yes, sir.'

'Not an accident?'

'No, sir.'

Barry Jones stared at her. He continued to stare at her for some time. He obviously had no idea what to say next. Eventually, he muttered, 'I don't believe it. Nobody would dare to kill Mattie.'

It was, on the face of it, a strange thing to say, but Hillary understood him almost at once. Mattie Jones was a mover and a shaker, a planner and forward thinker, a woman who got what she wanted. Her young neighbour Jennifer had called her clever. Vera Grearsley had made no bones about Mattie Jones's campaign to make her life a misery. Everyone who knew her reacted strongly to her. Even the stalwart Dorothea Grimmett had had to acknowledge a grudging respect for her.

She was not the sort of woman who would stand for being murdered.

Yet someone had obviously met the challenge head on.

'Do you know if your wife had any enemies, Mr Jones?' Hillary asked quietly, and Barry Jones dragged his eyes away from a spot on the wall behind her head and focused, with some difficulty, on her face.

'Enemies? Mattie. Well. Yes. No. I mean, she was a very hard woman to . . . I mean, she had a certain way of going about things that could put people's backs up, but I mean . . . murder? No. Nobody would want to murder her, surely?' Hillary knew she was not going to get anything more out of him right now. Either he was in genuine shock, or was acting as if he was. Either way, he could keep. After he'd stewed for a while, and had time to come to terms with his new situation, she'd be back.

'Well, that's all for now, sir.'

Barry Jones watched her, slack-jawed, as she got up. 'What? Is that it?' He sounded half scandalized, half relieved.

'Oh, there'll be more questions later, sir,' she warned him with a wry smile. 'When we've discovered more about the circumstances surrounding your wife's death. I must ask you not to leave the country, Mr Jones, at least not until things are sorted. We might apply to have your passport removed if you attempt to, and you must hold yourself available for further questioning. Do you understand?'

Barry Jones nodded. 'You think I did it.'

Hillary closed her notebook, and smiled at him. 'Does your wife have parents still living? Brothers or sisters?'

'No parents. She has a sister somewhere, but they don't get on. She was never invited over to tea, or anything,' Barry Jones smiled grimly. 'She wasn't even at our wedding.'

'Thank you, sir. I'll be in touch,' Hillary said, and walked to the door.

In the small anteroom outside, she paused for a moment, then walked over to the secretary. 'I have just a few questions, Miss Miller. Can you tell me what time you got in this morning?'

Rachel Miller shot her intercom a quick look, no doubt wishing she could ask her lover for instructions. Faced with Hillary's unwavering stare, she swallowed hard, and managed a forlorn smile. 'About eight thirty, I think. Maybe a few minutes earlier.'

'You live in Kidlington?'

'Yarnton.' A small village not far away. 'I still live with Mum and Dad,' she added reluctantly.

Interesting, Hillary thought. So why hadn't Barry Jones and Rachel Miller set up house together?

'And what time did Mr Jones get in?'

'Just a few minutes after I did.'

Well, that tallied. But then, if they were in cahoots, it would, Hillary thought. But again — if they were going to alibi each other, why not go the whole hog?

'And you left home — when?'

Rachel Miller dropped her eyes and reached out to straighten her desk tidier. 'About ten past eight.'

Probably a lie, Hillary mused. People tended to avoid eye contact if they meant to lie. 'Mr Jones and Mrs Jones are in the middle of a divorce, yes?' She changed the subject and kept it vague. As a rule, the more open-ended a question was, the more information could be milked from it.

But in this case, Rachel Miller simply reached for a pen and began to twiddle it between her fingers. She seemed unsure whether or not to answer, so Hillary became more specific. 'He left his wife, Matilda, for you, is that right?'

'I don't see that this is any concern of yours,' Rachel said tightly.

'Your parents don't approve. Is that it? Is that why you're not living together?'

'Barry and I will marry as soon as he's free,' Rachel said, again in that tight prim voice. Which instantly made Hillary wonder if she'd got the habit from her mother. She had an idea that when they ran a background check on Miss Miller they were going to find a strict upbringing and disapproval of divorce lurking somewhere around in the Miller family background.

'Well, I'll let you get on with your work,' Hillary said, and saw the younger woman shoot her a puzzled but grateful glance. No doubt she was dying to ask what this was all about, but wasn't going to.

Hillary nodded, and left. By the time she got to Puff the Tragic Wagon and climbed in, she could imagine the lovers were having a very serious talk indeed.

But about what, exactly?

* * *

Back at Bletchington, Keith Barrington was all but pacing up and down, waiting for Hillary to return. Through the open window he saw her park, and then head towards Gemma Fordham's vehicle, so he carried on pacing.

Outside, Hillary crouched down to look inside the car, and was just in time to see her DS bite down on a large salad sandwich. Gemma saw her at about the same time, and hastily held up a finger to pop a piece of escaping tomato back into her mouth.

'Sorry, guv,' she mumbled around her mouthful, but Hillary waved a vague hand.

'Didn't mean to interrupt your lunch. When you've finished canvassing, I want you to start on the background checks. Vic first, of course, but also Barry Jones and one Rachel Miller, his secretary.'

'Guv.' Gemma swallowed hard, and put the sandwich down.

'Might as well include Vera Grearsley in the mix as well,' Hillary carried on, knowing Gemma didn't need notes to remember it all.

'Neighbour with the crapping cat?' Gemma clarified. She'd obviously met the jewellery designer as part of her rounds.

'Right. Picked up anything interesting so far?' Hillary asked.

'Nothing on any vehicle, guv. I'm beginning to think whoever did it didn't come by car or any other motorized transport. It's odd that nobody at all noticed a car pull up outside the vic's house.'

Hillary sighed. 'Could be they were just all used to hearing cars starting and stopping around then. It was time for most people to be up and about and leaving for work.'

'All the more reason for somebody to see another car there, guv,' Gemma insisted stubbornly. 'The Jones's divorce was public property. A strange car parked up in front of the lady's residence would be bound to be a point of interest.'

Hillary frowned. 'True. So somebody on foot or bicycle maybe? Or they approached from the back?'

'No access from the back, guv, I checked.'

That was another thing about her new DS. You didn't have to keep checking up on her, and she was perfectly capable of good, solid, rational thinking without being prompted. It was just a pity that Gemma was out to screw her over, Hillary mused. Apart from that, she'd be the ideal second in command.

'OK. Well, keep at it,' she sighed. 'And let me know if anything interesting turns up.' She got up and walked away, not quite catching whatever it was that her DS muttered under her breath.

But she supposed it wasn't anything complimentary.

At the house, Barrington pounced on her the moment she walked in.

'Guv, you were right. I found these. They were hidden in her jewellery box, this big hand-crafted wooden thing. There was a secret drawer thingy at the bottom.'

He handed her his find like a chuffed retriever handing over a fallen pheasant. Hillary, careful to don thin rubber gloves first, took the offering of handwritten envelopes, and read the letters they contained, her eyebrows gradually rising.

Very nasty.

Somebody, who only signed themselves with the initials FC, really didn't like Matilda Jones. The language was blue, and the threats became more and more graphic with each successive missive. The sense of frustration fairly leapt off the pages.

There were six letters in all, all dated over the past five weeks. Luckily, their victim had kept them all in their original envelopes.

Hillary glanced at the postmarks on them. 'Chipping Norton, Oxon,' she read out loud. 'Good going, Keith.

You can help Gemma out with her background checks, but concentrate on anyone whose life touched our vic's, with the initials FC. And if you can track them down to Chipping Norton, start yodelling.'

CHAPTER FOUR

The death of a moderately wealthy woman, murdered in her own home, was always going to be news, and when Hillary returned to HQ early that evening, the media was out in force. Albeit looking a little nervous. The parking lot of a police headquarters, given the sniper killer's penchant for taking potshots at people in just such places, wasn't making for a happy atmosphere, but it was not enough to deter the diehards. Besides, if the sniper killer did kick off, just think of the TV footage!

Hillary was careful to avoid them as she kept her head down and walked straight for the main doors, aware that the press liaison officer gave her a wry look as she passed. But no doubt Paul Danvers, as nominal head of the investigation, had already given them a sound bite or two, so she was allowed to get away with it.

Upstairs, the large office was almost spookily deserted. At this time of day, all but a few of the day shift had gone, and although the night shift was beginning to trickle in, they were still mainly congregating at the lockers downstairs, or were up in the canteen, getting an early start on the tea and coffee.

She told Barrington to call it a day, not surprised to see that there was no sign of Frank Ross. Not that he ever needed to be told when it was time to clock off. She did find a terse report from him waiting on her desk however, full of interview notes that had probably been written up at the pub. She tossed them to one side, shucked off her lightweight jacket and reached for the first of the forensic reports.

It wasn't particularly encouraging. All the blood found so far belonged to the victim. Hillary, like any seasoned copper, knew that when a killer stabbed a victim, the killer nearly always managed to nick themselves with the knife as well, but there had been so much blood at the victim's residence, she couldn't see how forensics would ever be able to find a few drops of the killer's DNA amongst it. There had been no single spatter blood drops found at the very entrance to the door, where the killer must have stood when he or she started slashing, and the head boffin concluded the killer had probably worn gloves. A minuscule sliver of what appeared to be a leather-like substance *had* been found, and would be analysed, and if this corresponded with glove leather, then the hypothesis would be a relatively safe one. Which meant no fingerprints either.

But there was still a long way to go. The killer need only have shed one human hair for a DNA match, and Hillary knew from experience that some lab results could take months to come through.

She was just about halfway through the witness statements when she felt a presence loom up in front of her and quickly looked up. She smiled. 'Hey, Mel, you still here? I thought you newly married types were always in a rush to get home to the missus?'

Mel gave her a desultory smile in response, and pulled out a chair and sat down. He looked tired, almost rumpled, a phenomenon she'd hardly ever encountered before in her laid-back, sartorially elegant pal.

'This the murder in Bletchington?' He gestured to the mound of paperwork, and Hillary nodded.

'So far no one saw our killer arrive or leave. But I've a few files to get through yet.' She tossed the one she'd been reading on to the 'done' pile and leaned back in her chair, taking the opportunity of the break to stretch her cramped shoulders and arms. 'But you didn't come for an update on the Jones killing,' she said, making it a statement. Although Mel, as the team's superintendent, held overall charge of the case, he never breathed down her neck for results. 'Still the Myers case?' she hazarded softly.

Mel nodded grimly. 'Fell through. The judge had to rule the evidence gained on the misspelt warrant inadmissible. Gregg said that the old boy clearly didn't like doing it, and read them the riot act once the CPS withdrew the charges. Needless to say, the young thugs went wild. We're battening down the hatches for some bad press tomorrow.'

Hillary sighed heavily. 'They'll be pulled in for something else before long. Troublemakers like that always are. Especially when they get away with it once; it makes them cocky.'

'Which means some other poor girl is going to get attacked,' Mel snarled, then instantly waved a hand in apology. 'Sorry, I'm snapping at the wrong person, I know.'

Hillary shrugged. 'Snap away. I'm big enough, and mean enough, to snap back if I feel the need to.'

'The mother was devastated,' Mel said glumly. 'She was in court for the first time, even though we all tried to stop her going. And the girl's father looked daggers at Gregg. I reckon he probably threatened him too, but nobody's saying anything about it. Not to me at least.'

'Nobody wants to charge an anguished father with threatening behaviour to the police who let him down,' Hillary agreed flatly. Because they *had* let the Myers down. Every cop in the station house would be feeling and thinking the same thing. And although nobody would blame Mel, or even DI Gregg, it would still fester.

'Go home to Janine, Mel,' Hillary said tiredly. 'At least she'll understand. That's one good thing about marrying someone in the job.'

Mel nodded, and hauled himself upright. 'I suppose so.'

'And get an early night,' Hillary called after him.

He waved a hand in acknowledgement and was soon gone, and with a weary shrug, Hillary turned back to the witness reports.

* * *

In a pub in Witney, Gary Greene heard the man leaning at the bar beside him give a long, low whistle, and turned to see what was causing all the excitement. It was still early, and the pub was almost empty, but everyone there had turned to look at the blonde who'd just pushed through the doorway.

The short, spiky hair, so pale it was almost white, framed a bony but arrestingly attractive face with big grey eyes. She was tall, and the trousers and jacket in dove grey she wore only emphasized her lean, wiry build. Gary liked more curves on his women, but he knew class when he saw it. So he looked mildly surprised, then gratified, when the woman's gaze stopped at him, and she headed over.

'DC Greene?' she asked, her voice raspy and deeply sexy.

'Yes. Er, Sergeant Fordham?'

The text he'd received earlier that day had been somewhat ambivalent. A DS Fordham had wanted to meet him to talk over old times about his father, Ronnie Greene. The name of the pub and a time had followed.

Gary's first instinct had been to ignore it. His father's memory was more notorious than anything else, and it wouldn't be the first time a reporter, wanting to revive old scandals for a slow news day, had tried to wangle a 'family' interview. But it was a dull weeknight, and he was fed up of sitting in front of the telly with a boil-in-the-bag dinner on his lap, whilst his flatmates larked about.

Now he was glad he had come.

'Yes,' the blonde confirmed, running her eyes over him. 'You don't resemble your father all that much,' she mused, making him tense slightly. Because it suddenly dawned on him that the leggy blonde had been just his father's type, and there could only be one sort of reminiscence she had of his old man.

'No, I look like my mother,' he said flatly.

'Hillary Greene?' Gemma said, although she knew her boss had been Ronnie's second wife.

'That's my stepmother,' Gary explained patiently.

'Ah. Your mother not in the job then?'

Gary laughed. 'Hardly. Drink?'

'Apple juice, please.'

Gary ordered it, and then nodded towards a window seat at the back. Gemma took her drink from him and went ahead, letting him get a good look at her behind, which was rounded and firm, and always looked good in tight-fitting trousers. Gary took a gulp from his pint of Old Hooky as he went, and appreciated the show.

'I work for your stepmother,' Gemma Fordham said, once she'd settled herself down at the table, making Gary, who'd taken another mouthful of his beer, almost choke. 'That's why I wanted to talk to you.'

Gemma had sensed his antagonism, and guessed the reason for it. And she wanted to dispel, right away, any thoughts that she had been one of his father's women. Even though she had been.

'I only met your father the once,' she lied smoothly. 'When he was seconded to my old nick on a child abduction case. I'm from Reading originally, and when I got the chance to transfer to HQ in Kidlington I jumped at it. Especially since it meant working with DI Greene.

She's got something of a rep as an investigator, as you probably know.'

Gary nodded and smiled. 'Yeah, she's great.'

So, he's a fan, Gemma thought, with a pang of regret. She'd half been hoping that he would suffer from a wicked-stepmother complex. It would have made things slightly easier to quiz him if he'd been anti-Hillary. Now she'd have to be extra careful.

'Yes. A few years on her team, learning the ropes, and I reckon I could be DI.' Gemma took a sip of her drink. 'If I don't put my foot in it, that is. That's why I wanted to chat with you. I only know vague stuff about, well, what happened to her and your father. So I don't want to spoil my chances by doing or saying the wrong thing.' She gave him a full wattage smile. 'You know what it's like — you move to a new nick, and you know nothing: who to keep away from, who's doing what to whom, old scandals that are never referred to . . . The place can be a landmine.'

Gary nodded. 'You're ambitious to get ahead and don't want to step on any toes.'

Gemma nodded. 'You have a problem with that?' she asked, letting her voice go just a shade belligerent. 'Some men still don't like to see women get ahead.'

'Hell no,' Gary said, flushing slightly. 'It was my old man who was your typical male chauvinist pig. Not me. I saw what he did to Mum, and later, when I was older and understood things more, I saw what he did to Hillary. No, more power to you, I say.'

Gemma nodded. 'OK then. So, what really went on? I know my boss was investigated by the mob from Yorkshire. And now one of them's our boss. What the hell is all that about?' She rolled her eyes, glad to see the youngster relax a little and even smile.

'Yeah, Hill was hopping mad about that, I can tell you.' He grinned. 'But it's not complicated. My old man was bent. His best pal, Frank Ross, was bent. But my dad had brains, and they reckon he amassed a fair bit from this illegal animal parts smuggling operation he was running. He was about to get pulled in when he had his car crash and got killed — which probably saved him from jail time.'

Gemma snorted. 'No copper wants that.'

'Right.'

'But they investigated Hillary as well?'

Gary shrugged. 'I suppose they more or less had to. But by this time, Hillary had already left Dad and moved on to the boat — not so much because of the smuggling, because I don't think she knew anything about it, but because of his women.'

Gemma forced herself to remain relaxed, but it wasn't easy. To have herself lumped together under the heading of 'his women' was like having salt added to an open wound. It was one thing to know you'd been foolish as a nineteen-year-old, but another thing to have your face rubbed in it years later.

'So that was it,' she managed to say lightly.

'Yeah. It was,' Gary said flatly.

'Coming under investigation must have been hard on her.'

'It was. She was working her first murder case as SIO at the time. But they exonerated her. Later, one of them — Danvers — transferred from York to Kidlington, and a year or so ago became Hillary's DCI.'

'Charming. And you? Being the son of Ronnie Greene can't be easy,' she said sympathetically.

'Hell no. But none of us has it easy. And people are beginning to forget about him. I only ever have the odd reminder now. Like a few years back, when one of his old cronies from Bicester got in touch wondering what to do about the contents of his locker.'

Gemma caught her breath. 'Locker? I didn't know he worked out of Bicester. I thought he was stationed at Kidlington.'

'He was. Bicester was years ago. In fact, I was surprised he was allowed to keep a locker on there. I got the feeling a mate of his let him store stuff there on the sly. I don't know why he bothered. When I picked it up, it was only junk. Some old trainers, some . . .' He was about to say porn, and changed it at the last second. 'Magazines. Old deodorant and shaving gear. That sort of thing.' He shrugged and took a deep swallow of his pint. Was he imagining it, or was she coming on to him?

Gemma felt her heart rate drop in disappointment. 'So there was nothing personal at all?'

'Nah. Oh, only a book — he must have got it for Hillary. He wrote her this naff inscription inside. I dunno why he bothered, I thought at the time it was hardly her thing.' He pointed to her empty glass. 'Want another?'

Gemma shook her head. 'No thanks, I'm fine. What do you mean, not her thing?'

'Hillary took a degree in English literature, did you know?'

Gemma did, but shook her head. 'No. So what did your father get her? A comic book?'

Gary grunted a laugh. 'Might as well have done. No, it was one of those horsey thriller things. Like I said, not her sort of thing at all.'

'Dick Francis,' Gemma blurted out, suddenly remembering seeing it on Hillary's bookshelf when she'd broken in to the *Mollern* a few months back. She'd thought at the time it had looked out of place amongst all the Austen, Brontës and assorted poetry.

'Could have been,' Gary said with a shrug. 'I prefer Bernard Cornwell myself. Military history stuff, you know?'

Gemma did, and bought him another pint. Now that she'd got what she wanted from him, she was feeling good, and when they left the pub an hour later, young Gary Greene was feeling good, too.

He'd call her tomorrow and ask her out on a date.

On the drive back to Summertown, Gary Greene already forgotten, Gemma wondered how soon she'd be able to get back on the *Mollern* and take a closer look at that book. Unless she was well and truly on the wrong track, Ronnie Greene's inscription would be well worth reading. It was, after all, the ideal place to hide a clue as to the whereabouts of a lot of money.

Not that Ronnie ever intended Hillary to have it, of course. No, it would have been just his idea of a joke for the clue to a fortune to be stashed under his estranged wife's straight-as-a-die nose.

But this was one joke that could very well make her rich. She slipped in an old Eagles tape and hummed along to 'Hotel California.' Tonight she'd cook something special for Guy. The blind music don she was currently living with was something of an epicure, and she was feeling in the mood to please him.

* * *

Thursday 2 August came in slightly damp, but a freshening wind promised to blow the clouds away before the morning was out. Hillary, as usual, was first in, and shook out her umbrella in the lobby, wondering if people coming in to work felt a little bit safer with an umbrella over their heads. After all, a sniper couldn't get an accurate line of fire at your head if he couldn't see it. She wondered if she ought to put a notice up in the hall advising everyone it might be good to use one, come rain or shine, until the killer was caught, but doubted if the top brass, or the press liaison officer for that matter, would go for it.

The cops would look silly standing around under umbrellas in bright sunshine — the fact that it could save their lives probably wouldn't matter a damn.

Once at her desk she managed to get through the last of the reports before the first of her team came in. Gemma Fordham smiled at her briefly as she took a seat. 'Guv.'

'Gemma,' Hillary greeted flatly. It had been some months now since she'd learned that Gemma Fordham was an old flame of her husband's, and had almost certainly transferred to Thames Valley HQ in a bid to find a way of getting her hands on Ronnie's dirty loot. Thanks to her neighbour on *Willowsands*, Nancy Walker, she already knew the young DS had been on her boat once to have a look around. But she doubted that Gemma had realised the significance of the Dick Francis thriller on her bookshelf. And even if she had, she would be doomed to disappointment.

The money was already gone.

She could, she supposed, have gone to Mel and demanded that Gemma be transferred, which had, in fact, been her very first instinct. But then she'd had second thoughts. Gemma was a good, competent, and hard-working officer. After having to put up with Frank Ross as a DS, she was heaven-sent in comparison. And whilst Gemma still had hopes of becoming rich on Ronnie's money, she'd be very careful to keep on Hillary's good side, and more than pull her weight. So why not take advantage of all that? Hillary wouldn't have been human if she hadn't enjoyed the delicious irony of the situation.

Furthermore, Gemma had all the makings of a good DI. Personal feelings aside, Hillary knew the force couldn't afford to lose officers of Gemma's calibre. Not only did her martial arts training come in handy, she had brains and grit and a good analytical mind too. If only she would stop dreaming of dirty money and put her mind to it, she'd make a first-rate cop. And, in spite of everything, Hillary was enjoying teaching her the ropes.

The phone rang and Hillary reached for it, just as Keith Barrington came in. He nodded over at her as he took his chair and turned on his computer terminal. 'Thanks, Doc, I'll send someone over right away,' he heard her say. 'And many thanks for getting to her so soon. I appreciate it.'

He grimaced as she hung up, rightly guessing that Matilda Jones was imminently scheduled for autopsy. He looked at her, not exactly keen to go, but willing enough. It was part of the job, and one he'd have to get used to.

Hillary was looking at Gemma Fordham. 'Gemma, you can attend the autopsy.'

'Guv,' Gemma said, not a flicker of emotion showing on her face. Had he but known it, Gemma was more than happy to do the hated chore, because it meant that afterwards she could sneak off for ten minutes or so and pay a short visit to Thrupp. She still had the key to Hillary's padlock on the *Mollern*, having managed to get a cast of it a couple of months ago.

Hillary watched Gemma leave, and glanced at her watch. Still no sign of Frank. She was never sure whether that was a good thing or not. Next year he was eligible for early retirement, and she would be making it clear to Danvers, Mel, and Chief Super Donleavy that she expected everyone to put their oar in and make sure he took it.

She'd put up with him for long enough.

* * *

The last of the rainclouds had been swept away when a tall, dark-haired woman hurried across the car park and entered the building. Although a member of the public, she read the news too, and hadn't relished the thought of being so close to a police station when a maniac with a rifle and a hatred of the police was still on the rampage. But she was far too excited to stay away.

She'd only heard the news about Mattie late last night, and had been tossing and turning all night just thinking about it. On the one hand it was awful, horrible, of course it was. And nobody liked being mixed up in something like that.

But on the other hand, she had her duty to do. Or so she told herself as she walked towards the front desk and the friendly-looking middle-aged man behind it. When he glanced up at her, she smiled with the first hint of nerves.

'Hello,' her voice came out in something of a croak, so she cleared it, and said firmly, 'I want to talk to whoever is in charge of the Matilda Jones murder inquiry. I have information.'

* * *

Hillary Greene pushed open the door to interview room one, and smiled as the woman inside got to her feet.

'Please, sit down. Mrs Varney, is it?'

'That's right. Anthea Varney. Mattie Jones was my best friend.'

Hillary nodded across at Keith. 'This is DC Barrington, I'm DI Hillary Greene.' She took a seat opposite, and smiled across the table. 'Sorry about the room — it's a bit stark.'

'Oh, I don't mind,' Anthea Varney said, playing with several gold bangles at her wrist. She was anorexically thin, with shoulder- length, salon-perfect dark hair, plucked eyebrows, manicured nails and solid gold jewellery. She was wearing a long apricot- coloured skirt and a matching top with a scoop neckline worked in silver beads. She wore strappy high-heeled sandals, and looked as if she was about to go to lunch at the Randolph in Oxford. Her voice was well-educated, with just a hint of the Sloane Ranger.

Hillary could well believe she was best friends with the victim. Definitely birds of a feather.

'Thank you for coming in to see us, Mrs Varney. I'm sure a constable would have been calling on you in due course, once we knew of your existence, but this always makes it so much easier. You've known Mattie long?' Hillary asked pleasantly.

'Oh, ages. We were at university together. Her husband was in construction, and mine in boat-building. We had a lot in common.'

Hillary nodded. 'You saw her recently?'

'The day before she died. Tuesday, we had lunch. Browns.' She named one of Oxford's top cafés without a hint of name-dropping. 'She seemed fine. Her usual self and all that. We had a good old moan about Barry and that ridiculous bimbo he left her for. In fact, she showed me some photos. They looked ridiculous together.'

Hillary blinked. 'Photos?'

'Of Barry and his so-called personal assistant. Oh, didn't I say?' Anthea gave her hand a little wave. 'Mattie hired one of those deliciously down-at-heel private eye thingies. He trailed Barry for days, and finally got some shots of them shacked up together at one of those really awful motorway motel places. It made us laugh, I can tell you.' Hillary imagined it would. But why go to a motel when he had a one-bed flat of his own? Again, she had the feeling that Rachel Miller didn't want word of her presence at his flat getting back to her parents. In a way it was touching.

'I see. So Mattie was determined to come out on top in the divorce?' she prompted.

'Oh yes, you'd better believe it,' Anthea Varney confirmed. She fiddled with a long spiral-shaped earring, and her eyes became suddenly damp. 'I just can't believe she's gone. Who am I going to have lunch with now? We'd arranged to go away next weekend to one of these health-food spas. You know, for a bit of pampering and a massage by a Dolph Lundgren lookalike, that kind of thing. Mattie made sure they served cocktails at the bar — I mean eating salads is one thing, but going without a drink is something else.' She dabbed at her heavily mascaraed eyes. 'I'm going to miss her,' she added forlornly.

And Hillary believed her. She wondered if Anthea Varney had many other friends, but somehow doubted it. Which prompted her next question. 'Did Mattie have many friends?' she asked, and wasn't at all surprised when Anthea looked startled, thought about it for a moment, and then shook her head.

'No. I don't think so. It was always me, Vannie and Mattie at uni. We sort of fit, you know? But when Vannie married an Aussie and moved to the other side of the world, it was just us two.'

Interesting, Hillary thought. Why hadn't Mattie Jones made new friends? That's what most people did after leaving full-time education. You went on to a different world, with different rules, and different people. Perhaps she simply hadn't felt the need for friends. Or perhaps nobody wanted to be her friend. It made Hillary feel suddenly sad. 'So you don't know who'd have wanted her dead?' she asked quietly.

Anthea shuddered. 'No. Well, Barry, I suppose,' she said, looking at Hillary closely.

Hillary nodded, ignoring the silent request for information. 'Yes, we've already questioned Mr Jones, and his secretary,' she said blandly. 'Did Mattie confide in you about anything out of the ordinary? Did she ever complain of the feeling of being watched or followed, for example, or of receiving threatening letters or hate mail?'

'Oh no. Well, she was a bit paranoid about being followed, so she was always looking over her shoulder, but only because she thought Barry might do what she'd done and hire a PI. She was determined that his lawyers wouldn't get any naughty pictures of her to show the judge.' Anthea suddenly chuckled, showing deep laughter lines around the corners of her mouth. Crow's feet also appeared beside her rather deep-set hazel eyes, and Hillary guessed that she'd never laugh again if she knew how much it suddenly revealed her age. 'Perhaps that's why she was so coy about that weekend in July.'

Hillary's radar registered a distinct blip. 'Oh?'

Anthea waved a hand vaguely in the air. 'Oh, it was nothing much. Well, we'd had this long-standing arrangement to spend a week in Barcelona. You know, take in the shops, do a bit of café society, that kind of thing. We always take a week in July to go somewhere. Once we went to the Canaries, but it was too touristy.

We'd done Paris ages ago, so then we started picking a different European city each time.'

'Nice,' Hillary said, with a bright smile. And so it was. For some. The last time she'd been on holiday was three years ago. And that had been to Cornwall.

'Yes. Well, last month, she begged off,' Anthea said, still sounding somewhat aggrieved. 'When I pressed her, she said she was going away for a long weekend somewhere else instead, and we could always go to Barcelona in August. Well, I was a bit hurt at first, I can tell you, until I suddenly twigged. Well, she had to have got herself a man, right?' she said, when both Hillary and Barrington looked at her curiously. 'Why else would she put off our usual get-together? She denied it of course, but I could understand why. Until her divorce came through she had to be ultra-careful, didn't she? But I was sure she'd gone for a naughty weekend with a new fella.' She giggled suddenly, sounding shockingly young.

'Did she say where she was going?' Hillary probed patiently.

'No. But I got the feeling she wasn't going abroad.'

'And you have no idea who the man could have been?'

Anthea sighed, genuinely chagrined now. 'No. Mattie could be a secretive little cat when she wanted to be. And ferocious if you tried to cross her, let me tell you! When I tried to cajole a little info out of her, and I heard her voice get that edge to it, I backed off. But I know her type. He'd be younger than her, because she always said what was sauce for the gander and all that, and I know she'd think it funny to have a younger man now, after Barry left her for that tart. And he'd have to be well-off of course, or at the very least comfortable and independent. Mattie would never let a man sponge off her.'

Hillary wrote rapidly in her book.

'And he'd probably be dark. Barry was fair, but she'd always gone for the tall, dark and handsome type. That's why me and Vannie were so surprised when she settled on Barry. Course, we understood later. He made a real go of J&C Construction, allowing Mattie to buy that lovely place of hers. It had always been her dream to live in a big country house. Her father was a television repair man, you know,' Anthea said, as if it was something amazing. Which, in her world, it probably was. 'Mattie grew up in one of those little boxes on a housing estate somewhere. Can you imagine?'

'And you know nothing of her new lover?' Interesting though the information about their victim's early family life was, it wasn't as meaty as a new man.

'No,' Anthea said regretfully. 'But Mattie came back from her long weekend almost glowing.' And again she gave that annoying little-girl giggle.

'Was Mattie expecting a visitor yesterday morning, do you know?'

'No. She never said.'

'And she was much the same as usual?'

'Oh yes. Mind you, she'd been a bit tense for a few months now. But I suppose that was because the divorce was coming up and everything.'

Hillary nodded, and questioned her some more, but nothing new came to light. Apart from giving them a good thumb sketch of their victim's personality, lifestyle and habits, Anthea Varney had nothing else to offer them.

At the time her friend was being attacked, she'd been in bed with her husband, and Hillary, although she asked Barrington to check it out with the husband and neighbours, had no reason — yet — to doubt her.

Instead, she went back to her desk, giving serious thought to the victim's mystery lover. And how best to smoke him out.

CHAPTER FIVE

Hillary glanced across at Barrington, who was on the phone, arranging a meeting with Anthea Varney's husband. When he hung up, she leaned back in her chair.

'Keith, pretend you're a woman,' she said, making Barrington blanch just a bit. He shot her a startled, searching look, but she carried on without a quiver. 'And you want to arrange a dirty weekend with a toy-boy lover.' She knew he was gay, of course, but since he hadn't told her as much, she was not about to let him know that she knew. She understood only too well his reasons for wanting to stay in the closet, and wasn't about to put any pressure on him. Personally, she thought that his private life was his own affair, but she'd have been naive in the extreme not to know that it would affect her team, and team performance, if it became known. Frank Ross, for a start, would make the poor sod's life a misery. And she wasn't sure how Gemma Fordham would react either. So, for now, she was happy to keep the status quo.

'You're in the middle of a messy divorce,' she carried on, 'and you don't want to get caught. What do you do?'

'Book a room far away,' Keith said promptly. It was a typical, pragmatic response that made Hillary smile.

'Maybe. Or maybe you don't want to go too far. A long drive isn't necessarily something you want to have to put up with on a weekend break. It's tiring and boring. You want to get where you're going, and tuck into the strawberries and champagne.' Amongst other things.

Keith smiled. 'And it's not very exciting to sit in a car for hours on end,' he agreed wryly.

'Right. A little spice is always nice, and so the risk of getting caught, providing it's only a very *slight* risk, can add a certain piquancy.'

Keith swivelled his chair from side to side as he thought about it. 'Our vic liked the good life, so it would have to be a top class hotel.'

Hillary nodded. 'And somewhere close enough that she'd normally never think of bothering to go to but still somewhere with a bit of cachet and swank.'

'London?'

'Too noisy. Too crowded. Think seduction.'

'The seaside?'

'A dirty weekend in Brighton?' Hillary laughed. 'Not our vic's style, I think. No, I was thinking more in the region of the Cotswolds maybe. That's right on our doorstep, not too far to travel, but not somewhere you'd think about going to normally, if you lived so close.'

Keith nodded. 'Maybe the New Forest? That's only about an hour or so's drive away.'

Hillary nodded. 'Yes, maybe. Walks in the woods, feed the ponies. I want you to start running down her credit card receipts and transactions. See if you can find any for a hotel any time in July, even if it doesn't fit our bill. And get on to her phone records as well and start running them down.' Odds were more than good that Mattie Jones would have called her new lover on the mobile, even if not the landline. 'You're looking for anything that doesn't relate to business or any of the other usual things you might call on a day-to-day basis — specifically a lone male in a private residence. And hairdressers don't count.'

Keith grinned. 'Guv.'

* * *

Gemma Fordham parked her car barely a foot away from the Oxford Canal and climbed out. The tiny hamlet of Thrupp looked deserted, just as she'd hoped it would on a sleepy Thursday lunchtime. She could still smell the tang of antiseptic and the reek of formaldehyde in her nostrils, and took a long, sweet gulp of August country air.

The autopsy had been meticulous and gruelling. So many stab wounds. So much damage. Doc Partridge had been unable to pinpoint the exact killing lunge, since it could have been one of several, but cause of death was clear enough. At some point, the knife had entered the left ventricle of the heart, causing a massive bleed and an infarction. But the victim had lost so much blood, even if the killer *had* managed to miss the heart, or any other vital organ, she'd still have died from exsanguination. Time of death was still fixed between 7:00 and 8:00 yesterday morning. The victim had been in decent health otherwise — a non-smoker, her lungs had been in good shape, as had her liver and kidneys. So Matilda Jones had probably not been a heavy drinker. Her muscle tone was fair for a woman her age, which suggested a fitness regime, but she hadn't, according to Steven Partridge, been fanatical about it.

All in all, she should have lived to be ninety.

Gemma stood for a few moments in the warm sunshine, letting the chill of the morgue seep out of her bones, and thinking how good it was to be young, fit and alive. Then she turned and headed towards the little brick bridge that went over the canal, but under the main road into Kidlington. She walked for a few minutes before she began to feel a brief moment of consternation. The *Mollern*, Hillary Greene's narrowboat, was not there.

On her previous visit to the site, she was sure the boat had been moored only fifty yards or so from the bridge.

As a non-boat owner, she had no idea that any narrowboat was rarely left at the same mooring for any length of time. And for various reasons, Hillary Greene had moved the *Mollern* a number of times since Gemma's last visit. Once she'd motored up to Lower Heyford to make use of the facilities there to pump out her septic tank and fill her water tanks. Sometimes she moved because she needed to turn the boat around to head a different way, if she planned to take a short trip north. Sometimes she moved it just to find a shadier spot under some trees. In a midsummer heatwave, the boat could cook if left moored out in the full glare of the sun.

Although Gemma Fordham knew none of this, common sense told her that the *Mollern* couldn't be far away, so she carried on under the bridge and checked until the end of the line of boats, then turned and retraced her steps.

There must have been nearly twenty-five to thirty boats all told, and she saw the distinctive white, blue-grey and gold colours of the *Mollern* towards the back of the line, furthest from the village.

She glanced around casually before stepping on to the back of the narrowboat, but didn't see the curtains twitch on the boat called *Willowsands*, moored three up in the line.

Nancy Walker had lived on her boat for nearly a decade, and apart from a brief sojourn to Stratford-upon-Avon, had spent the majority of her time moored at Thrupp; it allowed her to trawl her favourite fishing grounds — Oxford University — for the young, clever and handsome men she preferred. Once before she'd seen this tall blonde woman on Hillary's boat, and knew from Hillary who she was, if not what she was after.

She'd become firm friends with Hillary Greene long before she knew the curvaceous brunette was a cop. Hillary's occupation had surprised her, but not totally dismayed her (she was careful to smoke pot only when Hillary wouldn't be around to smell it), and the friendship had gone from strength to strength. So when she'd mentioned to Hillary some months ago that she'd seen this Amazon of a blonde on her boat, Hillary had told her something of the story. Namely that she was her new DS, who'd almost certainly had a brief and probably disastrous affair with Hillary's late and extremely unlamented husband, and was definitely 'up to something.' Nancy suspected that Hillary knew exactly what that something was, but since she hadn't told her, Nancy didn't pry.

She'd have stood no prying into her own private life, and certainly no censure of it, and she liked to return the favour to her friends.

So, now she watched, curious and alert, as the blonde woman bent down, and Nancy guessed she could only be fiddling with the padlock to the *Mollern*'s only door. Then she reached for her mobile phone.

Gemma Fordham pushed in the small silver key and twisted it. Her fingers tingled because it refused to turn, and it sent a brief shockwave of near pain up her hand. She swore, shook her hand, and tried again, a little less hard this time.

The key still refused to turn.

She tried it the other way, although she knew that padlocks didn't open that way, and, of course, encountered further obstruction. She removed the key and tried it again. Nothing. She put the key in, then pulled it out a tiny fraction again, knowing that sometimes padlocks could be tricky.

No luck.

Eventually she pulled the key out and stood staring at the padlock. Her mind whirled for another explanation, but, of course, there was only one that made sense.

Hillary Greene had changed the padlock. Why?

Gemma felt a nasty chill creep down her spine, and once again felt paranoia nibble at the back of her scalp. Once or twice before, she'd caught — or *thought* she'd caught — Hillary Greene looking at her with knowing eyes. And now this.

Why else would her boss change the padlock unless it was because she suspected someone had been on her boat? Gemma took a deep steadying breath, and shook her head. OK. Perhaps she had, but that didn't mean she knew who it was. Copper's instinct might have warned her that her home had been invaded, but she wasn't bloody psychic. And she'd put enough villains away in her time for it to have been any number of ex-cons with a grudge. Get a grip, Gemma snarled silently at herself. You're imagining things.

Still, she stared at the key in her hand, and dithered.

Perhaps she was making more of this than need be? This was not any normal front door, after all, where a lot of effort would have to be made to change the locks. This was just a simple padlock job. Perhaps Hillary had simply fumbled the lock one night and lost the padlock over the side. It was easily done — a bit too much to drink, a passing craft tipping the boat to one side when she was opening the door, and hey presto, the padlock dropped out of her hand into the cut. And she was hardly likely to go fishing around for it, was she? Not in that murky, khaki-coloured stuff. No, she would have just gone out and bought another padlock, simple as that. They were cheap enough.

Telling herself that she was happy with that explanation, Gemma thrust the key back into her bag and jumped off the back of the boat. One thing was for sure — she was going to have to be careful. She didn't want Hillary Greene for an enemy. At least, not until she'd got what she came for and was well on her way again. She was still frowning to herself as she walked past Nancy Walker's boat. Back in her car, she started the engine.

She was being daft. After all, the alternative to all this was that Hillary Greene knew *exactly* who Gemma was, and what she was after. And if *that* had been the case, then Hillary would already have kicked her backside out of the team with a boot that would have made Beckham envious.

No. She'd just have to get another key made for the new padlock, that's all.

* * *

Hillary Greene listened to Nancy Walker's breathless greeting and sat quietly as she launched into a somewhat excited monologue. At her desk, she listened to a step-by-step description of her sergeant's activities, and when she was finished, smiled grimly.

'It's OK, Nance, she can't get on the *Mollern* again. I've changed the padlock.' She thanked her neighbour for her vigilance, promised to bring back a bottle of her favourite Chablis for them to drink that night, and hung up. And promptly wondered why Gemma had wanted to get back on the boat.

She must have given it a thorough going-over last time, which meant that she must have learned something new about Ronnie's dirty money since then.

But from where? Or whom? She doubted that Ronnie's first wife would have known anything, or would have talked about it if she had. But Gary was a different story. And it had been Gary who'd brought his father's book to Hillary from his old Bicester nick.

She glanced at Keith Barrington, then got up and went to the ladies' loo. Once it was empty, she took out her mobile and called her stepson.

Gary was pleased to hear from her, and assented readily to a drink sometime soon. Mention of her new DS brought forth a light, breezy response that told her instantly she was right. Gemma Fordham had pumped him for information. Gary was never offhand unless he was lying. With a vague semi-promise of meeting up in her local pub sometime that weekend, she hung up and went back to her desk.

* * *

In a small semi-detached house in the middle of Thame, a man searched methodically in a cupboard for an old personalized telephone and address book. He was sure it wouldn't have been thrown out, but added to the lumber of useless junk that 'might come in handy one day' and got stuffed in various caches around the house. Today he was glad of his wife's hoarding instinct.

The number of the man he wanted to contact would almost certainly be discontinued by now, but with it he might be able to persuade BT to track him down.

If not, there might be other numbers not out of use, belonging to members of his old team who might know where he could get in touch with the Mascot.

The Mascot could get him what he needed.

He finally found the old book wedged in at the back of an odds-and-sods drawer and called the number. It was, as he'd expected, answered by someone he didn't know, who told him that the person he wanted hadn't lived there for over four years. But he gave him a forwarding address. The fact that the new phone owner still had it after all these years only went to prove to the man that his wife wasn't the only one who kept worthless objects 'safe.'

He wrote it down, thanked his anonymous friend and hung up. Then, clutching the slip of paper in his hand, he walked out into the hall and paused at the bottom of the steps, listening intently. Nothing stirred. He couldn't even hear the sound of bedsprings creaking as his wife turned over in bed. Good. The pills the doctor had given her were working. With luck, she'd be unconscious for hours yet.

He walked to the front door and opened it, stepping out into a glorious day that he didn't notice, and walked briskly towards his local library, where they'd have reverse directories. Now that he had the address, he'd soon have the Mascot's new phone number. And after he'd got that, he could use the regular directory to find the location of his nearest gun club.

It was time to practise now. Time to brush up on old skills that were never really forgotten and hone them to perfection once more. It was time to get ready. It was time for the cops to pay.

* * *

Barrington rubbed his hands across his tired eyes and looked at the printed copy of the document again.

His stomach rumbled, telling him it was getting on for lunchtime, but he still had too much to do before eating. The trouble was, staring at a computer for hours on end, and talking on the phone to try and persuade faceless company watchdogs who 'valued customers' privacy' to hand over 'confidential' documents, took it out of you. After a while you began to hear a ringing tone in your head, and your vision blurred.

Now he reached for the coffee pot and poured himself another jolt of caffeine, and rested his eyes for a moment, before once more picking up the copy of Matilda Cartwright's birth certificate. Yes, the father and mother had the same name all right. He'd asked the database for any other hits with those names, and the printer had spewed one out. Now he looked at it again, just to make sure.

Yes. Fiona Jane Cartwright. Same mother, same father. Matilda Jones's younger sister. Had to be. He then found the listing in the census register, blinking his tired eyes to make the tiny print swim into focus again. FJ Cartwright, 18 Cheadle Close, Chipping Norton.

'Guv,' he said, glancing across the table, catching first Gemma Fordham's eye, then that of his boss. 'Those initials FC on the letters. Our vic had a sister, Fiona Cartwright. She lives in Chippie.'

He'd learned the local colloquial name for Chipping Norton from a PC in Traffic who lived there, and he was glad of the opportunity to use it now. It showed them all that he was fitting in, learning the beat, becoming a local. Frank Ross yawned, clearly unimpressed.

Hillary's eyes narrowed. 'I remember someone telling me Mattie had a sister that she didn't get on with.' She clicked her fingers. 'It was Barry, the hubby. He said Mattie never even invited her to the wedding.'

'But her own sister?' Barrington said doubtfully. 'Why would she write nasty letters to our vic?'

Hillary shrugged. 'Maybe she didn't.' There had to be hundreds of people living in Chippie with the same initials. Then again . . .

'Why don't we go and ask her?'

* * *

Chipping Norton stood on high ground. So high in fact that Chippie could have a few inches of snow in the winter, whilst the rest of the county merely made do with frost. It was regularly quoted by the weatherman as being the worst hit when rain or hail storms were passing, but right now the small market town looked happy dozing under a mellow midsummer sun.

Hillary always admired the huge factory on the outskirts of the town that had once represented a massive commercial endeavour, but which had long since been converted into luxury flats. Still, the sight of it — so massive, and with the tall chimney tower standing defiant — always roused feelings of respect. Nestled in the gently rolling hills, she imagined children saw it as a princess's castle.

But there was nothing magical about Cheadle Close. Right on the far north side of the town, it was a small estate of inevitable post-war council houses, and formed a semicircle with a litter-strewn green in the middle. A lone willow tree planted inside it looked very unhappy. A dog, lying under the shade of it, barked at them lethargically as they drove past.

Hillary counted down the houses — they ran in a straight order — and nodded to Keith to pull over. Number 18 was easily the worst-kept house in the close. She got out and looked around, hearing a dull roaring of traffic over to the left. Town or distant motorway? She wasn't sure. She could pick out the now privately owned residences at once. Most had well-kept gardens, neatly maintained fences and hedges, and were painted in various shades of cream and other pastels, whilst those still belonging to the housing association that had taken them over from the council were still the grim, depressing grey of the original render. At some point, PVC double glazing had been installed in those still rented out, but that was the only thing of worth on number 18. The garden was a mass of wild rampant squitch grass, nettles, thistles and a scraggly bush that might once have flowered, but was now over. The paving stones leading to the front door were cracked and uneven and weed-strewn. The door, once a deep shade of bottle green, now showed the original wood underneath, and it looked uncomfortably warped, as if the previous winter's rain had swollen it and left it bent permanently out of shape.

Hillary pressed a finger to the doorbell but heard nothing. It was obviously broken. She reached for the knocker, a plain black pitted iron thing, and rapped it down hard. After a few minutes, she heard the stirring of noise from inside, and a curtain in the front window twitched.

Silence again.

Hillary sighed and rapped the knocker again.

Still nothing.

'Keith, go around the back,' she ordered wearily. She waited until he'd disappeared from sight, then banged again, time after time, making it clear that she wasn't going away.

Eventually a voice from inside called petulantly: 'I don't want nothing. And I don't want to talk to no Jehovah's Witnesses either.'

Hillary took a step closer, putting her mouth up to the letterbox. 'We're police officers, Miss Cartwright. We just need to have a few words.'

Keith came back to join her. 'Locked up round the back, guv.'

Hillary nodded, then stood back a pace as she heard the sound of the door catch being clicked back. The door opened with a jerk, confirming Hillary's guess that it must stick. The woman holding on to the jamb peered around it — and one eye looked at them warily.

'If you're here about our Kevin, he's been going to school regular. It's summer holidays now, any road.'

'We're not truant officers, Miss Cartwright,' Hillary said patiently.

'Oh. If it's about our Jean, then she didn't do nothing. Men like to give her money to have a good time with, nothing wrong with that, is there? Our Jean's a pretty girl. Why shouldn't she have a good time?'

Hillary sighed. One juvenile delinquent for a son, and a prostitute for a daughter. And no partner in sight to help out. At this rate, she'd never talk her way past the front door.

'It's not about any of your children, Miss Cartwright,' she said patiently. 'We're here to talk to you about your sister.' The door began to shut, and Hillary stepped forward smartly, to prevent it from actually closing.

'Here, you can't do that!' Fiona Cartwright's voice, muffled but shrill, called from the other side. 'I know my rights. You got a warrant?'

Hillary, once she felt the pressure on the other side ease, relaxed a little, and nodded to Barrington, who'd stepped forward to help her, to back off.

'I don't need a warrant to talk to you, Miss Cartwright. Now we can either do this here and now at your home, which'll only take a few minutes, or I can send for a squad car, and we can do this at Kidlington, which will probably take all day. It's your choice.'

There was a moment of silence, indicating a brief internal debate, and then the door reluctantly opened, letting the daylight spill in, illuminating Fiona Cartwright more fully.

Hillary saw a woman who looked about ten years older than their murder victim, although she already knew from their birth certificates that Mattie Jones had been, in fact, three years older than her sister. Fiona was scrawny rather than lean like her sister, and her black hair was rapidly turning to grey. It was also long and uncut. Her skin had the yellow tinge of a dedicated smoker. Only the dark green eyes were the same. Hillary had noticed the victim's eyes from the photograph Barrington had copied. They hadn't been open whilst she'd lain dead in her large black and white hall.

Now those same eyes looked back at her from this woman's face, wary and hostile. 'Come on inside then if you have to,' she said grudgingly. 'Don't hang about giving the neighbours something more to gossip about.'

Keith shut the door behind him, and they found themselves squashed together in a tiny, rather smelly hall. Against one wall, a set of stairs led off, covered in green lino. The same lino, filthy underfoot from all the dirty shoes that had tramped across it, led through a doorway and carried on into what was a tiny kitchen.

Fiona Cartwright opened the second door that led into a small living room. The lino here was beige and patterned in squares and circles. A couple of rugs broke it up. The furniture was old and sagging, the art on the walls strictly of the charity-shop variety.

'I won't ask you to sit,' Fiona said flatly. 'This ain't a bloody hotel. So don't expect no cups of tea, neither. Tea bags cost money. So what the hell do you want then?' she asked pugnaciously. She stood beside an old-fashioned fireplace, the original 1940s installation, and Hillary thought how ironic it was that such things were now coming back into demand. She wondered how long it would be before the housing association would cotton on and come and take it out and install her a 'new, better one.' She was almost tempted to tell her about it. No doubt it would be levered out in a flash by the absent Kevin, and sold to somebody running a dodgy second-hand stall. But it would probably only go on booze or cigarettes. So she kept quiet.

'When was the last time you saw your sister, Miss Cartwright?'

'Her? Years. Why?'

Hillary blinked. 'You haven't read the morning papers?'

'Don't have papers. Papers cost money.'

It was, Hillary realised, a common litany in this household. Keith hadn't been able to find a listing for her in the phone book either, and now she knew why. Phones cost money. 'Radio?'

Fiona Cartwright snorted and glanced around. 'You see a radio? We got the telly — and that's rented. We go to the pub for music and stuff.'

Hillary could well believe it. Anything to get out of here. It felt damp and depressing even in the middle of summer.

'Your sister was murdered yesterday morning, Miss Cartwright,' Hillary said quietly.

Fiona Cartwright jerked. She looked at Hillary, then at Keith, as if seeking confirmation, then promptly folded her hands over her chest. She was wearing a pale green dress with a hand-knitted cardigan, and when she thrust her hands under her armpits and hunched forward a little, Hillary recognised the gesture immediately. Defensive. But the news, she was sure, had come as a surprise.

'Well, thanks for telling me,' Fiona muttered. 'If that's all, you can go.' She moved towards the door, but neither Hillary nor Keith moved with her.

'We have one or two questions for you, Miss Cartwright.'

'What? Why?' Her head reared back and she retreated to the fireplace, where she thrust her chin out belligerently. 'I already told you. I haven't seen Mattie for years. Don't ask me who'd want to do her in. I expect there were plenty, though.'

Hillary smiled. 'Really? Like who?'

Fiona shrugged, and tucked her chin back in. 'Dunno,' she mumbled. 'It weren't me, though, so why don't you bugger off, hey?' In spite of the language, her tone was more pleading than aggressive. She looked longingly at a cupboard under the telly, and Hillary guessed it housed alcohol of some kind.

'We'll be going soon,' Hillary said quietly. 'Where were you yesterday morning, from six o'clock onwards?'

'Six bleeding o'clock?' Fiona laughed. 'I was in bed, wasn't I? Where do you think I was? I heard our Kevin get up about eight. He made himself some cornflakes and was gone by about twenty past. I got up, cleared up after the lazy bugger, and had some toast. My daughter spent the night with friends, like. Then I went down to the shop, the greengrocer on the corner. I work mornings there. You can ask the Paki who owns it.'

Barrington winced.

Hillary nodded. 'Do you have a car?'

'You having a laugh?'

There was, Hillary knew, no train service, but a bus wasn't out of the question. But to get to Bletchington, Fiona would probably have to take one to Oxford, then change there. And it was unlikely that any would be running early enough for Fiona to get to Bletchington by seven in the morning. But she'd get Frank Ross to check. He could also ride the route and, with the help of a photo, see if any of the regular passengers or drivers recognised her. It would keep him out of her hair for another day or two at least.

'You said before that there were probably plenty of people who'd like to kill your sister? If you haven't seen her in years how do you know that?'

Fiona laughed. It was a grim, bitter laugh that again made Barrington wince.

'Leopards don't change their spots, do they?' Fiona said.

'Meaning?'

'Meaning our Mattie was a right conniving, thieving, selfish cow. She was when she was a kid, she was when she was a teenager, and no doubt she is now.'

'Is that why you wrote her those letters?' Hillary asked softly, and Fiona's large green eyes widened. Then she flushed.

'Don't know what you're on about. And now I want you to leave. Right now. Go on, sod off. I ain't having you in here no more. This is my house.' The words were born of guilt at being found out, and maybe temper as well.

Hillary nodded at Barrington to retreat. She knew people like Fiona Cartwright when they were in this sort of mood. Flushed with a self-righteous sense of grievance, and an instinct for self-preservation, they would get nothing further from her. Instead, she went back into the filthy hall and, once outside, the door slammed shut. But whether in anger, or simply the need to make the warped door close, she wasn't sure.

Walking slowly back to the car, she called Frank and told him what she wanted him to do. 'You'll have to get over here and take a recent photo of her first,' she warned him.

She heard him mutter, and knew she'd been right to prompt him. Left to his own devices, the lazy bugger wouldn't have bothered. 'Oh, and while you're at it, you can get a warrant for a sample of her writing, then ask the handwriting experts to compare it with the letters found in our vic's jewellery case.'

For unless she was totally barking up the wrong tree, she was sure that the victim's sister had indeed been sending her threatening letters.

The question was — had she followed through on her threats?

CHAPTER SIX

Hillary stood in line in the canteen queue and eyed the offerings with a sigh. She selected, with some reluctance, a herb omelette and salad, and resolutely kept her eyes away from the lasagne and chips. It was nearly two o'clock, and the canteen was emptying rapidly when she took a seat near the windows. The table, she saw, hadn't been used and was pristine, with none of the usual splotches of ketchup, smears of mayonnaise or scattering of crumbs. Then she noticed that all the tables lining up at the windows were in the same clean state, and realised that nobody had wanted to sit at them. They made too clear a target. Her lips twisted grimly.

No doubt about it, the sniper killer was beginning to get on her wick.

She sat down, feeling the familiar creeping sensation of near fear that tried to tug the scalp off her head, and refused to move. A couple of tables in, she saw two uniformed constables staring at her and whispering, and sighed. She was damned if she was going to move. If she got shot, they could just bloody well put something apt on her headstone. Something along the lines of what a stupid twit she was would do it.

She dug into eggs that were not quite so rubbery that she could patch a tyre with them, and reached for a newspaper on the table off to her left, which somebody had obviously abandoned. It was the *Sun*. Rapidly, she put it back. She was not that desperate for something to read.

She'd almost finished the last of the limp, slightly warm lettuce, when she noticed Barrington push his way through the door. He didn't look in the mood to eat, and when she saw his head begin to swivel, scanning the room to catch sight of her, she quickly picked up the last cherry tomato from her plate and bit into it. She was already gathering her stuff together to go when he spotted her.

'Guv, I think I've found the hotel our vic used for her dirty weekend,' he said by way of greeting as she walked towards him. Hillary nodded, shrugging into her jacket. 'It was in the Cotswolds, just like you said. Bourton-on- the-Water, in fact.'

Hillary knew the Gloucestershire village well — even though it was much beloved of tourists, and would normally have been a place she'd avoid like the plague. But she liked to visit the Birdland sanctuary there, where she especially appreciated the birds of prey. It also had a trout farm incorporated into it, and feeding the huge, silent fish had sometimes been a therapeutic way to wind down after a stressful day.

'OK. Name?'

'The Cloverleaf.'

'You can drive.'

'Guv.'

* * *

The Cloverleaf Hotel was not in the centre of the village itself, but right on the outskirts, almost closer to the neighbouring RAF village of Little Rissington in fact. But it had spectacular views overlooking a verdant valley, and large gardens complete with ornamental lake and roses galore. A sign, as they swept up the gravel path, gave it an AA four-star rating.

'Very nice,' Hillary commented, as Keith parked Puff under the shade of a weeping silver birch tree.

'Judging from the charge made to her platinum credit card, it should be,' Keith muttered sardonically. This was just the sort of place Gavin would have liked to stay in. Growing up the son of a wealthy entrepreneur father, Gavin liked a lot of things that Keith had never experienced. Fast sports cars, luxury cruises abroad, Cowes Week, the opera, you name it. And being in places like this, somewhere Gavin would take for granted, but which was so far out of Keith's budget that it might have been on another planet, only brought home to him what an odd couple they really were. And now, with Gavin's father facing trial on additional charges of fraud plus income tax evasion, as well as the smuggling of artefacts, Keith suddenly felt even more insecure than ever. Sooner or later, Gavin was going to demand that he leave the police force, if they wanted to stay together. Keith just knew it. And what would he do then?

'Constable?' Hillary said sharply, and Keith shot her a startled look, flushing when he realised she'd said something and he'd missed it.

'Never mind,' Hillary said shortly, and led the way towards the main entrance. Wide, shallow stone steps, done up in a half-shell motif, led up to a set of glossy bottle-green painted doors complete with gleaming brasswork. On a sunny August day they were stood open, and Hillary stepped straight into a lushly decorated foyer. The tiles underfoot were terracotta, but interlaced with little azure and deep green squares. The walls were a paler wash of cerulean blue, with splashes of accentuating colour. A woman on the oak reception desk glanced up at them, a professionally welcoming smile on her face.

Hillary wiped it off instantly by showing her ID card. 'Police. We just need to make a few inquiries. Nothing you need to worry about.'

The receptionist wasn't taking any chances, however, and buzzed through to the main administration office, requesting the presence of a Mr Phibbs.

Bernard Phibbs came quickly, and introduced himself as the under-manager (no doubt the actual manager was off on a golf course somewhere). He was a tall, lean, effortlessly elegant man. 'Inspector Greene?' he read her name off the card she held up. 'How may I be of help?'

'I want to inquire about a guest you had here, from the twentieth to the twenty-third of July inclusive. Her name was Matilda Jones.' Hillary got straight to the point. There was something about Mr Phibbs's smile that was making her feel antagonistic. Not that it showed on her face, which was as bland as his own.

Bernard Phibbs nodded at the receptionist, who retook her seat and tapped on the computer keys. She scrolled down a few screens, reading carefully, then shook her head. 'Sorry, we had no guests of that name during those dates.'

Hillary sighed. 'Fake name then,' she muttered, more or less to herself.

'Not Smith, guv,' Keith Barrington grinned.

'No. You got her credit card number there?'

'Yes, guv.' He pulled the relevant information out of his pocket and read the digits to the receptionist, who diligently typed them in, pulled up a different screen, then nodded.

'Mr and Mrs Fox. Registered two thirty that Friday afternoon. The Kingfisher suite. Ordered the special breakfast for their stay, papers—'

'Can you print me off a copy, please?' Hillary interrupted. 'Also, do you have records of any phone calls they made?'

The receptionist, a smart forty-something with an ash-blonde pixie-like haircut and triangular face, looked to the under-manager for guidance, and Phibbs visibly hesitated. 'We do, of course, have an obligation of privacy towards our guests, Inspector Greene. I'm sure you appreciate that?'

'I do, Mr Phibbs,' Hillary said, hoping the man wasn't about to tell her any. 'But Mrs Jones was murdered yesterday morning, so I doubt she'll be complaining to anybody about you giving out her relevant details.'

The receptionist bit her lip, and Bernard Phibbs blinked. 'Well, in that case of course. Amanda,' he turned to the other woman, 'I'd like you to give Inspector Greene and the constable everything they ask for.'

'Yes, Mr Phibbs.'

'Can I see the register please?' Hillary asked, stepping closer to the desk.

'Certainly.' The receptionist turned back the pages to the relevant place, and turned it around to face her. Hillary ran a finger down the line of names, and paused.

'They registered as a Mrs M and Mr T Fox,' she noted, and Keith quickly jotted it down in his notebook. Hillary smiled a thanks, and pushed the big leather-bound volume back towards her.

'We won't need to keep you, sir,' Hillary carried on smoothly, guessing that they wouldn't get anywhere with the staff with the intimidating presence of Phibbs hovering around. 'We'll only need to question a few of your people, those who served the, er . . . Mr and Mrs Fox that weekend. We'll be discreet,' she promised, before he could even open his mouth to ask. 'Your current guests won't even know we're here.'

At this, he relaxed a little, nodded graciously and withdrew. The way he did it reminded Hillary of the character Jeeves from the PG Wodehouse novels, and she wondered how they managed to teach that air of dignified obsequiousness at training college. Or did you have to be born with it?

'Were you on reception when Mr and Mrs Fox booked in, Mrs Reid?' Hillary asked, reading the name tag on the receptionist's dark blue jacket.

'Oh no. That would have been Janice. She's serving behind the members' bar this afternoon. We rotate duties, you see. That way, if ever we're short-staffed or someone calls in sick, we can cover for each other. If you'd like to go through the lounge, the members' bar overlooks the tennis courts.'

Hillary thanked her, and headed off in the direction of her pointing finger. The bar, at this time, was largely deserted, but the smell of real wood, leather, and expensive cigar smoke still hung in the air. Hillary sniffed, wondering if the guests at the Cloverleaf had ever heard of the non-smoking rule in public places.

The woman behind the bar was dressed in the same dark blue jacket and skirt as the receptionist. She had unnatural but striking Titian tresses done up in a bun on the back of her head, and a pleasant face, which smiled at them as they approached.

'Yes, sir? Madam?'

'Nothing for us, thank you,' Hillary said, once again showing her card. 'Don't worry, just a few routine questions,' she added, when she saw the smile begin to waver. Janice Bostock, as her name tag declared, had dark brown eyes and brows, and she looked around quickly as Hillary and Barrington sat on two of the bar stools.

'It's all right, Mr Phibbs gave us permission,' Hillary said, correctly guessing the reason for her unease. 'I understand you were on duty here from the twentieth to the twenty-third of July.' She waited while Janice mentally counted backwards, then nodded.

'That's right. On reception.'

'Do you by any chance remember a Mr and Mrs Fox, who checked in for a long weekend?' It was, Hillary knew, probably a long shot that she would — people in the leisure industry must see thousands of people pass through their manor, and remembering a pair of faces from the hoard was almost certainly asking too much. But to her relief, Janice nodded almost at once.

'Oh yeah! Fox by name, fox by nature.' She smiled. 'Well, he was. Like something out of a Hollywood movie, you know? Mind you, she was a bit of a pain. Glad I wasn't her waitress or chambermaid, I can tell you. She was the sort who always had to find fault with something — one petal on one rose in a huge flower arrangement was withered or something. You know the type?'

Hillary nodded sympathetically. 'Like that, huh? What else can you tell us about them?'

'Not a lot,' Janice said automatically, then really thought about it, and shrugged. 'She paid, I noticed that. Usually it's the man who coughs up with the old credit card, but not this time.'

Damn, Hillary thought. If Matilda paid for the room, she'd bet even money that she paid for everything else as well — all the drinks, and extras. Probably felt safer that way. Although she obviously wasn't the sort to let a man sponge off her, Mattie Jones must have decided, just this once, that it was safer to have the payments on her card. That way, if any nosy divorce lawyers or PIs came sniffing, there'd be no paper trail leading back to the man in her life.

'You say he was good-looking?' Hillary prompted.

'Oh yeah. I mean *really* good-looking.' Janice grinned. 'You don't see many men who are that nice on the eye, not in real life. But he was a hunk. About six feet tall, lean, dark — almost black — hair, and dreamy blue eyes. Slight cleft in his chin, everything.'

Hillary nodded. 'So if we got a police artist to sit down with you, do you think you could bring his face to mind well enough for him to get a good likeness?'

Janice Bostock frowned. 'Well, I suppose so,' she mumbled, looking from Hillary to Keith doubtfully. She didn't seem able to make up her mind whether to be alarmed or excited. 'Why, what's he done?' she asked.

'Perhaps nothing at all,' Hillary said blandly. 'But we need to speak to him.'

'Oh.'

'Anything else you can remember about them?'

Janice sighed. 'He was younger than her — mid-thirties I'd say. She was well preserved, though, know what I mean?'

'Yes.'

'And they could both play pretty good tennis. Sometimes, when things are slow around here, we watch the guests if they're on court. He was a fair athlete.'

Hillary nodded. 'Did you catch his first name?'

Janice opened her mouth, then closed it again. She smiled. 'You know, it's funny, but now that you mention it, I can't say as I ever did. She always called him darling, or sweetheart, or something like that. And he called her . . . oh, what was it now? He used a name, I know, I mean a specific, proper name, but I'm damned if I can think of it. Something rather ordinary, nothing like Camilla or Daphne or one of those sort of names that women like that usually have.'

'Mattie?' Hillary offered quietly.

'Yes! That was it. Mattie. Of course, mats!' Janice snapped her fingers. 'That reminds me.'

Hillary looked at her sharply. 'Mats? He called her Mats?'

'What?' Janice asked, startled, then smiled. 'Oh, no, no, it wasn't that. It's just, I was in here once, helping out at the bar, and he mentioned something about the mat. Sorry, I mean rug,' she quickly corrected herself, and nodded towards an impressive marble fireplace. 'See the original rug over there? He knew what it was. What it was called, what it was made of, even the name of the pattern.

I remember him telling her about it. She seemed unimpressed until he mentioned how much they sold for, then she took more notice. I remember thinking how funny it was for a hunk like him to know about mats. Rugs, I mean. And then when he called her Mattie, it sort of stuck in my mind.' She looked at Hillary hopefully, like a retriever coming back from the woods with a strange, unidentified bird. Not a pheasant or a partridge, but was it interesting? 'Maybe he was one of those interior designer chaps — you know, like you see on telly, doing makeovers for rooms?'

Hillary nodded. 'Thank you, you're doing very well,' she encouraged. 'I don't suppose they were particularly friendly with anyone else staying here at the time?'

'Oh no. Those two were wrapped up in each other and nothing else.'

Hillary sighed. 'All right, thank you. Keith, arrange for the artist to come and speak to Ms Bostock would you, at a convenient time for both?' She nodded to him to follow her and they wandered out through the open patio doors on to a large tennis court. Tubs of flowering geraniums lined the paved areas around the outer netting, but there was no one on court at present. 'Then, once you get a likeness have it distributed to the local papers. You know the sort of thing: "Have you seen this man?" And make it clear we only want to talk to him as a potential witness. No point in spooking him.'

Keith nodded.

'And make the rounds of the staff here. Find out if our mysterious Mr Fox ever used his credit card to pay for anything. I think it's a long shot, but we can't afford not to check up on it.'

'Guv. Shall I do it now?'

'Might as well, I have a few phone calls to make.'

Keith trotted off back inside, and Hillary pulled out one of those ubiquitous, but oddly comfortable, rounded white plastic chairs, and reached into her bag for her mobile. She dialled HQ and got put through to her own desk. It was answered quickly.

'DI Greene's desk.'

'Gemma. I want you to try and trace a Mr T Fox,' she said, by way of greeting. 'It's almost certainly an alias, though I wouldn't be surprised if the initial is right.' She paused for a moment, and shrugged. 'If you find any hits of a man in his early to mid-thirties, six feet tall — give or take a couple of inches either way — with very dark hair and blue eyes, follow up on it and see if any of them admit to being in the Cloverleaf Hotel with our vic on the twentieth to twenty-third of July last. Got that?'

'Guv,' Gemma said, without enthusiasm.

Hillary smiled wryly and hung up.

* * *

They got back to HQ at just gone four. As expected, Keith had had no luck in finding any member of staff at the hotel who'd even so much as caught sight of the hunky Mr Fox's credit card.

As she walked back to her desk, Danvers followed Hillary across the large open-plan office, and she gave him a quick but thorough rundown on the state of the investigation so far. As ever, Paul Danvers listened, quietly impressed and finding no reason for complaints.

'Sounds as if it's coming along,' he said, when she'd finished.

'Yes, sir.'

'Before you go, sir,' Gemma said, as Paul made moves to leave them to it, 'I'd like to invite everybody to dinner at my place this Saturday evening.' She smiled briefly, catching Keith's and even Frank's eye. 'I'm fully settled in at last, and Guy has been hinting about meeting my co-workers for some time. I'm a fairly competent cook, so I don't think you need to worry about your digestion. I thought Saturday night would be a good time for everyone — that is, unless something breaks on the case, of course.'

93

Danvers glanced across at Hillary, who shrugged. 'I'm free,' she said drily, and something in the way she said it made his heart leap. Had she ejected Mike Regis for good then? He hoped so. Oh yes, he certainly hoped so.

'So am I,' he said quickly. Even with all the gang present, a dinner out with Hillary Greene was something to look forward to.

'Yes, fine,' Keith said. 'Thanks, Sarge.'

'Frank?' Gemma said, and saw him give her a surprised glance.

'Yeah, OK,' he said, evidently surprised to be included. 'Ta,' he added, somewhat belatedly. Free scoff, after all, wasn't anything to be sniffed at. 'Bring a bottle, should I?'

'I'll be serving wine,' Gemma said flatly. Frank nodded, as if he'd known that all along and was only being polite.

'Right, I'll let you get on, then,' Danvers said and Hillary reached for the latest batch of reports, her lips twitching. Unless she guessed wrongly, Gemma Fordham had only issued the invitation because she expected, as those raised in a polite society do, that her dinner invitation would be reciprocated at some point. And Hillary was sure Barrington, at least, would push out the boat and make an effort to return the invite sometime soon, but Gemma Fordham would have a long wait in a very hot place indeed before she was ever invited on to the *Mollern.*

Gemma took her seat and did a quick double take. Was her boss smiling? She shot her a closer look, almost willing to swear she'd seen Hillary Greene's bottom lip twitch. But when she looked again, her boss was reading the latest forensic findings with a poker face.

Telling herself not to be paranoid, she began her hunt for the elusive Mr Fox.

* * *

Hillary managed to leave the office at a reasonable hour for once, and the town's church clocks had just finished tolling six when she pushed her way out the door. As usual, the car park was deserted. She was just about to set off across no-man's land, when she heard footsteps behind her. She turned and smiled. 'Hey, Mel.'

'I'll walk you to your car,' her old friend said, nodding across at the desk sergeant, who watched them go without much interest. Mel Mallow and Hillary Greene had been friends for donkey's years, so there was no gossip to be had there.

'Is this out of concern for my safety, or do you want something?' Hillary asked drily, as they set off across the forecourt. As usual, the spaces closest to the building were chock-a- block, whilst the spaces right out on the edges were all but empty. Only her old Volkswagen Golf, Mel's sporty Mazda, and one or two other hardy souls had parked further away.

'You know me so well,' Mel said drolly. A pair of sparrows were fighting in a yellow-flowering hedge, and out on the pavement she could hear children riding micro-scooters and shrieking with laughter. If it wasn't for the fact that she half expected to go down under a barrage of rifle fire at any moment, it would be a pleasant evening.

'What's up?' she asked, slowing down as they approached her car. She fished absently in her bag for the keys, then leaned against Puff's driver's door when she had them in her hand.

Mel, hands thrust down into his pockets, sighed. 'It's Janine,' he said finally, looking around, but seeing nothing interesting other than a wood pigeon perched on a telephone wire overhead.

Hillary bit back a quick retort. They hadn't been married six months yet. They couldn't be on the rocks already, surely? But what Mel said next totally took the wind out of her sails.

'She's pregnant.'

Hillary blinked, then blinked again, then managed a tentative smile. 'Well, that's good news, isn't it?' Or was it? Mel already had grown-up sons from his first marriage. Now, about to face the big five-oh, was he feeling too old to be a dad again? 'It is for me,' Mel said, promptly dispelling that particular theory. 'But I don't think Janine's exactly ecstatic.'

No, she probably wasn't, Hillary thought, picturing her blonde, ambitious, immature former DS.

'Thing is, I think she might be thinking of, you know, getting a termination,' Mel went on with a rush. 'I was hoping you'd talk to her for me.'

'Me?' Hillary squeaked, her voice going up into the stratosphere. 'Why me? You know we weren't ever really on those sorts of terms. I was her boss, yes, but she never really liked working for another woman, you know that. And it's not as if we had long cosy chats in the ladies' loo.' Cagney and Lacey they weren't.

'I know, I know,' Mel said testily. 'But she's always looked up to you. Trusted your judgement. And she hasn't really been at Witney long enough yet to get really close to anyone. And I don't think she's got the sort of relationship with her mother that would be of any help at a time like this. Oh hell, Hill, I just think she needs another woman to talk to. Help her get things in perspective, you know?' Mel wheedled.

Hillary did know. Mel wanted her to talk his wife into having a baby. It was useless. Hopeless. Janine would snap her head off and eat it for breakfast if she even tried, and who could blame her? She opened her mouth to tell her pal all this, caught the look of misery in his eyes, and sighed heavily instead. She saw his look change to one of hope and she shook her head helplessly.

'OK, Mel, I'll call her. Invite her for lunch or something,' she muttered. And that was *all* she was going to do. Have lunch. If Mel thought she was going to interfere in things that were strictly best kept out of, he had another think coming.

'Thanks, Hill. I know you'll help her see straight.'

Hillary watched him walk jauntily over to his car, and shook her head again. 'Men,' she muttered. The buggers simply had no idea.

* * *

The next morning Hillary awoke with a vague feeling of doom hovering over her. It took her a few moments to yawn and ease herself into the day, before she remembered her promise to her old pal. Muttering to herself, she took an ultra-quick shower, brushed her teeth, reached for a dark maroon two-piece with a pale pink blouse, and got dressed.

She told herself she didn't need breakfast, and ignoring her rumbling tummy, reached for the coffee jar. She flicked on the radio and spooned some instant into a mug, searching her fridge for milk. Someone further along the towpath was frying bacon. The bastard.

She came out of the fridge, not with milk, but an overripe pink grapefruit, which she cut in half, returning one half to the fridge and putting the other down on the table. She was just reaching for a spoon to eat it with, when the music — some tuneless pop ditty — came to an end and the familiar theme music to the local news came on.

It was the top story, of course.

The sniper killer had struck again — this time, far too close to home, in the town of Abingdon. Not twenty miles away. Hillary sat down with a bump, as the newscaster's voice, an accentless female announcer, swept on: 'Police have identified the latest victim as Superintendent Malcolm Gorringe. His family have been notified. Superintendent Gorringe was killed while arriving for an early meeting at Abingdon's Oxford Road police station. His wife and two grown daughters are being comforted by family members. '

Hillary put the untouched grapefruit back in the fridge and drank her bitter black coffee in bitter black silence.

The sniper killer was obviously escalating his campaign, taking less and less time between victims now. And Abingdon was so damned close. She rinsed her mug and set off along the towpath, dreading her arrival at HQ, where, given human nature, they'd no doubt already be suffering from a siege mentality.

* * *

As expected, it was eerily quiet when she pulled in to her usual spot on the outskirts of the parking lot. The law of averages said it was now exceedingly unlikely that the sniper killer would be set up and ready to pick off anyone at Kidlington — given that just a few hours ago he'd been bringing death to Abingdon — but she still felt queasy as she forced herself to walk steadily across the parking lot.

Inside the foyer, it was a lot noisier. Groups of uniforms and plain clothes stood in huddles, everyone talking. The desk sergeant instantly beckoned her over.

'Hey, DI Greene. Heard the news? They reckon the bastard made a mistake this time. I've got this mate who has a mate who has a brother who works out of Abingdon.'

Hillary nodded, knowing how the grapevine worked, and how surprisingly accurate it could be when you dealt with groups of people who'd been trained to deal with information properly. All around her she heard people falling quiet as they listened, although they'd no doubt already heard the desk sergeant going on about it.

'They say they got a witness who saw a bloke getting into a van. He was carrying a long bag — you know, like plumbers use. One of those things you need to hold something long and thin.'

'Got a number plate?' Hillary asked sharply.

'Partial, they reckon. And a description. If it's true, the Abingdon lot'll have him before long. You see if I ain't right,' the desk sergeant predicted grimly.

'I hope you're right,' Hillary said, her voice heartfelt. 'Superintendent Gorringe,' she added quietly. 'He got anybody here at HQ?'

The desk sergeant cottoned on at once. He knew that the job tended to run in families, and as they spread out it was more than possible that the latest victim of the sniper killer might have some relative or close friend here at Kidlington.

'Haven't heard anything yet, Hill,' the desk sergeant said sombrely.

'Well, if you do, tread lightly, yeah?' she said and heard someone shifting around behind her. It was now utterly silent in the large foyer.

The desk sergeant sighed. 'Yeah.' Hillary nodded, and headed for the stairs. She already felt tired, depressed, and still just a little sick to her stomach.

And the day hadn't even started properly yet.

* * *

In Thame, a man withdrew a lot of money from his bank. He saw the cashier give him a strange look, then saw one of the floor managers come across and talk to her. As he did so, a quick look of pity crossed the cashier's face.

So they knew what had happened already. But so what? He was beyond caring now. Let the whole damned world pity him if it wanted to.

He walked out and crossed the street, catching the number 5 bus. It took him, eventually, to the bus terminal where he got off and found a greasy spoon café. He ordered a full English breakfast, then sat staring at it as it congealed on the plate. A few minutes later, he sensed someone approaching his table and glanced up. A man slipped into the chair opposite and pinched a sausage off his plate.

'Hello, Clive. You look bloody awful, mate.'

The man shrugged. 'You look the same as ever, Mascot.' Clive was not sure why the guys in his old unit called Rear Gunner John Wilkins 'the Mascot.' He certainly looked like nothing of the kind. He wasn't cuddly, or cute, or even interesting. He looked, instead, like what he was. Brutal. Trained. A big-boned, flat-nosed, dead-eyed man with iron-grey hair and scarred knuckles. Perhaps they called him the Mascot for the same reasons that giant-sized men got called 'Tiny.'

'Surprised to hear from you after all these years,' the Mascot said, taking another sausage and munching it. A film of grease spread across his thickened lips, and, disgusted, Clive quickly looked away before the other man could see it. The Mascot had been the regimental boxing champion, back in the old days, and it wouldn't pay to get on his wrong side. Even now.

'You still in?' Clive asked, and the Mascot laughed.

'No, worse luck. Got in on the Gulf War first time round, but then I was mustered out. Missed the second show altogether. Pity that.'

Clive nodded, but without much interest, and leaned forward, dropping his voice to a bare whisper. It was pure habit — the café's only other inhabitants were eating their own food, reading newspapers and paying them no attention whatsoever. 'Thing is, I need a piece of equipment, Mascot,' Clive said. 'You know — a specialized piece of equipment.'

The Mascot picked up a piece of bacon and chewed it thoughtfully. 'The kind you used to handle?'

Clive nodded. 'Yes. Just like I used to handle.'

The Mascot's grey eyes narrowed slightly. 'I know a bit about your trouble, mate. You sure you want to go this route?'

Clive shot him a quick, hard look. 'Look, if you can't provide the goods . . .' he began, and the other man reached across and picked up the salt. Just that. But it clogged the words in Clive's throat to a choking silence.

The Mascot poured salt on the cold egg, then reached for the last piece of bacon and dipped it in. His fingers were now shiny with grease. 'Course I can fit you out,' he said flatly. 'Still got loads of contacts from the old squad. But it won't be cheap. Especially with the Old Bill in a palaver like they are. Sniper rifles ain't exactly easy to move right at the minute, know what I mean?' The Mascot smiled widely, revealing two missing teeth.

Clive nodded.

'But, yeah, I can get it for you,' the Mascot said. 'As I say, it'll cost yah.' Clive reached into his pocket and half withdrew a great wad of cash. The Mascot looked at it, unimpressed, and nodded.

'Yeah. That'll do for a down payment.'

CHAPTER SEVEN

Keith Barrington and the police artist arrived at the Cloverleaf Hotel bright and early, and were shown to a small, now obsolete smoking room that had been hastily but tastefully converted into a small library. Either none of the hotel's guests was feeling very literate that morning, or the management had deliberately steered them away from it, because the room was mercifully empty. What's more, they were promptly served extremely good coffee, on a tray, with sugar in a silver bowl and everything.

When the smiling waitress had left, PC Trevor Drudge looked at the porcelain cups as if they were a species of nearly extinct animal and whistled. 'You lot in CID have it cosy, dontcha?'

Keith grinned. 'Oh yeah, it's like this every day. Shall I pour?' He was just adding milk to his own, when Janice Bostock came in. She smiled at Keith and nodded, then cast a quick, curious look at Trevor. She'd never imagined she'd ever be asked to do anything like this, and was patently nervous.

Trevor smiled back reassuringly. After leaving school, he'd spent three years at art college and earned his BA, but had quickly decided he'd never be the next Damien Hirst and had joined the police force, more or less for a laugh. It had certainly made his fellow graduating students guffaw. Of course, he wasn't laughing now, after three years in the service, but sitting in a fancy hotel with a pretty girl and a drawing pad on his knee certainly beat riding around in a panda car, looking for trouble.

'Hello, I don't know if I'm going to be any good at this,' Janice introduced herself, sitting down next to Trevor Drudge, who smiled at her again over his coffee cup.

'Nothing to it, dar . . . er, madam,' he said cheerfully. 'You just describe the man you saw, and I try and draw him. Then you have a look and say, "No, that's wrong," or, "His chin's a bit more square," or what have you, and after a while, we'll have a likeness of this Mr Fox chap. OK?'

Trevor wasn't quite as good-looking as he thought, and he had, at the moment, a pimple on his chin that he was trying to hide beneath a bit of sticking plaster disguised as a shaving cut, but Janice wasn't fussy. At least he was tall and skinny, and had good teeth. Keith Barrington watched them flirt a little and decided to let them get on with it. Despite his youth and somewhat idiosyncratic way of working, Trevor was good at this part of his job, and more often than not came up with a good likeness of the man or woman they were after.

They started with the shape of the face — long, with a square chin, apparently — and progressed to the hair. As they worked, Keith questioned the witness lightly about the weekend Mattie Jones and her lover had spent at the hotel, and managed to tease out a few titbits that she hadn't mentioned before, but it was nothing earth-shattering. After about half an hour of solid work, Trevor began to hum, a sure sign that things were going well.

* * *

Hillary glanced up, surprised to see Frank Ross wander in at just a little after 9:30. He was even dressed in a clean suit, and had shaved. She watched him sit down behind his desk and reach for a file from his in-tray.

Wonders, it seemed, would never cease.

A few moments later, he grunted, and wheeled his chair over to hers. 'Documents, guv,' he said, not indicating the folder in his hand, but referring to the department that dealt with all matters paper. If you suspected a forged signature or you wanted handwriting experts to give something a once-over, you sent it to Documents.

Hillary took the folder and ran her eyes over the various reports. The letters found at Mattie Jones's house had been given a thorough examination, as had a piece of Mattie Jones's own handwriting, which had been included for elimination. It wasn't unheard of for people to write themselves letters, usually due to some kind of psychotic or stress-related incident. But Hillary didn't believe anything like that had happened here, and it was the first thing she checked. She was right. The handwriting was not Mattie's own.

They'd even included a personality reading on the victim's handwriting, just for good measure. Somebody, she mused with a smile, had been on a course, and was just itching to try out the latest theories. Hillary was always somewhat sceptical that a boffin could look at a line of writing and tell you all about the author, but she imagined that life in the labs couldn't be that much fun, and who was she to rain on anybody's parade if they came across an opportunity to do something a little out of the norm? She read the report with a pinch of salt, nevertheless, but in this case, they seemed to have hit it spot on. As well as confirming that the author had been right-handed, the report concluded that the writer was: 'almost certainly female, approximately 40–50 years of age, reasonably well-educated.' More technical terms about the upright strokes of Ts and loops on Ps, and so forth, led the expert to conclude that: 'the writer is very methodical and organised, with a strong sense of self-worth and preservation.' Hillary smiled grimly. That sounded like their murder victim all right. 'The subject also shows signs of being narrow-minded and self-absorbed. This may lead to the subject's inability to assess danger or pick up on, and accurately interpret, the signals of others.'

Hmm. Getting into the realms of fantasy there, Hillary thought, but then shrugged. Or maybe not. Mattie Jones certainly hadn't seemed to realise that somebody wanted her dead. They'd come across no signs that indicated that she'd known she was in danger — no recently reinforced doors or newly installed window locks. No personal alarm gizmos or pepper spray canisters. So perhaps the boffin had it right. She'd simply been too engaged in enjoying the good life to realise that she'd hurt or pissed off somebody enough that they wanted her dead.

She turned the page, and saw that the piece of Fiona Cartwright's writing that Frank had secured was half shopping list and half to-do list. Naturally, there were no complete sentences, no punctuation or anything else of much use.

Plonker, she thought grimly, and read the analyst's report with interest: 'Despite the somewhat scrappy contents of the specimen sample, in my opinion, this was definitely written by the same hand as the following letters, labelled A–F respectively . . .'

Hillary flipped the page over, to check that the letters referred to were in fact the threatening letters they'd found at Mattie's house, then went back to the report.

'Again, the writer was a woman, maybe a few years younger than that of the murder victim, but I would say with a considerably lower IQ. The author of examples A–F has low self-esteem and anger issues.' Again Hillary read, without fully understanding the complications arising from Ss that leaned to the left, or the significance of uncrossed

Fs and open-ended Ds, before cutting to the summary: 'The author shows signs of depression, but also, in direct and somewhat baffling contrast, a growing sense of euphoria.' In conclusion, the expert advised, somewhat drily, that the investigating officer might like to consult a mental health expert when questioning this witness.

Hillary grunted and tossed it all back to Frank, who read it with his habitual sneer. 'Shrink, my arse,' he finally said, making her mind boggle for a few seconds, before she realised that he was, in fact, talking about the likelihood of Fiona Cartwright getting her own private psychiatrist to sit in on any subsequent interview.

'Bring her in,' she said curtly.

* * *

Keith Barrington, clutching his newest acquisition, made his way from the Cloverleaf to Osney Mead, the home of several Oxfordshire newspapers, where he distributed the triumphant result of Trevor Drudge's artistic endeavours. It was, he had to admit, a masterly piece of sketching. Unlike some police-issued e-fits, which would have made Frankenstein's monster blanch, this was a sensitive, clever drawing of what looked like a real flesh-and-blood man. Even the editors he approached, begging for an inclusion of it in their next issues, looked impressed. One even thought he knew the man, which made Keith's heart flutter, until he was told the man in question was gay, and only five feet two.

He did the rounds of other newspaper offices not located in the city, then headed back to HQ. When he went upstairs, only Gemma Fordham was at her desk, busy working on updating the Murder Book. When she saw him, she nodded. 'Good, you can help me with Mattie Jones's background check,' she said. She caught him looking at Hillary's empty desk and chair, and smiled grimly. 'She's interviewing Fiona Cartwright again. Apparently she did write those letters to her sister.' She filled him in on the handwriting report, and saw the flicker of disappointment in his eyes when she told him Frank was sitting in on the interview. She knew how it was. He'd been in on the initial interview with the sister, and wanted to follow it up. Well, life wasn't like that. She wasn't totally without sympathy for him, but it was part of her job to toughen him up. 'I've got as far as the vic's divorce proceedings on her hubby. You can take her solicitor if you like.'

'Right, Sarge,' Keith sighed, and punched the law firm's name into the database. He doubted that Mattie Jones's divorce lawyer had been driven to taking a knife to her out of sheer frustration, but you never knew. Their victim had doubtless pushed her solicitor hard, and would have demanded the results she wanted. It seemed to be her way of doing things.

And Hillary Greene wasn't the only one who was slowly becoming convinced that it was this hard-headed, narrow-minded vision that had got her killed.

* * *

Hillary Greene looked across the table at Fiona Cartwright and sighed. 'Would you like a cup of tea before we start?'

'No thanks,' the other woman said sullenly. She was wearing a dark grey skirt and a pale pink T-shirt, slightly frayed around the neckline. She wasn't wearing make-up and kept pushing a strand of greying hair back over her left ear as she talked. Her fingers drummed and fidgeted nervously on the table top, their ends nicotine-stained and shiny.

'I would, if I were you,' Hillary warned her. 'We're likely to be here some time, and you'll start getting dry after talking for an hour or so.'

Fiona Cartwright flicked a nervous green-eyed glance over her, then shrugged. 'I ain't got nothing to say, so I can't see that coming off,' she muttered belligerently, and glared at the NO SMOKING sign on the wall. 'What do you do if I light up? Arrest me?' she asked, then laughed. For some reason she seemed to find that really funny, and laughed for a long time.

Hillary let her wind down, wondering what it was. Booze? Possibly, but she couldn't smell alcohol on her breath. Drugs were possible, but she didn't quite have that manic twitch of the junkie coming down off a high. It could be down to sheer nerves. Or maybe she just had a peculiar sense of humour.

When she had finished laughing, Hillary took the samples of letters found at Mattie Jones's house and put them on the table. Even in their plastic protective sheeting it was obvious what they were, and Fiona eyed them like a wall-eyed horse spotting Becher's Brook after accidentally wandering into the Grand National.

'You may remember my sergeant here taking a sample of your handwriting away, Miss Cartwright?'

Fiona glanced at Frank, paled slightly, and glanced away again. 'Prick,' she muttered.

Frank smiled, not at all offended.

'Our handwriting experts compared it with these letters we found at your sister's place,' Hillary went on smoothly. 'Can you guess what they said, Fiona?'

'Couldn't care less,' the other woman responded instantly, sitting back in her chair and folding her arms over her chest, looking bored and sullen.

Hillary sighed, and leaned back in her own chair. This was going to be like pulling teeth. OK, time to try a new angle.

'Not that it's really surprising,' Hillary mused, 'that you hated her, I mean. Mattie was a gorgeous woman, wasn't she? Well groomed, graceful, clever.' Hillary let her tone become admiring. 'From the things people say about her, she turned heads wherever she went. It's hard to believe you're sisters.'

Fiona Cartwright flushed, and, as Hillary had expected, instantly took the bait. 'Huh! I'd be gorgeous too if I had thousands and thousands of pounds to spend on make-up and clothes and beauty treatments and whatnot.' She stopped abruptly, and shot Hillary a sly, considering look. 'Think you're clever, don't you?' she said. 'Getting me to talk and all that. I know you lot. I ain't as daft as people think. I may not have got O levels, like precious Mattie did, but I got O levels in life, that's what I got. Nobody cheats me or does me down, I can tell you. And I raised my kids the same.'

Fiona's face suddenly lit up in a beatific smile. 'That's something Mattie never had, ain't it? She never had no kids around her. Nobody to love her, to really care whether she lived or died. For all her fancy house, and her fancy car, and her 'flair for colour' and all her poncy words and faffing about . . .' She was almost shouting now, and once again she abruptly stopped, panting for breath. Then she looked at Hillary through narrowed eyes, and smiled. 'You won't find anybody who's sorry she's dead,' she said coldly, suddenly eerily calm. Then she reached into her bag and got out a packet of cigarettes. Hillary waited until she'd put it between her lips and flicked a lighter on, before reaching across and taking it from between her startled lips.

'Tell me what you meant in these letters, Fiona,' Hillary said quietly, laying the cigarette down on the table between them. 'Take this one, for instance.' She turned the evidence bags around and read from one at random. '"Don't think you're going to get away with stealing from me. I know what's mine by right, and I'll have it back. I'll have it all back." Now what, exactly, did your sister steal from you?'

Fiona blinked, and looked at her unlit cigarette, then back to her still flaming lighter, then back to the cigarette, then to Hillary, wondering if she dare pick up the fag and light it. She seemed to waver for a moment, then shrugged, flicked the lighter shut and put it back in her bag. After a second's thought, she picked the cigarette up also, and put it back in the packet in her bag.

All this was accomplished in a deadly silence. When she'd finished and looked back up, she seemed surprised to find both coppers watching her. She snorted a laugh. 'What?' She looked from Frank to Hillary, then snorted again. 'I ain't talking to you lot. Ain't you got that yet? I got nuffink to say.' She wiped her nose on the back of her hand then folded her hands under her armpits again.

Hillary nodded. 'You know, when I read that letter, I thought it might be from a disgruntled employee at first,' she said casually, although she'd thought nothing of the sort. 'You know, someone from J&C Construction. We knew that Mattie had worked as a sort of bookkeeper and staff manager. And I could just see her cutting some poor devil's benefit or sick leave or what have you. Maybe promising them a bonus for working late or hard, and then not following through. She had a tight grasp on money, didn't she, your sister?'

Fiona opened her mouth, then grinned a wide, Cheshire cat smile and wagged a finger in front of Hillary's face in a you-can't-get-me-that-way-again gesture. Frank shifted in his seat, obviously wondering if the handwriting boffin hadn't got it right after all; the woman was definitely renting out parts of her belfry to a bat colony.

Hillary, ignoring the finger in her face, carried on. 'Then I read some more of your letters, and I quickly realised that *that* scenario didn't really fit. It was much more personal than an employer–employee spat. This had real venom behind it.'

She pointed to another of the letters and read out loud. 'You think you're so clever, living in your millionaire's house, drinking those dainty little cocktails. But one day, one of them will choke you.' Hillary put the plastic envelope down, and frowned. 'But Mattie didn't choke, did she?'

'So you say.'

'Somebody stabbed her.'

'It wasn't me.'

'Somebody who really hated her. She was stabbed so many times, she left a pool of blood nearly twenty feet in circumference around her,' Hillary carried on, her voice soft, almost soporific now.

'Plenty of people hated her,' Fiona Cartwright snorted. 'Anybody who knew her, I bet.'

'Why did *you* hate her?'

'She stole from me.'

'What? What did she steal?' Seeing her witness's face start to return to her usual mulish expression, Hillary took a wild stab in the dark. 'Was it Barry? Was Barry Jones going out with you first?'

Fiona's smug grin grew into another Cheshire cat impersonation that culminated in another bout of hysterical laughter. By the time she was finished, she was flushed and panting again. 'Barry Jones? That loser? Give me a break. I wouldn't have looked at him sideways.'

'Hardly a loser,' Hillary pointed out. 'He gave your sister a fine standard of living, after all.'

'Hah! Just shows what you know,' Fiona crowed. 'He'd have been nothing without Mattie. She was the one who pushed him, and nagged, and got her way. Worked the poor stupid bastard until he dropped. No wonder he left her for his secretary,' she said, and began laughing again.

Frank Ross looked across at Hillary uneasily. Any more of this weird laughter and they'd have to call in the men in white coats to come and take her away. Hillary too glanced nervously at the silently whirling tape recorder, and could just imagine what a good defence lawyer would make of it all. But if they wanted to get to the bottom of all this, they had no option but to push on and hope for the best.

'Who told you he'd left her, Fiona?' Hillary asked quietly, and the laughter abruptly stopped. Fiona's brightly shining green eyes blinked.

'Eh? What?'

'Who told you your sister was getting divorced?' Hillary repeated patiently. 'From what you've said before, you never talked to your sister, never kept in touch, never even went to Bletchington. Both your parents are dead, and you have no other close relatives, so they couldn't have kept you informed. So how did you know she was getting divorced?'

Fiona licked her lips. 'You know, I will have that cup of tea now.'

Hillary nodded to Frank, and spoke into the recorder. 'DS Ross is leaving the room.'

They sat in silence for the three minutes it took Frank to come back with one of those white polystyrene cups that could make a 1962 claret taste like creosote. He set it down in front of their witness, as Hillary intoned for the tape, 'Detective Sergeant Ross returns at twelve thirty-two p.m.'

Fiona took a sip and grimaced. 'No sugar.'

Frank reached into his jacket pocket and withdrew a handkerchief, suspiciously crusted together in the middle, a lint-flecked roll of Polo Mints, a paper clip and a small envelope of sugar. He handed over the sugar, considered the Polo Mints, then opened them and popped one in his mouth.

Hillary sighed. 'Why don't you want to tell us what it is that your sister stole from you, Fiona?' she asked, with infinite patience. 'You know we'll find out in the end. This is the age of the computer, you know. The information highway and all that jazz.'

Fiona muttered something around her tea, then shrugged. 'OK, fine,' she snarled. 'We had this aunt, see, mother's twin sister. Married some rich geezer years older than her. When he died, instead of living it up and having a high old time, she remained a widow for, like, sixty years or something. You know the kind, a dozy old bat. Never went out, kept four cats, and scared the neighbourhood children silly on Halloween night by wiring up an electric buzzer to the doorbell. You know, gave the little sods a mild electric shock. Had you lot round to her, they did. Dozy old bat, should have been put away years ago.'

Hillary smiled. 'Sounds like you were really close,' she said drily.

Fiona Cartwright flushed. 'Yeah, well, me and Mattie were her only relations. Her hubby hadn't got any, and by the time she finally got around to popping her clogs even Mum and Dad had gone. So we should have got equal shares, right? In her will?' she asked, chin jutting out, her voice genuinely aggrieved now.

Hillary nodded, seeing it coming a mile off. 'But her will wasn't like that, was it?'

'No, it bloody well wasn't,' Fiona growled. 'She left everything to Mattie, didn't she? Course, most of the spending money was gone by then, but that wasn't the point. There was still her house — a big detached thatched cottage, with acres of old orchards and even a stretch of river with its own private fishing rights. Worth a bloody fortune, wasn't it, even all them years ago.' She paused, panting with sheer frustration. 'When the solicitor read out her will, I knew exactly what my bloody thieving sly bitch of a sister had been up to! The old lady even said it. "For all her tender care of me . . ." That's how she put it, silly old cow. As if Mattie had really cared about her. Bollocks, she cared. She just cosied up to her, calling in regular like, taking her boxes of bloody chocolates I dare say, and treats for those flea-bitten moggies of hers . . .' By now, Fiona Cartwright was on the edge of her seat, all but shouting into Hillary's face. Flecks of spittle flew on to the table top, and Frank Ross was also perched on the edge of his chair, ready to grab her if she became violent.

But Hillary remained seated, making no threatening movements of her own, and kept her voice level and calm. 'Your sister knew you were the only family she had left.' Hillary nodded. 'And made sure that she was the one who inherited. Clever, wasn't she?'

Fiona suddenly slumped back in her chair, mumbling, the fight gone out of her. 'She sold the cottage, right off, but not the land,' she said, yawning widely. 'By then she was engaged to marry Barry, and after the wedding she decided to build five bungalows on the site with the money from the sale of the cottage. Of course, she made Barry change the company name to Jones and Cartwright. But they sold them bungalows for another fortune, and then there was no holding her back, was there? But half of it should have been mine.'

Fiona Cartwright's tight, white, baleful face glared at Hillary Greene. 'Don't you see? Mattie had it all — and I had nothing. I had a shitty life, while she played the Queen of bloody Sheba. She never gave me nothing — not a helping hand, nothing. I could have rotted for all she cared.'

'Is that why you killed her?' Hillary asked softly.

And Fiona once more gave her that Cheshire cat look. It made the hair on the nape of Hillary's neck stand on end. No two ways about it; Fiona Cartwright was borderline crazy all right. But there was also something gleeful in the way she laughed. Something knowing. 'No, I didn't see her then, clever clogs,' she jeered. 'I was out shopping that morning before I went in to work. The local Spar shop, you just ask them. I always do my midweek shopping on Wednesday morning. It took ages for them to do my receipt at the checkout because of all the coupons I cut out. Amazing what offers you can get from the papers and stuff. They'll remember me all right.'

And Hillary was sure they would. But she remembered that Fiona had told them during their first interview that she'd gone straight to work. An obvious lie.

Hillary knew some people lied all the time, and often for no particular reason. For all her vitriolic, simmering hatred for her sister, there was a wild, repressed excitement about the woman that spoke of euphoria. Her hated sister was dead, and the cops weren't going to be able to touch her for it, because she hadn't done it. That was the vibe Hillary was getting from Fiona Cartwright, and she had the sinking feeling that this new alibi of hers was going to hold water.

'We'll take a break now, Miss Cartwright. Give you a chance to calm down. As I said at the start of the interview, you can have a solicitor present any time you want.'

'Don't need one,' Fiona shot back triumphantly. 'I didn't do nothing.'

Hillary nodded vaguely, and motioned Frank to follow her out. Outside, they both took a long, deep, much-needed breath. 'Bonkers,' Frank said in disgust.

Hillary sighed. 'Maybe. You had any luck finding anyone on the buses who saw her that morning?'

'No, guv. Not passengers, not the regular bus drivers. No one recognised her.'

'All right. Get down to her local Spar shop and see if she really was there, and what time she arrived. I doubt it'll be as early as the time the murder was committed, but even so. If she only got there at nine, nine thirty, we're going to have a hard job putting her at her sister's place an hour earlier. You're sure she doesn't have access to a car?'

'No,' Frank said shortly. 'Not only has she never had one, she can't drive either. Never passed her test. I checked with the DVLA.'

Hillary grunted. 'She's got two teenage kids, Frank,' she pointed out. 'Either one of them could have access to an old banger, and could have driven their dear old mum over to Bletchington that day, licence or not. I want you to put the fear of something into those two, and track down all their friends with access to a car. Check speed cameras, the lot. If there was any way Fiona Cartwright *could* have got to Bletchington that day, I want to know about it. And whilst you're at it, I think the nearest railway station to Mattie's house is in Tackley. Take a picture of Fiona to the village and show it to anyone you can find in the general vicinity of the railway.'

Frank muttered something grim, and shuffled off.

Hillary sighed, and went back to the interview room. But as soon as she saw Fiona was back to sitting with her arms crossed aggressively over her chest, and wearing that now familiar mulish look, she knew, with a sinking heart, that she wasn't going to get anything more out of her that day.

CHAPTER EIGHT

When Hillary got back to her desk, she pulled up the background check on Mattie Jones that Gemma was still working on, and read what they had so far. She was sure there'd been something that Fiona Cartwright had been hugging to herself gleefully, back in that interview room; maybe some sort of family secret, maybe some mistake Mattie Jones had made in her otherwise perfect life. She glanced across at Gemma and cleared her throat.

'Guv?' Gemma responded instantly.

'I want you to concentrate your research on our vic to her immediate family. Father, mother, and especially sister. Dig out any skeletons rattling in the family closet — interview their neighbours back at the old homestead, see what kind of dirt you can dig up. Leave the husband and his lover for a while; they'll keep. I got the distinct impression during my interview with Fiona Cartwright that there was something she knew that I didn't. And I don't like it.'

Gemma nodded. 'Guv.'

Hillary looked across as the door to the office burst open, and three uniforms from Traffic bustled in. 'Did you

hear? They've arrested him — they've got the bastard.'
The speaker was the oldest of the trio, a heavyweight, grey-haired man, and he was talking to Sam Waterstone, the sergeant whose desk was nearest the door.

'What? Who?' Sam asked, bewildered, then a huge grin spread over his face. 'The sniper?' he yelled, and the rest of the office gave up a ragged cheer.

'Yeah, Abingdon pulled him in at lunchtime. Got him from the partial van number and witness description. They've just put it out over the radio.' This time it was the youngest member of the group who spoke, a dark-haired sprog straight out of training college. 'Usual, "helping police with inquiries" line, but my mate, whose sister works out of dispatch at Abingdon, says they definitely reckon they've got him. The search warrant for his house has come up with ammo and everything. And they reckon they know where he's got the rifle stashed.'

The room began to buzz with excitement, and Hillary felt the tension in her shoulders slowly seep out. It puzzled her for a moment, because she hadn't realised she'd been so tense. But that was probably true of everyone. Now, it felt as if a steady, bearable, but nasty weight had been lifted from her shoulders, and it felt wonderful. She saw the same easing of movement from everyone in the office. Even Frank Ross managed a smile — which scared the chap behind the desk next to him.

For a while the talk was of nothing else, but eventually Hillary got back to work, and started by checking her emails. There a message awaited her from Janine Tyler, now Mallow, turning down her offer of lunch tomorrow, but saying she could probably meet her for coffee later on that day, as she had to conduct an interview in Yarnton at four o'clock. Hastily, Hillary sent off a reply, agreeing to a 3:30 meeting in the coffee shop in the big garden centre in the village. It would only take her five minutes to get there.

Opposite her, Barrington was following up on his notes, ticking off the little question marks that appeared in the margins as he cleared up possible loose ends. He frowned at one such loose end, wondering what he'd meant by: 'Crapping cat woman. Neighbour mentioned her car in garage. Follow up.'

He squinted at his shorthand notes, but was sure that's what they said. Crapping cat woman? His mind boggled for a moment, then he twigged. Of course. One of Mattie Jones's neighbours had fallen out with her over her cat getting into her garden. Who was it now? He turned back the pages of his notebook, feeling as if he should have the whole contents of it memorized by now, so often did he refer to it.

Vera Grearsley, that was it. He frowned, remembering now. It had been during the initial canvassing, on the first morning of the murder. There'd been a group of people congregating on the village green, talking about the latest sensation. He'd wandered around, listening, putting in the odd question, just absorbing the mood of the crowd. And someone, talking about something else, had mentioned that Vera Grearsley hadn't been able to take her cat to the vet that day because her car was in the garage.

Keith sighed, rubbing his eyes tiredly. So what? Why had he made a note to himself to follow it up? He went to the Murder Book to read Hillary Greene's notes on her interview with the woman, and suddenly realised that Vera Grearsley had said she was driving her car to work at the time Mattie Jones had been killed. Some story about showing a necklace to some Oxford don.

But how could she if her car was off the road? He smiled, nodded, and reached for the keyboard. Time to find out who Ms Grearsley insured her car with. From that, he could probably find the name of the garage, or mechanic, she used. And if she'd been caught out in a lie, his boss would want to know why.

* * *

Superintendent Mel Mallow looked up as his PA came through the door. Her normally smiling face looked sombre, and a worried frown tugged her eyebrows down in the middle. 'Sir, there's a phone call for you on line one,' she said, puzzling him even further. Why hadn't she just put it through? 'It's from DI Gregg, sir. I think it's bad news,' she added tactfully.

Mel groaned. The Myers case again. How much more bad news could there be concerning it? Already the police handling of the case had been savaged in the local press. He nodded grimly, and his PA withdrew, still looking troubled. He felt a shaft of acid indigestion lance through him as he put the receiver to his ear.

He was probably getting an ulcer. And no wonder, with this job.

'Gregg?' he said curtly.

'Sir.' The voice of the man who'd led the Myers inquiry sounded old and tired in his ear. He knew, as well as Mel, that this case would probably blight his career for years to come. 'It's Mrs Myers, guv,' Gregg said, coming straight to the point. 'She's taken an overdose — her husband found her this morning. She's in intensive care. Paracetamol, apparently,' he added flatly, needing to say no more. Most cops knew how bad a paracetamol overdose could be. Cruelly, most victims seemed to have a chance of recovery, but the damage already done to vital organs meant, all too often, that suicide victims died long after the actual desire to die had passed.

'Will she make it?' Mel heard himself ask, and realised at once what a bloody stupid question that was.

'I don't know, sir.'

Mel closed his eyes briefly, then opened them again. No point sounding off at Gregg. 'All right. Keep me informed,' he said curtly, and hung up.

He got up and walked to the window, for the first time able to do so without worrying about getting shot at. The scuttlebutt from Abingdon was coming in loud and clear — they'd got the sniper killer all right. The last phone call from a DCS over there had informed their chief constable that the rifle had been recovered, and ballistics were already working on confirming it. The man was a Yank, of all things, one of those hunters from the northwest who liked to kill deer then drape the carcasses over the hood of their cars. Exactly why he'd come to England to shoot policemen hadn't yet been established, but no doubt it would be soon enough.

But the view of the sunlit car park did little to dispel the sense of gloom he felt. The Myers girl was already in a mental home, unable to face the ordeal of coping with what had happened to her. Her rapists had walked free. And now her mother might be taken from her. What a mess. What a miserable, damnable mess.

He reached for the phone and dialled Hillary Greene's extension number.

Her breathless voice answered a good thirty seconds later. She had, in fact, been halfway to the door to leave. 'DI Greene.'

'Hill, it's Mel. You got a minute?'

'Actually I was just off to see your missus for a coffee,' she said, the faint reproof in her voice reminding him of the favour he'd asked of her. He felt his gloom deepen.

'Oh, in that case, don't let me stop you,' he said. 'And thanks.'

Hillary grunted something, then said quietly, 'Something up?'

Mel gave a dry laugh. 'It'll keep,' he said softly, and hung up. And went back to his now safe but unhelpful view of the outside world.

* * *

Janine Mallow, newly promoted to DI, looked up as her old boss joined her at the table. Janine had failed her Boards the first time around, when she'd worked under

Hillary, and she'd always felt, rightly or wrongly, as if she'd been forced to walk in the great woman's shadow. But now, holding the same rank at last as her one-time mentor, Janine felt none of the antagonism that Hillary Greene could sometimes engender in her. Instead, she noticed that her old boss had that tired, strained but concentrated look that she remembered of old. As she sat down opposite her, a black coffee in her hand, Janine smiled. 'Murder case?'

Hillary nodded and glanced around. The place was half empty, but probably not the ideal place to discuss a gruesome stabbing. 'Let's not talk shop,' she said wearily.

'Hear they got the sniper killer,' Janine said with a grin. 'About bloody time. Everyone at Witney's been acting so squirrelly, I've felt like bringing in bags of peanuts.'

Hillary laughed out loud. This was the Janine of old. Acerbic, confident, just slightly blinkered. 'Know what you mean,' she said, rolling her shoulders and sighing. 'It's nice to take a decent breath again.'

Janine nodded, stirring her cup of mocha, then glanced up at the older woman with a tight smile. This was the first time they'd met up since she'd left HQ, and she somehow didn't think Hillary missed the old days and wanted to catch up. 'Mel put you up to this, didn't he?' she accused flatly, and somewhat to her surprise, Hillary nodded.

'What the hell he expects me to do, I don't know,' she confirmed grimly.

Janine grinned. It was odd, talking to Hillary Greene as an equal, and not as a junior officer. It made her feel both reckless and almost resentful at the same time. 'It's none of your business, you know,' Janine said, taking a sip of her mocha, then grimacing. 'Hell, this is sweet. I don't usually have a sweet tooth.'

Hillary lifted an eyebrow and took a sip of her own bitter black brew. She could point out that pregnancy was famous for giving the mother odd food cravings, but doubted Janine wanted to hear it. 'Witney working out OK then?' she asked instead.

Janine shrugged and glanced at her suspiciously. 'Aren't you supposed to be giving me advice? You know, the older woman, steering me gently towards the right path?'

Hillary Greene grinned. 'The right path being the one a certain Philip Mallow wants you to follow?' And when Janine gurgled with laughter over her cup, Hillary grinned back. 'Sod him.'

Janine sighed and put down her cup. 'You know, it's not as if I don't want kids. I'm just not sure I want them now.'

Hillary nodded. 'You think there'll be plenty of time later. When you've had a few years of being a DI under your belt. Got a few good cases in. Showed the brass what you're made of, so they don't forget you during maternity leave.'

'Exactly,' Janine huffed. 'But try telling Mel that.'

Hillary nodded and took a sip of her drink. She could tell her that, sometimes, there wasn't enough time. Sometimes, it was already too late and you had to grab opportunities with both hands. But Janine was young, and well armoured, and still inexperienced enough to think nothing could hurt her.

After a moment, Janine looked at her. 'What? No two pennies' worth you want to put in? No words of wisdom?'

'As you said, it's none of my business,' Hillary muttered.

Janine laughed. 'I'll bet that's not what Mel expected you to be saying.'

'Mel's going through a hard patch,' Hillary said, and Janine pulled a face.

'The Myers case,' she agreed, instantly contrite. 'What a balls-up,' she added angrily. 'He's getting all the flack, and it's not even his fault. What the hell do we pay law clerks for if they can't even get a simple warrant right?'

Hillary could have told her that it *was* a superintendent's job to take the flack, but she doubted Janine wanted to hear it right now. Instead she leaned back in her chair and wondered what Fiona Cartwright was doing at this moment. If she did get some legal representation, it would be hell on wheels trying to re-interview her. Any brief worth his salt would start singing for a psychiatric evaluation the moment she opened her mouth. Then they'd have to have shrinks present, social services maybe, and the organ grinder and his monkey, as well, probably.

'It's not fair to expect me to put my career on hold just to make Mel feel better, right?' Janine's resentful voice pulled Hillary back from her gloomy thoughts.

'No,' she agreed shortly. 'But then, he's your husband. You might actually *want* to make him feel better.'

Janine blinked, opened her mouth to make some sort of comment about Hillary's less than saintly marriage to Ronnie Greene, and how she was hardly in a position to spout crap like that, then found herself closing her mouth, her words unspoken. For some reason, she couldn't quite meet Hillary Greene's eyes. 'You're thinking I should have the kid,' Janine said flatly. 'Aren't you?'

'Actually, I was thinking of ordering a slice of that coffee and walnut gateau,' Hillary said, looking over Janine's shoulder at the cakes adorning the glass counter by the tea urns. 'And what a bad idea it would really be.'

Janine laughed suddenly. 'But as an expectant mum, I can now order it and get away with it.'

Hillary blinked. 'Cow,' she said softly, and Janine began to laugh. It was then that Hillary knew her old friend had nothing to worry about. Janine would have the baby, and carp on about it, and generally make Mel's life miserable for the next nine months, but then, he was a man. He deserved it.

When she got back to the office, Keith had an air of badly repressed excitement about him. Noticing it, Hillary didn't even bother to slide her handbag off her shoulder, as Barrington leapt to his feet when she approached.

'Guv, I've found a discrepancy in a witness statement.' Succinctly he told her about Vera Grearsley. 'I've checked with the garage she uses, and her car, a Clio hatchback, was brought in two days before the murder of Mattie Jones. Apparently there's a big problem with the transmission. They say she won't be getting it back until after the weekend. They're waiting on parts.'

Hillary nodded and glanced at her watch: 4:45. No doubt most people would be thinking of clocking off work about now. The thought made her smile. She caught Frank's eye, who hastily turned away. He intended to be gone at five on the dot, no doubt.

'Right then, Keith, let's get back to Bletchington,' she said. She saw Gemma Fordham smile, and wondered vaguely how the blonde woman's search for her husband's millions was going on. She almost had it in her to wish her luck. Almost, but not quite.

* * *

Vera Grearsley was twisting two strands of silver together to form a Celtic knot when she realised the light from the open doorway had been abruptly cut off. She pulled back the tweezers quickly, knowing from bitter experience just how easy it was to make a hash of silver, and lifting the magnifying goggles from her eyes, she pushed them on to the top of her head in a gesture of habit.

She recognised the policewoman in charge of Mattie's murder inquiry immediately. 'Oh hello.' She got up from the work bench and joined them at the door. 'Let's have a seat.' She pointed to a wooden garden bench pushed up against a wall festooned with a dark purple clematis. Bees droned in the wild woodbine that was growing up a nearby fence post. Her garden was messy, blooming, and a wild creature's delight.

'Mrs Grearsley.' Hillary smiled briefly. 'I just want to clear up a few things. You told us before that you had to leave early the morning Mrs Jones was killed, in order to go to Oxford.'

'That's right.'

'To see a female don who wanted to buy one of your jewellery pieces?'

'Right again.'

'And, as far as you could tell, at around the period of time that Mrs Jones was killed, you were stuck in a traffic jam on the road to the city.'

'Again, yes. You know how the traffic backs up to that first roundabout?'

'We've since learned your car is off the road, Mrs Grearsley,' Hillary said, still in a pleasant, conversational tone.

Vera blinked. 'Right again.'

At this point, Hillary felt Keith Barrington stir in some agitation beside her. But, unlike the green young constable, Hillary wasn't so convinced that Vera Grearsley was playing silly buggers with them. Or even that she was being openly defiant.

'I was on the bus,' Vera Grearsley said. 'Sorry, didn't I make that clear?'

Once outside on the road again, Keith muttered something and blushed slightly when Hillary told him to confirm her story with the bus driver. 'And see if you can find any regular passengers who might remember her,' Hillary ordered. 'You'll find a lot of people who use the morning work bus have been doing so for years. They're as likely to remember a new face to the morning commute as not.'

'Guv.'

'And don't look so miserable,' Hillary advised with a smile. 'It was well spotted, the apparent paradox in her story. This time it didn't work out, but remember, it's details just like that one that sometimes break a case wide open.'

'Guv,' Keith said, far more happily now, and slipped into the driver's seat. Puff the Tragic Wagon turned over, coughed once — tragically — then died.

Hillary sighed. 'What was the name of that garage Vera Grearsley uses?'

* * *

Puff redeemed himself and started on the second try, but didn't sound all that happy all the way back to Kidlington, and Hillary resigned herself to having him overhauled, yet again. Although she could easily afford a new car, it simply never occurred to her to go out and get one.

Gemma Fordham was still at her desk when they got back, although the whole office was rapidly emptying. Most of the day shift were heading off to the local pub to celebrate the catching of the sniper killer, and Hillary received several offers to join them as she made her way across the room. Promising to drop in later, she'd just taken a seat behind her desk when her phone rang.

It was the desk sergeant.

'DI Greene, ma'am,' he said formally, letting Hillary know at once that there was a member of the public with him. He was never usually so polite. 'There's a lady here wants to talk to you about the Matilda Jones murder inquiry.'

'I'll be right down,' she said at once. She hung up, then nodded to Gemma to join her. Keith, somewhat gloomily, returned to his computer terminal in search of the bus company that would have run a service to Bletchington last Wednesday morning.

* * *

Marie Whitman looked around the interview room nervously. She was a lean, slow-moving woman, somewhere in her mid-fifties Hillary guessed, and she noticed she wasn't wearing a wedding ring. She was dressed in a powder-blue jacket and matching skirt, with a cream blouse, and had the look of a self-sufficient working woman. Not a high-flying career woman — but something steady and, in its own way, rewarding. Hillary could see her as the manageress of a flower shop, or something of the sort.

'You have information for us, Ms Whitman?'

'Yes. Well, perhaps. I mean, I don't know how important it might be.' Slightly myopic pale blue eyes looked at Hillary anxiously. 'I work at a dental surgery in Headington — I'm the office manager. I come through Bletchington every morning — I live in Tackley, you see.'

Hillary nodded, not really needing the details, but preferring to let the witness dictate her own pace.

'On Wednesday morning, I was particularly early. It's the annual audit, and . . . well, that doesn't matter.' Marie ran a harassed hand through her dyed, corn-coloured hair. 'I was passing the green at Bletchington, oh it must have been just before seven. Maybe even a quarter to. I didn't really take any notice — well, there was no reason to, was there, not at the time? But later, when I read in the papers about the murder there . . . well, it suddenly jogged my memory.'

Hillary nodded patiently. 'You saw someone?' She led her to the point gently.

'Oh no. I saw a car, that's all. Parked on the green,' Marie corrected her swiftly. 'There's nothing really unusual in that, I know. I mean, at that time of the morning, not everyone had already left for work. No, what caught my eye was that there was someone sitting in it, leaning sideways, as if peering through the passenger window.'

'Could you see what they were looking at?'

'No. Well, there was only the house. The murdered woman's house, I mean. The car was parked opposite it.'

'Could you describe the person in the car?'

'Oh no. I was gone and past in a few moments. I think it was a woman — but I'm not sure. I just didn't get the impression of the bulk of a man, if you see what I mean.'

Hillary nodded. 'Colour of hair?'

'Fair,' Marie said definitely. 'It's what showed up the most. And perhaps you think of women as being blonde more than men, don't you? Although why, I'm not sure.'

Hillary smiled. 'Can you describe the car?' she asked, and wasn't at all surprised by what Marie Whitman said next.

'I'm not very good with makes and models and that sort of thing. My nephew, now, had he been with me, could have told you everything from the year it was made to its horsepower, but . . .' Marie Whitman shrugged. 'It was white. And not huge — sort of like an Astra, or something that size.'

Beside her, Hillary caught the faintest of sighs from Gemma, and knew how she felt. A potential lead, at last, a solid sighting, and it was all but useless.

'Of course, it was the number plate that stuck in my mind the most, because of my sister,' Marie Whitman said, with a smile.

Hillary blinked. 'You remembered the number plate?' she asked, disbelievingly. The number of times she'd wished a witness could remember a number plate didn't bear thinking about. And always, but always, no witness ever did.

'Well no,' Marie said, and didn't understand why the policewoman gave her such a wry smile. 'Only some of it,' she carried on, determined to get it all out. It had taken her some time and some courage to come here, and now that she had, she wanted to unburden it all. 'Because of Anne, you see. My sister's name is Anne.'

Hillary blinked.

'And when I saw the car, I thought — well, it reminded me of one of those personalized number plates you can buy, and how good it would have been for Anne,' Marie burbled on, realising that she wasn't making sense, and beginning to feel like an awful fool. 'It had AN and then something else, numbers obviously, and NE at the end. Making out Anne. You see what I mean?' she asked hopefully.

Hillary heard Gemma scratching it down quickly in her notebook, and smiled. 'You're doing fine, Ms Whitman,' she soothed. 'Now, did you see this person — this woman, you think — get out of the car? Approach the house at all?'

'Oh no. Like I said, I was driving by. I just sort of noticed it, all quick, like. You know — white car, someone peering at the house from inside, and the ANNE thing. Just sort of flashed across my mind, and then I was gone past.'

Hillary nodded. 'It's been a couple of days now, Ms Whitman,' she probed gently. 'Did you not think of coming in with this before?'

Marie Whitman blushed. 'Sorry. But we've been so busy at work, I haven't had a moment to myself. Haven't read the newspapers much, or had the television on. But as soon as I remembered, I came straight here,' she added defensively.

'And you're sure it was Wednesday morning?' Hillary pressed.

'Oh yes. It was the beginning of the audit — don't worry, I haven't got the dates mixed up,' Marie said with a shiver. 'I dread the annual audit. I mean, I'm always ever so careful with the books, but all it takes is just one little mistake, and, well . . . the inconvenience and worry!'

Hillary thanked her, and saw her out, and Marie Whitman looked pleased to go. Hillary could have pressed her for more details, maybe even sat her down with PC Drudge, the police artist, to see if they could come up with a sketch of the woman in the car, but she knew it would have been pointless. Even worse, misleading. A witness, wanting to be helpful, would often make up things, all unawares, in an effort to be useful. And could subsequently lead an investigation up a blind alley.

'Well, the partial number plate will help,' Hillary said to Gemma, as they climbed the stairs back to the main office. 'And we've got the colour. See what you can find.'

'Guv,' Gemma said, a small frown tugging at her brows. As soon as she got back to her desk, she began rooting through her notebook.

Hillary nodded across at Keith. 'Call it a day, Keith. You might want to get up early tomorrow and catch the bus from Bletchington—'

'It's Saturday tomorrow, guv,' Keith pointed out, then bit his lip, realising he'd interrupted her. 'Sorry, guv. I've pulled up the timetable — it's not the same on weekends.'

Hillary nodded. Hell, she must be more frazzled than she thought — that should have occurred to her. 'Just talk to the bus driver then, and do the route on Monday morning.'

'Guv.'

He was just shutting down his computer terminal when Gemma Fordham gave a ladylike snort. Her rough, throaty voice sounded particularly pleased as she said, 'I thought so. That partial number plate, guv, I knew it rang a bell.'

Hillary lifted one eyebrow as Gemma Fordham, super-sergeant, grinned. 'Rachel Miller, the husband's new lover. Drives a white Megane. Licence number,' and she rattled off letters and numbers. The letters, when put together, spelled out ANNE.

'Well, well,' Hillary mused. 'That puts them right back in the frame. Bring the girl in tomorrow. Pick her up from her parents' place and make sure they see you. Don't let her ring Barry Jones,' Hillary ordered. It was time to rattle a few cages.

Gemma nodded happily. At last, things seemed to be moving.

CHAPTER NINE

Saturday morning, Hillary woke slowly. At first she felt a rocking motion, then a soft, low drone, and realised a boat was passing by, its gentle wake shifting the *Mollern* at her moorings. She rubbed her face and yawned, reaching out for her watch which she kept on the bottom of the narrow rim surrounding the round porthole of her bedroom window. It was just gone seven.

She sighed and rolled over, wondering if she should have brought Rachel Miller in last night. She'd sensed that Gemma Fordham had been surprised by her decision to wait until the next morning. But she'd been tired, as had her team, and sometimes it paid to be cautious. She didn't think Rachel Miller was going to go anywhere, and, at this point, didn't think speed was particularly of the essence. Of course, if Barry Jones's secretary-cum-lover had done a runner in the night, she'd be shuffling files in Records until her retirement.

That particular thought chased all possibilities of going back to sleep out of her mind, so she sighed and rolled up and over into a sitting position on the edge of the narrow bed. She knew Mike Regis had always hated her bed. No room to manoeuvre, he'd complained, his green gaze shimmering, the crow's feet appearing attractively at the corners of his eyes. She sighed once more and got up, took a quick shower and changed into a pair of tailored beige trousers and a bright amber blouse.

Padding along the narrow corridor to the tiny galley, she put the kettle on and popped two pieces of bread into the toaster. Tomorrow, it being Sunday and officially her day off, she'd have to take the boat to get the toilet tank pumped out, and fill the water tank. And she needed to recharge the generator. So much for a day of rest.

Perhaps Mike had a point. Perhaps it was time to get off the boat. After all, she'd only started living on the *Mollern* as a last resort, when she'd left Ronnie, and he'd been such a pain about selling the house. But now her old marital home had been long sold, and the semi-fortune it had sold for was doing nothing but accumulating interest in her bank account. She could easily afford to sell the boat and find herself a small bungalow somewhere. Or a two-up two-down cottage that needed a bit of TLC.

Then the toast popped up, and she reached for the Oxford marmalade. Her breakfast made, she took it and her mug of coffee to the tiny table beside the large rectangular window and sat down. Outside, the pretty pink rosebay willowherb flowers stirred on a late-summer breeze; gossamer of seed heads and spiderwebs floated out across the water, and in the field opposite, a combine harvester was kicking up a layer of dust as it gathered the barley and attracted an ever-growing flock of seagulls. Underneath her window, Barney, an Aylesbury duck, a white diamond amid a flotilla of brown mallards, quacked for his breakfast, and Hillary knew she wasn't going to be leaving the boat any time soon.

She absently patted the bulkhead nearest to her, as if she might have given her home a small fright by thoughts of abandoning it, and shook her head with a smile. She was going soft in her old age. She tossed the remains of her toast out the window to Barney, left Thrupp just before eight, and was at her desk by ten past.

The office was still quiet. Weekends could be odd at HQ — quiet, or filled with rioting football hooligans. It was calm when a lot of people opted to actually take their days off, or chock-a-block if there was a labour-intensive case on. This morning the building seemed almost peaceful as most of the officers working the case were out on interviews. A couple of uniforms were over in one corner, talking excitedly about the sniper killer, who had been officially charged last night. Ballistics, it appeared, had made a match on all five victims.

'I heard he was married to an English girl, who left him for a copper. That's what set him off,' Hillary heard one of them say, and grimaced.

Pity the poor sod who'd fallen for the wife then, Hillary mused. What was his life going to be like from now on, knowing that his private life was the cause of getting his fellow officers shot? She couldn't see the relationship with the killer's wife lasting, and she sure as hell couldn't see him staying in the force either. Even if he got more pity than recriminations from his friends and colleagues, guilt alone would probably make his life miserable.

She sighed and refilled her coffee mug, feeling vaguely depressed.

* * *

Hillary Greene wasn't the only one feeling that way. A few miles to the south, Keith Barrington sat down abruptly on the edge of his bed. He was still living in the small, rather dingy bedsit in Summertown that he'd first moved into on coming to Oxfordshire, and was finding it hard to move out. The university city, awash with students and the support system workers needed to prop up the giant education industry, made it a nightmare to find decent accommodation at a price a jobbing copper could afford.

But today it was not his surroundings that were bringing him down, but the voice in his ear.

'But, Gavin, you knew it was going to be hard going,' he said, hating the sound of whining he could hear under his oh-so- reasonable tone. 'And your father's a tough man, so if it doesn't bother him, why are *you* so mad?'

He heard a heavy, sardonic sigh filter down the phone line, and felt his stomach clench. When he'd left London — hell, was it only three or four days ago? — Gavin had seemed resigned to things. Now, Keith listened as his lover laughed grimly and felt his private life teeter on a knife-edge.

'I'm not my father, plod, as you might have noticed.'

Keith winced. Whenever Gavin used his not very affectionate nickname he knew he was in serious trouble.

'I expected to be playing in the Harrogate charity tournament this week. Not trying to support my dad against his vicious bloody so-called chums on the board.'

Gavin, young, fit, and a ferocious player, had long since harboured a semi-serious dream of turning tennis pro. Harrogate, as Keith had fast learned since becoming his lover two years ago, was a top-notch venue on the amateur tennis circuit. Wimbledon scouts and top-ranking trainers were always in attendance, looking for the next Andy Murray. And Keith knew how much Gavin had been looking forward to playing there. He'd been training hard, and had been over the moon to be invited to play.

Now this.

'Look, did they actually vote your dad off the board?' he asked quietly, and heard Gavin sigh ostentatiously.

'No, but only because they couldn't. Dad's got a massive load of stock, and he's been rallying around everyone who's loyal to vote with him. But what happens when the publicity really kicks in? When the trial starts, and his name seriously becomes mud, I doubt he'll survive another coup.'

Keith swallowed hard. 'Gavin, why does any of this mean we should take a break, as you like to call it, from each other? You're already living in London whilst I'm in Oxford — we can't take much more of a break from each other than that. If you want to break up, just bloody well say so.' He heard the hard edge of anger in his voice now, and felt like kicking something. Gavin maybe. Himself, certainly. It was a good job there wasn't a cat around.

'You want to split up, don't you?' He heard Gavin's accusing voice rise hysterically on the other end of the line, and closed his eyes in despair. What was it about Gavin Moreland that could tie him up in such knots?

'No, I don't,' he said flatly. 'You're the one who called me, remember, laying all this guff on me about "taking some space", whatever the hell that's supposed to mean.'

'You are such a Neanderthal!' Gavin spat. 'I'm going through hell, and this is all the sympathy I get?'

Keith laughed grimly. 'Gavin, your father's been caught with his hand in the till. If I know your dad, and I do know people just like him,' Keith said bitterly, thinking of all the businessmen who played the system and got away with it, 'he probably won't even be convicted. And even if he is, he'll be put in some cosy open prison somewhere and have a little nest egg salted away in Jersey or wherever for when he gets out. It's not the end of the world. Your trouble is you've always had it too easy. If you had to see—'

He heard the dialling tone drone in his ear, and slammed the phone down hard. Well, that was that. The writing had been on the wall for some time, he supposed. He felt like bursting into tears, something that horrified him. Gavin could weep and wail, but that had never been his way.

He got up abruptly and stepped over to the washbasin, forcing himself to wash and shave, then dress, then get in his car and go to work.

But he felt numb. Sick inside, and resentful. Why had he had to fall for a spoilt little rich boy anyway? He must have been out of his bloody mind.

As he got out of the car he wondered bitterly where the sniper killer was when you really needed him. Right about now, a bullet in his head would have been welcome. Then he felt instantly ashamed of himself for the self-pity that allowed him to think such a thing, and that in turn made him angry. He strode grimly into the foyer, ignoring the cheery greeting of the desk sergeant, who, despite a monumental hangover was feeling good that morning, and made his way to the office.

* * *

Gemma Fordham slipped on a pair of knee-length brown leather boots and stood up. 'You sure you have everything you need for tonight?' she asked, looking down at Guy, who was lying in bed with a forearm over his eyes. Why he did that, she was never sure, and had never felt like asking.

'Of course. I've got Mrs Freeman to come in tonight to help. Don't worry, we're having a high old time planning the menu and doing stuff.'

Gemma nodded. Guy liked to cook, but, of necessity, he was somewhat limited in what he could do. Blind men, sharp knives and open flames didn't exactly mix.

'OK. See you then. I might get in early today, I'm not sure. Depends on what turns up, and how the interview with the witness goes this morning.'

'You think the secretary did it?'

'I'm not sure,' Gemma hesitated. 'She must have lied about what she was doing that morning. And if she *was* there, it puts her right at the murder scene around the time Mattie Jones was killed. She was the "other woman" and from what we've learned about the victim, I don't think Mattie Jones would have been very civilized about her. They might have had a mother of all cat fights.'

'So why don't you sound more convinced?' Guy asked, genuinely curious. When he'd first started dating Gemma Fordham, he'd asked his friends to describe her, of course. And their description of a tall, spiky-haired, judo-trained, kick-ass pale blonde woman sort of fitted in his mind with the gravelly voiced, finely honed body that slept in his bed at night. But the closer they became, the more aware he was of her frailties. Her confidence masked just a few cracks of insecurity. Her ambition was always tinged by a touch of anxiety.

Was Daddy proud of her?

When Guy had learned that her father was a fireman, as were all her brothers, he'd known instantly how that had played a large part in shaping his lover's psyche. But since she'd moved from Reading to Kidlington, he'd also sensed a different kind of angst in this complex, hard-to-love woman who'd carved a place in his dark world. And it revolved around her boss, Hillary Greene.

When Gemma had told him she'd invited her 'team' to dinner tonight, he'd been both surprised and slightly wary. Now he was going to meet this woman, this Hillary Greene, for himself. Guy had always been a good reader of people — probably because he was, of necessity, a good listener. And if something about Hillary Greene made Gemma Fordham nervous, he wanted to know what it was.

Now he smiled, feeling the bed depress next to him, and knew she was leaning over him. He lifted his face for a kiss, and gasped as she stuck her tongue between his lips. 'Something to remember me by.' Gemma's husky, damaged voice ended in a wicked laugh, and Guy shook his head.

'Be careful,' he said, and meant it. He knew the sniper killer had been caught, of course, and many of his friends yesterday had remarked on how relieved he must have been. But he knew, as of course did all the loved ones of serving officers, that the sniper killer was only the most famous and recent of dangers. There were still the domestic fights that could suddenly turn on the police officer sent to calm them down; teenagers with flick knives, high on skag; bank robbers with guns; villains with cars that they drove like dodgems; thugs with bats and spades and lead piping. And Gemma, a martial arts expert, would be expected, more than most, to do her fair share of tackling them.

Sometimes, he wished she'd quit the force and join the fire service. She'd probably be safer, with all those older brothers and her daddy to look after her.

He listened to her run lightly down the stairs, then heard the clack of her boot heels on the hall floor, then the opening and slamming of the door.

Guy Brindley lifted his arm off his face and opened his eyes, and met, of course, with the same old darkness.

* * *

Rachel Miller looked surprised to see the tall blonde woman and the red-haired man on her doorstep. Back in the house, her parents were sitting down to their bowl of porridge — the same breakfast they'd had ever since they got married — and she instinctively took a step outside and closed the door behind her.

'Detective Sergeant Fordham, Detective Constable Barrington,' Gemma said curtly, showing her ID. 'Miss Miller, we'd like you to come with us to Kidlington Police Station please. DI Greene has some further questions for you.'

Rachel Miller blinked. 'Today? It's Saturday,' she heard herself say, and then felt stupid. She looked around nervously. No neighbours were coming to the doors yet, and so far not a single curtain had twitched, but they would.

'Look, can I meet you there?' she asked helplessly. 'I need to change and—'

'What you're wearing is fine, Miss Miller,' Gemma said, obeying to the letter Hillary's instructions. Polite but firm.

'Look, what's this—' Rachel broke off as the door behind her moved, making her suddenly lurch forward. Gemma took a correspondingly quick step backwards, trod on Barrington's foot, mainly because he wasn't paying attention, and Rachel gave a gasp of dismay.

'Rach, what is it?' The voice belonged to a handsome middle-aged man. Gemma recognised the same eyes and chin as the suspect, and realised this must be Miller's father.

'Dad, it's nothing. I just have to go out,' Rachel said quickly, casting a pleading look at Gemma, who looked back stony-faced.

'Are these friends of yours, chick?' Tony Miller asked. He was a tall, fine-boned man, with short-cropped dark hair and large, fine eyes. His mouth, though, was slightly deformed, and Gemma realised he'd probably been born with a cleft lip, and had surgery to correct it. It was probably why she found him so attractive. She knew she liked a quirk in her men, a physical or sometimes mental defect, that allowed her to feel comfortable with them. Sometimes she wondered if she should see a shrink about it, but whenever she did, some atavistic inner voice warned her that it was probably not a good idea.

Now she smiled, like a shark scenting blood in the water. Her boss wanted some cages rattled — well, now was as good an opportunity as any.

'DS Fordham, sir.' Gemma, ignoring the pleading puppy-dog look in Rachel Miller's eyes, flashed her ID. 'We just need to ask your daughter some questions concerning the Matilda Jones murder inquiry,' she said pleasantly. She might have added the usual cachet that there was 'nothing to worry about' or it being 'only routine' but she didn't.

Tony Miller shot his daughter a quick look, then stood to one side, allowing a small blonde woman to duck under his arm. Here was the other parent, Gemma observed. The one who did a lot of charity work, as her own research had shown. Gemma wondered how much charity had begun at home.

'What's everybody doing gossiping on the doorstep?' Cynthia Miller asked, brightly and nervously. 'Why don't you come in and have a cup of tea?'

'Can't stop, Mrs Miller,' Gemma said firmly. 'We won't be keeping Rachel long,' she added, although, in fact, she had no idea how long they would be. It all depended on what she had to say, and what Hillary Greene made of it.

'Keep her? Where are you going?' Cynthia Miller asked sharply, fear ratcheting her voice into a higher volume than she normally used. She must have heard it for herself, because she instantly lowered her voice as she added, 'Who are these people, Rachel?'

'They're the police, Mother,' Rachel said miserably. 'And, like they said, they need me to help them.' She gave a pretty little shrug, kissed her mother smartly on the cheek and all but grabbed Gemma's arm to lead her back down the path.

Once in the car, Gemma reached for her seatbelt and smiled grimly. Her eyes met those of Rachel Miller, ensconced in the back seat with Barrington beside her, and then looked away as she reached to turn on the ignition.

The Millers, Gemma noticed, watched them until they were out of sight, arms around one another, for once oblivious to the curtains twitching in the houses around them.

Gemma had never been more glad in her life that she lived in a mansion in North Oxford with a blind music don. Living a respectable life in the suburbs would be the death of her.

* * *

'But I've already told you what I did that day,' Rachel Miller said nervously, ten minutes later. They were in interview room two, a blank-faced constable at the door, a tape player revolving on the table in front of them, radiating all the menace of a loaded gun. Opposite her sat the woman who'd visited the office Wednesday morning, and the bitch of a police sergeant who'd picked her up.

'Yes, but I'd like you to tell me again, please,' Hillary said. 'For the benefit of the tape this time.'

Rachel bit her lip and stared at the tape. When she'd first entered this room, she'd listened numbly to this woman telling her she had the right to have a solicitor present. At the time, she'd hardly taken it in. It was unreal, like something from the telly. Now, suddenly, she felt afraid. Very afraid. Why did they want to ask her about Wednesday morning again?

'Perhaps I should have a solicitor after all,' she heard herself say.

* * *

His name was Gunther Mohl. Rachel didn't know him at all, but when DI Greene had asked her who she should contact, Rachel had been at a loss. She didn't have a solicitor, of course. She hadn't made her will yet, so she didn't even have a contact with a civil lawyer. So she'd asked them to call Barry, and get him to arrange legal representation for her.

She didn't know why, but she'd half expected them to refuse. Instead, Hillary Greene had smiled, nodded and left, leaving her for nearly half an hour on her own. During that time, the red-haired constable had come in with a cup of tea, but she'd barely sipped it, her hands shook so much.

Then they'd all come back with this stranger in tow. A German, by the sound of his name, although when he spoke, he spoke with a totally accentless voice. Another product of Oxford, probably.

'Miss Miller, I'm Gunther Mohl.' He held out his hand, and Rachel took it automatically. He was a short, squat, sandy-haired man, with boiled-gooseberry eyes and a tight-lipped smile. 'I've had a chat with DI Greene here. Before we begin, Inspector, I'd like a few words with my client?'

Hillary Greene nodded, and left. Rachel watched her go, wondering why she seemed so pleasant. It made her feel more scared than ever. When the door closed behind the police officers, she leaned forward across the table and began to whisper furiously.

Outside, Hillary and Gemma Fordham waited at the desk sergeant's counter, marking time and making small talk, until the consultation was over.

'Think she's going to cop to it, guv?' Gemma asked curiously, as the desk sergeant, eyes gleaming, looked to Hillary for her answer.

'Doubt it,' Hillary said. 'Although stranger things have happened at sea.' It was one of her father's many sayings, and seemed appropriate. It certainly made the desk sergeant snort with appreciation.

'She's rattled,' Gemma observed.

'Oh yes,' Hillary agreed. 'She's been telling us porkies all right.'

'I hate it when they ask for a solicitor,' Gemma said. They tended to take so much fun out of things.

Hillary shrugged. 'One of the many things you'll have to get used to, I'm afraid.'

Outside, in the newly safe car park, a plethora of nicotine addicts smoked in blissful peace. It made Hillary feel slightly better to see things getting back to normal. 'What's the latest out of Abingdon then?' she asked the desk sergeant, who was only too happy to tell her.

* * *

'My client wishes to make a statement, Inspector,' Gunther Mohl said, the moment they'd walked back inside and set the tape rolling again.

Hillary sighed. 'Oh yes?' In her opinion, a carefully thought-out statement couldn't hold a candle to a good, gruelling question-and-answer session.

Rachel Miller cleared her throat, looked at Hillary, and then quickly down at the table. 'I went to Matilda's house that morning,' Rachel said, and cleared her throat again. 'I got up about six fifteen, and was out the house about ten minutes later. I drove to Bletchington and parked outside, on the green.'

Hillary crossed her feet at the ankles and nodded. 'Go on.' Her voice, like her face, was expressionless.

'I never got out the car,' Rachel said at once. 'I just, well, watched the house for about twenty minutes, and the moment I saw Mrs Jones moving around inside the kitchen, I left.'

Hillary raised an eyebrow, glanced across at the solicitor, then back to Rachel. 'That's it?' she asked, letting her voice rise a little in disbelief. 'That's the entire statement?'

'It's the truth,' Rachel Miller said levelly, meeting her eyes at last. 'I'm sorry I didn't tell you so to begin with, but I didn't realise then that she'd been killed. I mean, that that was why you wanted to talk to Barry. I didn't realise how, well, important it was.'

'Or incriminating?' Hillary asked drily, and Rachel Miller bit her lip.

'I didn't kill her, Inspector,' she insisted again, then spread her hands helplessly. 'Why would I? I had no reason to. Barry was mine — he was going to marry me as soon as the divorce became final. I had no reason to want her dead.'

'Oh come now! She was threatening to sue Barry for more than half the business. If she succeeded, J&C Construction could have been sold out from under you.

Your lover would go from managing director of a successful company to just another building labourer looking for a job.'

Rachel flushed. 'That's exaggerating things,' she said angrily. 'Barry's a great builder, and he has contacts and friends all over the construction world. Even if he *had* had to start again, we'd have managed,' she said aggressively.

Hillary smiled. She certainly didn't like her knight in shining armour being maligned, did she? Ah, what it was to be young and in love. Rachel Miller had all the zeal and certainty of a Juliet all right.

'So, why did you go to the house of your lover's wife, Miss Miller?' Hillary deliberately phrased the question provocatively, and glanced across at Gunther Mohl as he shifted uneasily on his chair.

Rachel Miller flushed. 'I don't have to answer that, do I?' She, too, looked at her solicitor, who after a moment's hesitation, shrugged.

'You don't have to answer anything,' he said patiently. 'But it would probably be for the best.'

Rachel looked down at her hands, then at the tape rolling remorselessly on, then closed her eyes. 'I just wanted to be sure she was alone,' she said, making Hillary Greene blink. For a moment she wondered how Rachel Miller had known that Mattie Jones had a secret lover. And why she should care.

The next instant, of course, sanity returned, and she twigged. 'You thought Barry might be there?' she asked.

Rachel winced. 'No!' she squeaked, protesting too much. Her shoulders slumped a little. 'I mean, no, not really,' she added reluctantly. 'I just wanted to be sure.'

Hillary watched her for a few moments, assessing the situation. She could push her, perhaps get her to admit to all sorts of doubts about her relationship with Mattie's husband, but that might be counterproductive. 'What time did you leave Bletchington?' she asked instead.

Rachel looked relieved, and even smiled. 'I don't know. About seven twenty, something like that? I'd seen her draw back the curtains and put the kettle on and when I was sure there was no one else there with her, I left.'

'And went where?'

'Like I told you. To work.'

'Any witnesses to that?'

Rachel stared at her, then smiled. 'The cleaners. Two ladies, I'm not sure of their names — one of them was Jamaican. They work for the cleaning service. I chatted to them on the way in — they were nearly finished in the outer lobby, and had already done all the offices.'

Hillary nodded, thinking furiously. Of course, she could have gone into the house and killed Mattie Jones, but then she'd have been covered in blood. Would she have had time to go back to her parents' house, wash herself unseen, drive back to Kidlington and be on time to meet the cleaners before they left? She somehow doubted it. 'Did you see anyone else hanging around the house, anyone watching it, as you were doing?'

'No.'

'How about when you were leaving?'

'No. Only a woman on a bike, about a mile or so outside the village. Otherwise, it was pretty quiet.'

'All right, Miss Miller, that'll be all for now,' she said, then nodded pleasantly across at Gunther Mohl before getting to her feet. Outside, she walked slowly across the lobby. 'Check with the cleaners,' she said flatly to Gemma, who sighed.

'Guv.'

Like Hillary, she was inclined to believe Rachel Miller's story. It was just too lame not to be true. And, also like Hillary, she'd gone over the logistics of it in her head, and had come to the same conclusion. Moreover, it would have meant that Rachel Miller had gone to the house with a knife, intending to kill.

And for what?

Like Hillary, she recognised her as a naive young woman with stars in her eyes. The girl was head over heels in love with Barry Jones, and in her eyes, he was Superman and Romeo and the Easter bunny all rolled into one. When she said she thought he could start a whole new company by himself, she believed it. And who needed dirty, sordid money when you were in love? No, the only thing Rachel Miller had wanted to know was if Mattie Jones had been trying to lure her husband back. A less insecure woman would have known just how unlikely that scenario was. And since she'd been reassured about that, why kill her?

No, with no real motive, and an alibi of sorts, it looked as if the Miller girl was off the hook.

Upstairs, Hillary Greene was reading the latest witness statements from Uniform. Some had come in late, due to call-backs, some had gone back for second interviews. And one of them also made mention of a woman on a bicycle.

She sat up straighter and ringed it, waited until Barrington had got off the phone, then tossed him the report. 'We need to find the woman on the bike,' she said crisply. 'She was probably biking to work, or maybe the shops, and she'd have been passing Bletchington well within the time limit for the murder. She might have seen something, and a bike is almost silent. If anyone *had* been lurking around Mattie's house, they'd have stayed hidden at the sound of a car, but might not have noticed the bike.'

'Why hasn't she come forward?' Keith asked, and Hillary smiled grimly.

'Why indeed? Perhaps she didn't read the papers. Perhaps she'd left for a fortnight in Lanzarote that same day. Perhaps, like the vast majority of the great British public, she just didn't like to get mixed up in murder investigations.

'Re-interview the witness, get a description, ask around the village, find out if she was a regular. She sounds like a "green" to me — hardly anybody else uses pushbikes nowadays. Unless she's recently lost her driving licence or never had one.'

'Right, guv,' Keith said, with a distinct lack of enthusiasm in his voice. Hillary glanced at him sharply. Now that she thought about it, he seemed unusually down in the mouth today. She was just about to ask if everything was all right, when her mobile rang. She reached for it and pressed the green button.

'DI Greene.'

'Hillary.'

For a second she couldn't place the voice, then she blinked. 'Mike,' she said, knowing she sounded as surprised as she felt, and wishing she hadn't.

Mike Regis laughed in her ear. 'I can tell from the sound of your voice you haven't exactly been pacing the floor waiting to hear from me.'

Hillary felt herself tense. Because his words were heart-rendingly true. She *hadn't* given him much thought these last few days. Hardly lover-like behaviour when you'd just split up. But damn *it,* she'd had a murder case dumped on her. She couldn't be expected to pine and hunt a killer at the same time.

'Mike, look . . .'

'No, don't worry, I'm only teasing. I just didn't like things ending the way they did. We want to stay friends, right? I just wanted to call to ask you out for a drink tonight. You know, chat a bit, smooth over any rough edges. After all, we might have to work together again some time, so I don't want us to feel awkward.'

'Yes,' Hillary said. 'That would be nice. Oh damn! I can't, not tonight. I'm going out to dinner.' She'd suddenly remembered they were all going to Gemma's. 'I . . .'

'That's fine,' Mike Regis said abruptly, and hung up.

Hillary took a long, slow breath, and hit the red button. For a moment she let the phone rest, heavy and accusing in her hand. She could always ring back and explain that it wasn't a date. That she hadn't leapt into Paul

Danvers's lap, or anyone else's for that matter. It was just a team effort, a social gathering at her sergeant's place.

Yes. She could always do that.

But really what was the point?

* * *

Clive drove slowly down Kidlington's main street, looking around him carefully. He saw largish residential houses, the road lined with trees, a few shops dotted about here and there, several sets of traffic lights. When he'd gone from one end to the other, he reversed his car and drove through again. People, sunshine, traffic. The usual Saturday lunchtime snarl-up.

He didn't mind the clogged roads. He was in no hurry. He had nothing to get back home to now. The bed upstairs no longer creaked with the weight of his wife turning restlessly on it. He slowed as he drove past the entrance to Kidlington Thames Valley Police Headquarters.

He looked at the houses surrounding it. Then he nodded.

After that, he drove his car to a deserted stretch of marsh and woods not far from Charlton-on-Otmoor, and, miles from anywhere, set up his target practice butts. As he loaded a fifteen-year-old but perfectly serviceable high-powered rifle, the bullets felt like familiar friends in his hand. He attached the telescopic sight, lay down on the ground, fitted his belly flat against the grass and listened to a reed warbler over in the marsh call to its mate. And fired his first round.

It missed.

But that was to be expected. He fiddled with the sighting. Those Hollywood films that had handsome assassins load up a gun from its component parts, sight and kill someone all within three screen minutes were pure myth.

It always took time. Patience. Skill. Practice.

He fired a second time.

And missed.

He smiled patiently, readjusted the scope, readjusted the lay of his belly, pressed against the warm, scented summer grass, and fired again.

And missed.

He took a screwdriver, a tiny thing, and adjusted the grip. Took a long slow breath. He was rusty. He needed to practise. He could practise all day. He had nothing else to do.

He took aim and fired. And scored.

Patiently, he reloaded, tried again. Missed. Tried again. Scored.

The reed warbler had long since fallen silent when the man from Thame fired again.

CHAPTER TEN

Hillary slowed down as she approached the turn-off, wondering if she'd made a mistake. But Gemma had definitely said it was the house just past Squitchey Lane, and the next driveway with three monkey puzzle trees out in front. So she shrugged and turned into a short gravelled drive. Frowning, she switched off the engine and climbed out of Puff to look at the house in front of her.

She wondered if it qualified as a mansion.

Perhaps not. Not quite. Mansions brought to mind sprawling lawns, gardens, and deer parks with gazebos and statues sprinkled about. This was a house in North Oxford, sandwiched between the Woodstock and Banbury Roads.

But what a house. Huge, with a white facade, and covered with wisteria that was going through its second summer flowering. Diamond-paned windows glinted in the late evening sun. It had a fancy tiled roof and an oak front door with genuine nineteenth-century brass knocker, knob and hinges. Golden-leafed spotted laurels lined a large lawn. There was even a small pond with genuine koi.

It had to be worth at least two million on the current market. Hell, maybe even more.

Hillary looked around again, not seeing Keith's old jalopy, or Frank's car either. But Paul Danvers's smart new Megane was parked at the furthest edge of gravel. So she was in the right place then.

Hillary blew out her cheeks, wondering what she'd let herself in for, and was suddenly glad that she'd dressed up for the occasion. Normally, dinner at her sergeant's digs wouldn't have warranted a pair of black tailored trousers, strappy black sandals, and a raw-silk blouse the colour and luminescence of pearl. She'd even swept her bell-shaped cut of hair up on to her head with two tortoiseshell combs and had added a pair of pearl stud earrings, which her mother had insisted she have last Christmas. Granny's pearls, she'd always called them.

She glanced down at the bunch of fragrant freesias in her hand, and shrugged. Well, if she'd known, she'd have bought a bloody orchid!

She rang the bell, and smiled as Gemma opened the door and stepped back. She was wearing a peacock-blue trouser suit, with a turquoise and silver necklace, earring and bracelet set to go with it. Her spiky, near-white blonde hair had been recently styled, and she was wearing a perfume so expensive Hillary's nose actually twitched. Gemma Fordham made her feel instantly underdressed and dowdy.

'Gemma,' Hillary said wryly.

Gemma Fordham smiled and stepped further back. 'Please, go right on through — you'll hear the voices from the piano room. Guy invited some of his friends from college over, so of course they're all piled into the smallest room in the house.' She rolled her eyes and smiled.

Hillary smiled tightly back, but wondered how small any room in this baronial pile could possibly be, and walked through a pleasantly cool hall, following the sound of voices to a delightful hexagonal-shaped conservatory-cum-music room.

She smelled the academia before she even set foot through the door. Some of the guests were even wearing gowns. The reason for this was quickly explained, when the first person who saw her come into the room pressed a glass of champagne on her, and whispered that most of them had just come from a ceremony at the Sheldonian that had overrun shamefully, leaving them no time to change.

Hillary, feeling somewhat relieved, took a sip and caught Paul Danvers's eye. He was looking totally at home in this environment and he beckoned her over at once. She, somewhat reluctantly, joined him on a comfortable window seat overlooking a small but well-maintained back garden.

'Sir. This is a bit of a surprise,' she greeted him. 'Did you know Gemma lived in a place like this?'

'Gemma's chap, Guy Brindley, is the Fellow of Music at St Barts,' he said, explaining everything in that one short sentence. But added anyway: 'Old money.'

'Ah,' Hillary said.

'He's over there,' Danvers lowered his voice. 'The thin, good-looking one in the dark glasses.'

Hillary blinked. Sunglasses?

'He's blind,' Paul Danvers said a shade grimly, remembering the sensation of shock he'd felt when Gemma had first introduced them about ten minutes ago. Guy Brindley had smiled and thrust out his hand — about forty degrees to the left of where Paul had been standing. It had left him feeling totally out of his depth. 'I wish she'd given me some warning.'

Hillary smiled. 'Not our sergeant's style, I think.'

Paul nodded then glanced at her sharply. 'I thought you two were getting along all right?'

'We are,' Hillary said blandly, taking another sip of her champagne. It was good stuff.

Paul grunted, and catching the eye of the man standing beside him, introduced himself. A mutual interest in rugby was quickly established, and Hillary heaved a sigh of relief. She'd never been particularly good at making small talk.

Perhaps because there was a lull in the conversation, or perhaps because Hillary simply had very good hearing, a few moments later, as she sipped her champagne, she heard through the murmur of general conversation a pleasant male voice say mildly, 'I think Gemma's boss has arrived. Not the man, the woman.'

It intrigued her enough to look casually across the rim of her glass. The man speaking was a corpulent, grey-haired, somewhat cherubic-looking man, and he was speaking to their host.

'Really?' Guy Brindley replied. 'What does she look like?'

Hillary, knowing she was about to be looked at, turned slightly on the window seat to glance outside.

'Quite a looker, really,' the cherub said, making Hillary's lips twitch. 'Tallish, with that nice shade of dark hair tinged with auburn. Sorry, old son, means nothing to you of course.'

'No, it's giving me a visual picture. Go on.'

'Well, mid-forties, I suspect, but looks well on it. Actually got a figure, you know, curves and everything. Not that your Gemma isn't stunning, in a different sort of way.'

'Eyes?'

'Dark brown. Very fine, too. Dark brows. Good high cheekbones, a strong chin. Like I said, a very handsome woman indeed. She's a bigwig in the police, is she? Can't say I'm surprised. She looks strong. I mean, she has character. Damn, I dare say the poetry chappies would have a quote on the tips of their tongues. Us astral physicists are a bit short when it comes to describing things. Unless you want a first class description of a blue quasar?'

Hillary wished they'd move on and discuss something else. Or that she could stop earwigging. Although it was nice to hear complimentary things about herself, it was beginning to make her feel uncomfortable.

'Why the interest?' the cherub asked curiously.

'Oh nothing really. It's just that she's Gemma's immediate boss, and she's never worked under another woman before. She seems a bit antsy about it. You know how it is . . .' Guy Brindley's voice lowered, and the person Paul Danvers was talking to laughed loudly, and she missed the next bit.

At that point, Hillary saw Gemma's reflection in the window approaching her, and she turned and got to her feet, smiling. It was only then that she realised she was still holding the flowers.

'They're Guy's favourite,' Gemma Fordham said, with a smile that was just a bit annoyed. Did Hillary Greene never put a foot wrong? 'Having no sight, he tends to go for scent, and those,' she pointed at the brightly coloured flowers in Hillary's hand, 'and wild violets are his favourites,' she explained.

'Did I hear wild violets mentioned?'

Hillary let her eyes slide from Gemma's shuttered grey gaze to the black-glassed obstructions in front of Guy Brindley's, and smiled. 'I wasn't able to find any of those, not in August,' Hillary mused. 'But my sergeant's just informed me that these might do. Thank you for the invitation to dinner.'

She didn't try to force the flowers on him, but stepped closer, just close enough to allow him to feel the slight pressure the flowers made on his arm. With his other hand he groped for them, and already smiling, brought them clumsily up to his face. One bounced off his nose and he laughed. 'Heavenly. I've been meaning to write an oratorio dedicated to scented flowers for years.'

Gemma, who'd been looking forward to the meeting between her lover and boss, fully expecting it to be as awkward and uncomfortable as it usually was, found herself grinding her teeth.

'So why don't you?' Hillary asked, allowing the smile to creep into her voice.

Guy Brindley laughed. 'Time.'

'Like the wind, goes a-hurrying by,' she murmured, quoting a song she vaguely remembered from the sixties. She realised that none of the academics who'd overhead her remark had been able to place it — no doubt they were thinking along the lines of Keats, Leigh Hunt or one of the Romantic poets, rather than an obscure, probably American, sixties songwriter.

Guy Brindley laughed. 'What a voice that man had,' he said, and Hillary, with a jerk of surprise, realised that of course music in all its forms was this man's thing.

'I've never heard him sing anything but that,' she said, because she hadn't, then abruptly noticed Gemma looking puzzled, and not best pleased. 'I can see Barrington,' she said, her voice suddenly crisp and businesslike. 'He's looking a bit out of his depth. If you'll excuse me a minute . . .' She made no attempt to touch Guy, either to shake his hand, or press his arm or anything else. She simply walked away.

Gemma drew in a deep breath, and Guy, hearing it, smiled tightly. 'You really don't like her, do you,' he whispered, reaching down to her, and fumbling a kiss on to the side of her face.

'Actually, I don't know,' Gemma said with a sigh. Which, of course, only made things worse. 'It's just that nothing ever seems to faze her.'

'And that annoys you?'

'Hell yes!' Gemma said, then had to laugh.

The dinner, of course, was splendid. Altogether, they were sixteen in number, but the long mahogany dining table fitted them all with ease. Pinks, gypsophila, love-in-amist, and fern fronds made up the pretty flower arrangements that ranged down the length of the table, and the fine silver and number of cutlery items made Frank Ross distinctly nervous. The eight courses made him even more so, but he managed to eat them all without spilling anything. The woman on his right was a librarian at the Bodleian, who found him both fascinating and repellent in equal measure.

Keith, after several glasses of Château Lafite, began to feel better about life in general. Good wine tended to do that. Hillary, who was driving, watched him with a thoughtful eye, until he mentioned that he'd walked here from Park Town, and would be walking back.

Danvers was watching Hillary with appreciative eyes, and she carefully pretended not to notice. She knew once it became generally known that she and Mike were no longer an item, she might have trouble with her good-looking boss.

The conversation, as ever at a gathering like this in Oxford, was intelligent, witty and slightly back-stabbing.

She enjoyed herself, to a degree, but was glad, in the end, to go.

* * *

Sunday was a glorious day. It started warm and stayed that way, with none of the burning heat of high summer, but also with none of the warning coolness on the wind that spoke of approaching autumn. The swallows swooped their paths along the canal, scooping up water, and a pair of swans with five grey cygnets mugged the *Mollern* for some bread. Hillary, still full from last night's feast, was happy to laze on top of her boat with nothing more than a glass of orange juice and a novel, tossing the swans and the other river pirates that passed by the odd crust of bread from a stale loaf.

Her mood was blighted a while later, however, when her mobile rang, and Mel's terse, tight voice answered her greeting. She listened gloomily, and with a growing sense of unease, as he told her that Valerie Myers had died as a result of her overdose.

'I think they're going to set up an internal inquiry,' Mel added gloomily. 'I can't see how they can avoid it now.'

Hillary groaned. More pointless politics. 'But what's the good of that? Warrants are the ultimate responsibility of the law clerks. Yeah, they might slap Gregg over the wrist for not reading it more closely, but everyone knows that coppers aren't lawyers. And you'll be safe enough, surely?'

Mel's sigh came grimly over the wire. 'I suppose. But that's hardly the point, is it? It's the father I feel the most sorry for. His wife's dead, and his daughter's in a mental hospital. Last year, he had it all. What's he got now?'

Hillary tossed the last of the bread to a moorhen family, and sat up, bringing her bare knees under her chin. She was wearing a pair of beige shorts and an old white tank top. Her arms and legs were gratifyingly tanned, but right then she hardly noticed.

'Mel, there's nothing you can do about it but grin and bear it. And try to remember — it's not your fault.' But her words felt hollow, even as she said them, and she knew they'd be of no comfort. Instead, she changed tack. 'How's Janine?'

It worked, to a certain extent. He chatted happily for a while about becoming a father again, and when he at last rang off, Hillary sighed and lay back against the towel, letting the sun wash over her. And thought about Mattie Jones.

She might be wrong, but Hillary had the distinct feeling that she hadn't met the killer yet. Not that she thought it was a random slaying or anything like that. No, there was definitely a connection to someone, somewhere — but she hadn't found it yet. She just didn't get the sensation of something nibbling away at her. Of something nebulous, some clue, some word, some gesture, being out of place.

She sighed, and rolled over to tan her back.

Sometimes, you just had to leave the work at the office.

* * *

Less than a mile away from where Hillary Greene blissfully sunbathed, Phyllis Clayton shoved a pallid-looking chicken into the oven and turned the heat up to 180. With the potatoes peeled and ready for roasting, the cauliflower and carrots cleaned, seasoned and waiting in the pot, she was at last able to put her feet up and take it easy.

It was not that she was sorry to be back at work full-time again. After all, both the kids had left the nest, and her Harry looked as if he might be made redundant from the plant any minute. So taking the secretarial course at the Tech to buff up her old secretarial skills had probably been the smartest thing she'd ever done. And she quite liked everybody down at Fullbright and Peabody — well, apart from Mr Hadshaw, of course, but nobody liked *him*.

But it did mean that the weekends tended to be a bit of a nightmare, what with all the household chores she hadn't got around to doing in the week. Then there was the gardening — still, at least Harry did the lawns and the hedges, and washed the car. Even so, it often felt like she couldn't get a decent moment's peace to herself.

But now, with Harry down the pub and the Sunday roast seen to, she could sit down at last with a mug of her favourite coffee and yesterday's *Oxford Mail*, which she hadn't managed to read yesterday. She liked the Saturday edition best.

She stretched back in her favourite recliner — nearly twenty years old now, but it still worked — and read the front page. She took a sip and turned the page, and started to read about the latest offering at the Oxford Playhouse.

She liked a nice musical, but this was about something depressing: Ibsen. She sighed and turned quickly to the next page.

She saw at once the police artist's sketch of a Mr Fox, whom the police wanted to talk to.

'Well, stone the crows,' Phyllis Clayton said.

* * *

In accord with Sod's Law, the next day's weather was a repetition of the day before. With everyone returning to work with the Monday morning glums, the sun shone and the birds sang, and the bees buzzed in the buddleia. Everyone would rather be outside than in, and for once, the patrol-car johnnies smiled and gave the finger to the CID and office workers who were stuck inside all day. With the sniper killer caught, charged, and safely banged up in Abingdon, life was once more good.

Upstairs in the main office, Hillary nodded to Keith as she passed by his desk, and glanced cautiously across at Gemma Fordham. For once, Hillary was the last in — well, Frank Ross had yet to show up, but that didn't count — and she glanced at her watch surreptitiously as she tossed her bag on to the desk and sat down. No, it was still only 8:45.

'A nice dinner Saturday, Gemma,' Hillary said mildly.

'Yeah, Sarge, great stuff. I liked the stuffed partridges,' Keith said, but only because that had been the only thing he'd recognised. He had a vague, uneasy feeling that he'd also eaten venison at some point, and guilty images of Bambi had been haunting his dreams all that weekend. Well, Bambi and an irate Gavin.

'Glad you enjoyed it,' Gemma said briskly. 'Guv, I've come across this chap.' She reached forward with a piece of paper, a transcription of an interview she'd followed up Friday night. 'When you told me to interview the neighbours and any friends of Mattie's mum and dad, I came across an old girl who remembered the boyfriend

160

before Barry. Well, the only serious boyfriend before Barry. Apparently Mattie's mother had high hopes of her marrying him, but Mattie had been eighteen at the time, and went off to university instead.'

Hillary nodded, listening and reading at the same time. 'Apparently this George Philby was something of a golden boy?'

'Well, that didn't say much, not for around there. He had a job and all his teeth, but that's about it,' Gemma said flatly, and seemed surprised when Hillary laughed.

'Right. Well, it's ancient history all right. I don't see . . . oh. Wait a minute.' She was coming to the end of Gemma's precise but detailed notes. 'The break-up was bad?'

'I got the feeling it was more than bad,' Gemma said, recalling the glee in the old lady's eye as she talked about 'Mona's girl.' 'The old woman I spoke to had a daughter herself of around Mattie's age, and I got the feeling there was a bit of rivalry going on. Of course, Mona Cartwright won hands down when Mattie got a place at university. Nobody around there had ever gone before, and certainly not the daughter of a television repair man.'

'So she was inclined to dish the dirt?' Hillary said, a shade warily. You had to be careful of vindictive old women.

'Yes,' Gemma said, instantly catching on. 'But it was not what she *said* that rang the alarm bells, so much as what she didn't seem to know, but resent.'

Hillary frowned, leaning back in her chair. 'Not quite sure I follow that, Sergeant,' she said drily.

Gemma smiled briefly. 'Sorry, guv. I got the feeling that the old dear knew there was more, much more, to the George Philby/Mattie Cartwright break-up than met the eye, and was frustrated that she didn't know what. She said Mona Cartwright had been "acting like a cat on a hot tin roof" for months, and she scented some sort of scandal.

The fact that she never found out what it was still rankles, nearly thirty years later.'

Hillary nodded. 'Well, there's nothing to say that the reason for Mattie's death doesn't lie in the past. Sometimes ancient history can come back to bite us. See if you can locate him and—'

'Already done, boss. Philby never left the area. In fact, he still lives in Carterton, where they all grew up. Works as a mechanic out at Kidlington airport.'

Hillary nodded. 'Good work. OK, let's go and see what he has to say about things.'

* * *

George Philby was a heavy but still good-looking man, with a full head of quiffed brown hair and piercing blue eyes. The extra weight sat easily on his large frame, and even in oil-stained blue overalls Gemma could see why women would fancy him. At eighteen, he must have been really something. They drove to Kidlington airport in less than five minutes. The airport catered mainly to light executive aircraft: Learjets, Cessnas, that kind of thing. They went in Gemma's car, since Puff was still acting tragically, and made straight for the administration offices.

Rather than let civilians — even if they were coppers — roam loose around a busy working airport, the office manager had George Philby paged, and when he showed up, left them alone in his office without too much fuss. But he was obviously intrigued, and gave the puzzled mechanic a sharp, thoughtful glance as he went out.

'DI Greene. This is Sergeant Fordham.' Hillary showed him the ID, and was about to ask him to sit down when she realised that the office manager probably wouldn't want the mechanic smearing engine oil all over his clean, beige, ergonomically designed office chair, and smiled briefly instead. 'This is simply routine, Mr Philby.'

'Call me George,' George Philby said at once. 'Makes me nervous being called Mr Philby by you lot. Er, no offence or anything.'

Hillary smiled again. 'None taken.' According to Gemma's research, Philby didn't have a criminal record of any kind, not even traffic violations, but Hillary wouldn't have been surprised if he hadn't, in his time, lifted a few easily saleable bits and bobs from the hangars, and sold them on the quiet.

He certainly seemed wary.

'You may have read in the papers that a Mrs Matilda Jones was murdered at her home in Bletchington last Wednesday?' she began.

George's mouth dropped open a bit. 'Eh? Yeah, yeah, course I read about it in the papers, like.' He looked at Gemma nervously, then back to her. 'I don't get it.'

'We just wanted to talk to you about your relationship with Mrs Jones.'

'Eh? What relationship?' George blustered. 'Look, I'm a happily married man, I am. My Jenny's a gem — I wouldn't do nothing to hurt her. And my kiddies — I wouldn't do nothing to risk losing them, let me tell you. I ain't gonna become no weekend dad, taking 'em out to the zoo once a month. If someone's been saying different, the bastards are lying!'

Hillary realised the problem at once. 'You've misunderstood, sir,' she said, before he could work himself up into an even more self-righteous head of steam. 'We're talking about when you were both eighteen or thereabouts. Matilda Jones, or Matilda Cartwright, as she was then. I understand you were engaged to be married?'

George Philby leaned suddenly against the wall nearest to him, his face going pale. 'Mattie? That were Mattie Cartwright?'

Hillary nodded. 'You didn't know?'

'No. Well, it said she was Matilda Jon . . . of course! After a while, she upped and married Barry Jones, didn't

163

she? I knew that — one of her mum's friends told my mum. I should have put it together. Matilda Jones. Mattie Cartwright. Oh hell.'

He looked around for a moment, as if trying to focus on something, then in the end simply allowed himself to slide down the wall and sit on the carpet. The carpet was dark brown. Which was probably just as well.

'Sorry, but this has sort of taken the stuffing out of me. I was right fond of Mattie. And knowing she's been murdered, and I read about it in the papers and all, and didn't even know what I was reading. It's given me a right funny turn, I can tell you.'

And he did look a nasty colour. He'd turned from pale to a green-tinged sallow.

'A glass of water, Sergeant,' Hillary said, and Gemma nodded, going over to the water cooler near the door. One of the perks of management, no doubt. The cup, though, was the same thin white plastic that made everything taste just slightly synthetic. She nudged it against the black plastic tap until it was half full, then took it over to Philby, who was still sitting with his back to the wall. He looked up, seemingly surprised by the offering, although he'd watched her fill it, then accepted it gingerly, as if not used to taking presents from women.

'Er, thanks.' He took a sip, and then a bigger gulp. 'Bugger me, this isn't how I expected my day to go,' he said, and tried out a laugh. It didn't quite work, but his face began to lose the green tinge. 'Sorry, you wanted to talk about her? I can't see how I can help. Last time I saw her . . . bloody hell . . . must have been, what, well, I was eighteen, and I'm forty-seven now. Hell, I can't even do the maths. Feels like someone turned my brain off.'

Hillary nodded. She knew the signs of shock all right. 'Just a few questions, sir. We're still trying to build up a picture of Mattie. Her life, what she was like, that kind of thing. So, was the engagement official?'

'Oh yeah,' George said at once. 'I bought her the ring and everything. A tiny diamond thing.' He laughed suddenly. 'All I could afford at the time — saved up months to afford it. Mattie never gave it back when she dumped me. But then, that was Mattie. She probably sold it and bought herself something nice with it.'

There was something so candid and genuinely amused about the admission that it made Hillary's heart beat just a bit faster. At last, here was a witness without an axe to grind. Someone who knew the victim of old, and had nothing to lose or gain by talking about her.

She took the chair from in front of the manager's desk, brought it over to rest a few feet from him and sat down. Instantly picking up her cue, Gemma walked further away to sit behind the desk itself, where she could take her notes without him seeing her, or interrupting the flow of the interview.

'You don't sound as if you mind. Most men would have found that annoying.'

George blinked, his thoughts obviously long ago in the past and far away, and laughed again. 'Yeah. Well, not much point in that, is there? I mean, you don't blame a dog for pissing up a tree, do you, or a cat for scratching the curtains. That's just the way she was. I knew her at school, see. Grew up with her. I knew just what she was like. But I didn't care. There was something . . . better about Mattie. Better than the crappy comprehensive we were in. Better than the old council houses we went home to. Better than, well, anything. Telly, cider, footie even. She was like someone from Hollywood. She dressed better than anyone else. She was smart and funny, and yeah, she had claws. Surprised the hell out of me when she said yes when I asked her to marry me. Should have known it wouldn't last. Well, it didn't, did it? She got a place at Northampton, and that was that. She was off.' He shook his head admiringly. 'Never looked back.'

'So it was just the fact that she got a university place that split you up? There was no other man — perhaps older, married, rich? Anything like that?' Hillary asked, mindful of the whiff of scandal that the neighbours had detected.

'Nah. Not that Mattie wouldn't have gone for it, though.' George's handsome face split into a grin. 'But there was something of a shortage of sugar daddies in Carterton.'

Hillary laughed along with him. 'Only, my sergeant over there was talking to an old neighbour friend of Mona Cartwright, Mattie's mum, who seemed to think there was something a bit dodgy about you two breaking up.'

George nodded wryly. 'Nosy old cows, ain't they? Middle-aged women neighbours. Nothing like 'em for sniffing out the dirt. Yeah, well, I suppose they got whiff of the baby. Though how, I dunno. Mona was dead clever about that — as was Mattie, really.'

'Baby?' Hillary said sharply. Nothing had come up in the investigation about a baby.

'Yeah, I got her up the duff, didn't I?' George said, half shamefaced, half proud. 'Back then, us kids didn't really know much about stuff. Not country kids like us. Nowadays, blimey — gynaecologists, half of 'em, before they even hit puberty.'

Hillary grinned.

'Mattie was madder'n hell, I can tell you. And when she got accepted at Northampton, I thought she was gonna have an abortion. Didn't want a kid in the way, slowing her down, ruining her life, did she? That's the way she put it. I tell you, it sort of turned my stomach that did. Luckily, her mum put her foot down. And in the end, Mattie agreed to have the kid, but to have it adopted out as soon as it was born. I never got to see it. Dunno, even, what it was. By then, I was persona non grata, as they say.' He sighed, and looked down into his empty white plastic cup. 'Would have been nice to hold it, though,' he said softly. 'Just once, like.'

Hillary let the silence linger, then asked him all the usual routine questions. But at the time of the killing, he'd already been at work, doing the early five till one shift. A fact the office manager confirmed later.

Outside, Hillary leaned against Gemma's car and absently watched a white functional-looking aeroplane take off. Its engine drone made conversation impossible for a moment, but once it was far enough away, she turned to Gemma. 'We need to speak to Mattie Jones's son or daughter pronto.'

'It might be hard finding the right adoption agency after all this time, guv, and you know what all of them are like about client confidentiality,' Gemma pointed out.

'Get a search warrant if you have to,' Hillary ordered.

'Guv.'

'And read the small print,' she added bitterly.

When they got back to HQ, the desk sergeant, who was talking to somebody about a poisoned dog, immediately beckoned her over. 'Got someone waiting for you in three,' he said shortly before turning back to the irate and tearful owner — or former owner — of a noisy Jack Russell.

Hillary nodded. To Gemma she said, 'Send Keith down. I want you to get cracking on the other thing right away.'

Gemma nodded, a shade surprised. She couldn't quite see why Hillary Greene was so hot to talk to someone who, if their adopted parents hadn't informed him or her that they had birth parents knocking around the planet somewhere, might not even know that Mattie Jones had existed.

But she was coming to realise that Hillary never did anything without a reason.

Frowning thoughtfully, Hillary made her way to interview room three. Inside, a plump woman in her mid-fifties watched her come in and half rose to her feet. Hillary waved her back down.

'Hello, luv. I'm Phyllis Clayton. Did the man on the desk tell you I wanted to see someone about that picture in the papers?'

The desk sergeant hadn't, but Hillary nodded. 'This is about Mr Fox?'

Phyllis snorted. 'Mr Fox, my eye. That's old Mrs Kershaw's son. I thought as much as soon as I saw it, so I did.'

The door opened and Keith walked in. Phyllis eyed him somewhat suspiciously. Whether it was his youth or the red hair, Hillary wasn't sure. But she indicated him to take a seat quickly.

'Let's all get comfortable, shall we? This is DC Barrington, Mrs Clayton, he'll take notes. I hope that's all right? It's just that we like to get things clear.'

'Oh yes, luv, that's fine. Don't want the police making no mistakes, do we?'

On anybody else that might have sounded facetious, or at the very least double-edged, but Hillary didn't even wince. She already had Mrs Clayton's measure. And she meant exactly — and only — what she said.

'Right then. You saw the police artist's sketch in — which paper was it?'

'*Oxford Mail*. Saturday's edition, 'cept I only saw it yesterday. I didn't think you'd be open on a Sunday, like, so I waited until this morning to come in. Hope that's all right.'

Beside her, she saw Keith's head shoot up, obviously wondering if she was taking the mickey, but Hillary nodded quickly, and said smoothly, 'That's fine, Mrs Clayton. I wish all our witnesses were as thoughtful.'

Phyllis smiled, relaxing against her seat. She hadn't expected to like coming down to a police station, and her Harry had said she ought to leave it well enough alone but she knew she had to speak up. Besides, she'd always wanted to see inside one of these cells.

'And you recognised the drawing as . . . ?'

'Old Mrs Kershaw's son. The one she's always going on about, and is so proud of. Timothy his name is.'

'Timothy Kershaw,' Hillary repeated. 'And you think it's a good likeness, do you?'

'Oh yes. Can't mistake him. Well, he is a handsome lad, I have to give him that. Mind you, according to his mother you'd think he could be a Hollywood film star or something.'

'Well, I expect all mothers are proud of their sons,' Hillary said, and Phyllis blushed a little.

'Yes, of course, you're right. I say the same about my two.'

'You don't happen to know where Mr Kershaw lives, do you?'

'Oh no, luv. He must have left home, what, a good ten years ago.'

'But you can give us his mother's address?'

'Oh yes, luv,' Phyllis said happily, and spelled it out slowly and carefully, so the youngster could get it down properly.

Keith gritted his teeth and patiently copied it down. When he was finished, Hillary thanked Phyllis politely, shook hands, and saw her outside into the car park. Phyllis, chuffed, trotted off towards the entrance, where she could catch a bus back into work. She didn't like taking the morning off, but she knew her boss would be interested when she told him where she'd been. And the other ladies in the office would want to know all the details as well.

Back inside, fully aware of having made Phyllis's day, Hillary went back to her desk. 'Check out Timothy Kershaw,' she told Barrington. 'First see if you can get a picture ID — driving licence is the obvious way to go.' No point bringing him in unless he looked something reasonably like the sketch.

'Guv,' Barrington agreed happily.

Hillary leaned back in her chair, feeling happier herself. She'd just gone from no leads to two solid leads in the space of as many hours. Sometimes it just happened like that.

Who said Monday mornings were the worst?

CHAPTER ELEVEN

Barrington had no difficulty obtaining a copy of Timothy Kershaw's driving licence. In fact, a red flag showed up on his computer the moment he typed in the name and such details as he had. He quickly printed it off, then studied the photocopy of a tiny digital image of a man's face.

For once, Timothy Kershaw's good looks counted against him. It was pretty hard to disguise the handsome square-shaped face, the piercing blue eyes or dark, thick hair. The picture — poor quality though it was — was a dead ringer for DC Trevor Drudge's sketch.

'Guv, I think Kershaw's our man,' Barrington said, handing over the copy to Hillary, who looked at it, then nodded.

'I agree.'

'Notice the red flag, guv?'

Hillary had. Timothy Kershaw had lost his driving licence three months ago, after a second drink-driving conviction. So Mattie Jones must have driven them to the Cloverleaf Hotel for their little romantic getaway. 'Current address?' She looked across at Barrington, who'd already scribbled it down in his notebook.

'Middleton Cheney.' Barrington didn't know it — he was still finding his feet, and his way, in his new county.

'Out by Banbury,' Hillary said, guessing his difficulty, and glanced at her watch. They could stop for a pub lunch on the way. 'Right, let's go.'

Replete after a meal of home-made vegetable soup, crusty bread and a fruit salad, Hillary was happy to let Barrington drive. They were in his car, a twenty-year-old rust-bucket of a Volvo with a totally knackered suspension, but the day was glorious. With her window wound down, she heard the odd corn bunting singing away from the tops of the hedgerows they passed. Combine harvesters were out in force gathering in the crops, and on the roadside verges they passed several stalls selling late-summer soft fruit and assorted vegetables.

She might have Barrington stop at one on the way back and pick something up. It beat eating out of a tin for a change.

Middleton Cheney wasn't quite a town, yet it was too big to be a real village. They found Kershaw's address on the east side, in the mock Tudor belt. The house was new, with modern landscaping in the gardens and a double garage. Barrington parked out front and stared at it, not sure whether to feel envious or disparaging.

Hillary climbed out and looked carefully around. There were two sixty-something men, both mowing their lawns, probably taking advantage of early retirement, and making the most of the warm sun to get the garden chores done. Being August and still the school holidays, three children, obviously all siblings, were racing along the pavement on small identical scooters.

She was aware of being watched from next door as she walked up Kershaw's garden path, pausing to admire a dwarf magnolia tree that held pride of place in the front garden. When it was in bloom it would probably be spectacular. At the door, she rung the bell and waited. Of course, at this time of day on a Monday, he'd probably be at work, but it was the season of summer holidays, and they had to try here first. Besides, if the twitching curtains from next door were any indication, they might get a bit of intelligence on Timothy Kershaw before actually having to interview him.

Sure enough, there was no answer to the doorbell summons, and turning away, she heard the door to the next house open. 'We don't buy or sell at this door.' The woman who stood there looked at them firmly. 'Nor religion, either.' She was a tall, lean, white-haired woman with a jutting chin and rather fierce white eyebrows.

Hillary smiled. 'We're looking for Mr Kershaw, madam,' she said, wishing she had a ten-pound note for every time she'd been mistaken for a Jehovah's Witness or seller of insurance. 'Police,' she added, just as firmly, reaching into her bag for her ID.

Barrington reached into his pocket for the same, but already the woman had closed the door behind her and was walking towards the neat wooden fence that separated her from her neighbour. Hillary obligingly stepped off the path and walked across the lawn to meet her.

'You won't find him in,' the woman said, looking at Hillary's ID closely.

'At work is he?'

'Don't think so. I saw him climbing into a taxi Saturday afternoon, about six or quarter past. Had a suitcase with him.'

'On holiday then,' Hillary said flatly. Damn. Just her luck.

'Suppose so,' the woman, who had yet to identify herself, said dubiously. When Hillary cocked her head, she shrugged. 'He had his two weeks abroad back in June though. I remember him talking to Geoff, my husband. He went to one of them islands in Greece.'

'Some people take more than one holiday,' Hillary pointed out, and looked at the house behind her. Especially if they could afford a place like this.

'Ah, not him,' the woman said emphatically. 'He owns his own business, a textile company out Chippie way. He's always going on about how hard he has to work. Just has the two days off over Christmas and New Year's Day, and forget Easter. He's always going on to Geoff about the hours he has to put in. And, to be fair, he doesn't often miss a day's work,' the woman added, a shade reluctantly, Hillary thought.

'I don't suppose you know where he went?'

'No. Sorry.' The woman looked as if she was working up the courage to ask her what they wanted with him, so Hillary thanked her quickly, and turned away.

Back in Barrington's roasting car, Hillary held the door open and rolled down the window before getting back inside. Then she looked across at Barrington thoughtfully.

'Do me a favour. Go back and ask the neighbour if she knows what papers Kershaw took.' She seemed the kind of observant, not to say nosy old biddy, who would probably know.

Barrington nodded, wondering why she wanted to know, thought about it for a few seconds, then smiled widely. 'Right, guv.'

He came back a few minutes later looking pleased — whether with himself and his growing powers of deductive reasoning, or whether with the news he brought, Hillary wasn't sure.

'He takes the *Guardian*, the *Banbury Cake* and the *Oxford Mail*, guv.'

'And the picture of himself came out in the *Oxford Mail* on Saturday?'

'Yes, guv. It's delivered in the morning. But Kershaw always does his shopping on a Saturday morning, and probably didn't get around to seeing it until the afternoon.'

Hillary nodded. 'Good — asking the neighbour about his Saturday morning routine showed initiative.'

Barrington beamed. 'So, he sees the sketch of himself and legs it. Doesn't look very good, does it?'

'No, guv. You think he's our man?'

'Perhaps. Or maybe he's just a bit chicken,' Hillary mused. 'He reads that his lover's been murdered, but doesn't come forward. Remember his convictions for drink driving? And the neighbour's told us he's obviously stressed out by his business, so maybe alcohol's become something of a crutch for him. People like that don't tend to cope well with added problems.' She put on her seatbelt and tapped her fingers on the nylon strap thoughtfully. As Barrington followed suit, she carried on theorizing. 'Perhaps he was hoping that the cops didn't know about him — after all, Mattie would have gone to a lot of trouble to keep their affair secret, and she must have stressed over and over again the need for discretion, because of the upcoming divorce. It's been a few days since Wednesday, so perhaps he starts to feel safe when there's no knock on the door, bringing the constabulary to ask him what he's been up to. Then, wham. Suddenly his face is plastered all over the local press as a person of interest.'

Barrington started the car, and picked up the thread. 'And perhaps he's just the kind to panic. He's the lover, ergo, we'll immediately want to put him in the frame as being the killer?'

Hillary shrugged. 'Whatever. We're going to need to find him. Tell you what, drop me in town and I'll take the bus back. You scout around here — remember, he hasn't got a car, so he'll have to rely on public transport. Find the taxi firm that picked him up and see if they have a record of where they dropped him off. My guess is Banbury station. If so, pull the surveillance tapes for Saturday if you have to, to see which train he got on. Better yet, he might have paid for his ticket with plastic, in which case it'll be easy.'

'Guv,' Barrington said, smiling happily. He loved this bit. Using his brains to track someone down, feeling as if the case was actually moving, perhaps speeding up to a conclusion. And it beat sitting in the office, punching the keyboard and thinking about Gavin.

Who still hadn't phoned him back.

* * *

Gemma hung up the phone on the eighth adoption agency, and crossed it off her printed list. She sighed and punched in the numbers for the next.

She was not feeling particularly happy that morning. After the last of the dinner guests had left Saturday night, she'd immediately asked Guy what he'd thought of her boss. She was still smarting that Hillary Greene, on leaving, hadn't even mentioned returning the favour and inviting everyone around to dinner on the *Mollern*. It was just the right weather for a barbecue on the towpath, after all.

And what Guy had to say next hadn't improved her mood at all.

She knew Guy was one of the best judges of character around — probably because of his lack of sight. He never saw the concealing smiles, the masks behind which people hid. He only heard voices, was aware of the movement of the body, heard the way the breathing quickened, or was caught, measuring the nuances of their reactions, analysing the meaning behind the tone. Gemma always felt that he knew when she was lying to him, and had cultivated the habit of distracting him. But she also knew he was aware of that tactic.

So when she asked him for his assessment of Hillary Greene, she was prepared to listen.

'Well, she's intelligent of course, you don't need me to say that. Fairly self-confident, but sort of rueful with it. Like she's well aware of her own weaknesses and foibles, and is almost amused by them. That's rare — both the awareness and the reaction to that awareness. It makes her incredibly strong. In her mind, I mean, and character.'

Gemma had felt then the first creeping of dismay.

'And because she knows herself so well, I would imagine it's just a short step for her to be able to read other people as well. Is she well known for her interview technique?'

The question shook her. Not only because it was so pertinent, but because of the answer she knew she had to give. 'Yes. Several people have remarked on it. She can interview any kind of witness, villain or victim, and get straight on to their wavelength. I was talking to Superintendent Mallow not so long ago, and he told me it used to drive Janine, his wife, crazy the way Hillary could winkle information out of people. The way she could instantly become their friend, or worst nightmare, depending on which scenario would get the most information. And the way she used to see things other people didn't. You know, make connections that aren't obvious to everyone else.'

Guy had nodded. 'I rather think, my pet, that she's got your number.'

Gemma had gone cold. 'Why do you say that? What do you mean?'

Guy had reached for her, holding her close, his fumbling hands running gently across the tops of her arms. 'As for what I mean, you're in a better position to say than I am. I know you've got your own reasons for transferring to Kidlington, and . . .' he added quickly, sharply, as she made to remonstrate, 'I don't care. It's none of my business if you don't choose to tell me. As to why I say that — well, it was just the way she sounded whenever she talked to you. Her tone altered, just a bit. It became sort of . . . knowing. Patient. Perhaps even a bit guilty.'

Her lover's words had meant that Gemma had spent a largely sleepless night that night, and Sunday had dragged. Now, back at work, she still couldn't make up her mind if she was just being fanciful. And putting too much trust in a blind man. But what if he was right? What if her boss really did know what she was up to?

'Hello?'

The voice in her ear jolted her out of her morose maunderings, and she quickly went into her spiel. Unfortunately, the agency had only been in existence for twelve years. Trying to be helpful, they were able to give her the name of some who'd been in the business for half a century or more, and Gemma thanked them and hung up.

She sighed, and picked the names out of the list of over thirty she had in front of her. Might as well try them first.

* * *

Frank Ross was feeling pretty smug with himself. Not because he'd been doing anything specific, but just because he'd been the only one in the room available to answer the telephone when it rang at 2:15 that afternoon. The boy wonder and the boss were out, chasing down some lead, and the blonde kick-boxer was making her already raspy voice sound almost sandpapered by talking endlessly on the phone.

So, when he reached across to answer Hillary's phone, and found himself talking to a Mr Arbuckle of the Melson and Blythe insurance company, his boredom quickly fled.

'And that policy is for how much exactly?' he asked, then whistled between his teeth as he wrote it down. He lowered his voice and glanced across at Gemma, who was busy yacking away about adoption dates, and paying not the slightest attention to him.

'No, we're still investigating, obviously,' Frank murmured. 'But if I were you, I'd hold off making out any payments just yet.' This was obviously welcome news to Mr Arbuckle, who, not unnaturally, was looking for a way out of parting with so much of his company's profits.

When Hillary got back, two bus rides later, Gemma was busy scribbling into her notebook and looking relieved. But it was Frank who instantly caught her attention. He was looking pleased with himself. Something that always made her stomach clench in alarm. 'Frank,' she said cautiously, tossing her bag on to the desk top.

'Guv. While you've all been gallivanting about, I've come up with something solid at last.'

The likelihood of that was so remote that for a moment, Hillary wondered if he was actually joking. Frank flushed sullenly, so the disbelief must have been writ large across her face.

'Did you know that Barry Jones stands to come into a whopping half a mil in life insurance on his wife's death?'

Hillary didn't. Although she'd have probably found out sooner or later. Either from Mattie's solicitor, whom she was due to interview about the contents of her will, or from the insurance agency themselves who'd certainly want to know whether or not . . .

Hillary smiled widely. 'Insurance agency just got in touch have they, Frank?' she asked sweetly, choosing to ignore the way Ross's fists began to clench and unclench on top of his desk. 'Well, better have Jones in then. You can do that, Frank, since it's your lead.'

Ross got up without a word and walked stiffly out. It was only then that Hillary became aware that Gemma Fordham was watching her like a hawk. She glanced across at her.

'When you've been here a bit longer, you'll get used to the way Frank's mind works,' she said. But suspected that Gemma was already well aware of it. She wondered, for a fleeting moment, if the blonde kung-fu expert thought she'd been too hard on him, then shrugged it off as irrelevant. 'Got something for me?'

Gemma blinked. 'Er, yes, guv. Got the agency that handled the Mattie Cartwright adoption. They're being a bit cagey over the phone.'

'OK, we'll go talk head to head.'

'Warrant, guv?'

'Let's not bother with that unless we have to.'

'Guv.' Feeling a little shaky, Gemma grabbed her bag and followed Hillary across the floor. That little scene with Frank Ross had opened her eyes to several things she'd missed before. Or, not missed, exactly, but simply hadn't bothered to seriously consider. Now, she was wondering if that had been a serious mistake.

Hillary Greene was tough. She had to be. Not only to do the job she did, but also to put up with Ross for nearly six years. How many people would have been able to do that? She never let the little bastard grind her down, and never let him get the best of her. Then she'd survived the disaster that was her marriage to Ronnie, and the subsequent investigation into her possible corruption.

As she got behind the wheel of her car, and waited until Hillary had strapped herself in, Gemma began to believe that maybe, just maybe, Hillary Greene knew all about her. That Hillary Greene had read her like a book. That all this time, it was Greene who'd been playing her. And not the other way around.

She turned the engine on and pulled out of the parking lot, her face feeling hot, her hands feeling cold.

* * *

Barrington struck gold fairly early on. There weren't that many taxi firms that regularly dealt with the inhabitants of Middleton Cheney and, unusually, he struck lucky the first time. What's more, the driver's log did indeed show that he'd dropped Mr Kershaw off at Banbury station.

It was there that he hit his first snags. The ticket office computer listed tickets issued, but not names. It was, basically, an aid to the accountants, to ensure that ticket operators couldn't pocket any of the fare money. As an aid to tracking down individual passengers it was useless. He couldn't ask for, or access, Timothy Kershaw's credit card transactions from his laptop computer which he carried with him in the car. He needed to be logged on at police

HQ to do that — as well as get the necessary paperwork and permission.

But mindful of Hillary's instructions, he did ask to see the platform surveillance tapes. Luckily for him, he had a narrow timeframe of reference from the taxi driver, who'd dropped Kershaw at the station at 6:25 exactly.

Unluckily for him, Saturday evening was one of the busiest times of the week. The tapes showed a veritable crowd of people milling about. But, once again, Timothy Kershaw's good looks made him stand out, and, with the aid of the CCTV operator, he was able to track him from the moment he stepped out on to the platform. When he boarded the third train to come in, he had the operator rewind the grainy tape until he could see the front of the train, with the destination and number lit up just above the driver's window.

His heart sank: Birmingham.

Shit. The second most populated city in the damn country. He sighed, thanked the CCTV operator and left.

It would be back to the computer after all. He had to access those credit card transactions and just hope that, wherever he was, Timothy Kershaw was busy spending his money. And hadn't thought to take a lot of cash with him.

* * *

The adoption agency was run out of a tiny office on South Parks Road in Oxford. Hillary and Gemma were shown into a cupboard-sized office, so tiny it only had two chairs. A name plate resting on the desk informed them that a Mrs Rowena Tomkinson was in one of them. Hillary took the other. Gemma leaned against one wall and opened her notebook.

'This is about the Matilda Cartwright adoption, I take it?' Mrs Tomkinson said, after carefully scrutinizing their ID cards, and then actually ringing to confirm their authenticity. She was a short, compact sort of woman, with a carefully cut, permed ball of hair of that indeterminate colour when fair hair morphs into silver. She had deep-set dark eyes and a rather prominent nose. She would have made a terrifying headmistress of a girl's private school.

'I have to tell you that, had any of the parties concerned indicated that they wanted complete privacy to be maintained in this matter, I could not legally tell you anything without a court order,' she began, making Gemma's heart sink. 'However,' Rowena Tomkinson continued, 'you're probably aware of the initiatives that were implemented some years ago, whereby both the adopted child, and the birth mother, could opt to leave a letter lodged with the agency, giving permission for their identity and a telephone number to be given out, should either one wish to get in contact with the other.'

Hillary nodded.

'It's usually the children who want to know most, of course,' Mrs Tomkinson said, 'when the adopting parents inform them of the existence of birth parents. Of course, quite a few mothers come to regret their decision, and write in also.'

Hillary couldn't see Mattie Jones ever regretting her decision to have her child adopted. She could, after all, have had more children at any point in her marriage, had she felt the need for them. 'And in this case, who was it who wanted to get in touch?' she asked.

'Oh, both of course,' Rowena Tomkinson said, as if surprised. 'It has to be, for the system to work. It was designed so that children and birth parents *both* wanting to find each other were able to do so.'

Hillary blinked. 'I see.' There was something off here, but now was not the time to be distracted. She'd have to think about it later. 'Perhaps we can get some facts first. Matilda Cartwright gave birth when exactly?'

Rowena Tomkinson reached for the file that had been lying closed in front of her and opened it up. '1 March 1980.'

'And the sex of the baby?'

'Girl.'

'And the name of her adoptive parents?'

'I'm afraid I can't give that out without an order. It violates *their* rights to anonymity, you see.'

'Can you tell me the baby's name?'

'Tabitha. That was the adoptive parents' choice. There's no indication here that Miss Cartwright named her baby. Sometimes they do, you see, and the adopted parents can then choose whether or not to keep it.'

'And Tabitha's surname?'

Mrs Tomkinson gave her a long, level look.

'Miss Cartwright later became Mrs Jones,' Hillary said flatly, 'and last Wednesday was brutally murdered in her home in Bletchington. You may have read about it.'

Rowena's face tightened and she dipped her head slightly in acknowledgement.

'Now, for obvious reasons, we need to get in touch with Tabitha to find out if she ever *did* contact her mother. She might have vital evidence in a murder inquiry.'

'I understand that, but I simply can't give that kind of information out without the proper authority.'

Hillary sighed, knowing a dead end when she met it. 'Very well,' she said wearily, and got to her feet.

Outside, she rolled her shoulders and shook her head. 'OK, Gemma, the hard way it is. Get the warrant.'

When she got back to HQ, Frank was waiting in interview room one. She left Gemma to get on with it, and pushed her way inside.

Barry Jones looked up warily, and beside him, a grey-haired man in an old-fashioned dark blue suit watched her approach with a poker face to die for. He looked bored out of his skull and semi-comatose.

'Mr Jones asked for his solicitor to be present, guv,' Frank said flatly, fiddling with the tape and setting it recording. Hillary waited whilst he stated the date and time, and then they all listed themselves as present for the tape.

'Now, Mr Jones, we have a few more questions for you regarding your wife's murder,' Hillary began.

Barry Jones nodded. 'I didn't think it was about anything else, Inspector,' he said, then looked as if he immediately regretted it. 'I didn't mean that to sound flippant,' he added quickly, looked down at the tape recorder helplessly, then sighed and shrugged.

'I understand, sir,' Hillary said, not willing to get confrontational just yet.

'I want you to tell me about the insurance policy.' She let him have it without any fanfare, and saw him frown in puzzlement.

'Insurance policy?'

'The one on her life that will leave you half a million pounds richer, Mr Jones,' she said, letting her voice become disbelieving now. 'Melson and Blythe insurance company. Ring a bell?'

Barry Jones stared at her blankly for about two seconds, then began to smile. He saw her eyes narrow, and the smile instantly went. Then it seemed to creep back again, as if he couldn't hold it off. He put his hand over his mouth to hide it, then closed his eyes and shook his head.

After a few moments, he laughed out loud. 'I'm sorry,' he said, but laughed again, shook his head, waved his hand about somewhat helplessly in front of his face, then gave in and continued laughing. He laughed until his face began to redden with the effort, and his solicitor watched him with some alarm and perhaps the beginnings of interest.

A possible fat legal fee looked as if it might be in the offing after all.

Hillary, knowing mild hysteria when she saw it, simply waited. Eventually, Barry Jones got himself under control.

'I'm s-sorry. Really I am. It's just so damned f-funny. Mattie would be furious. In fact, she'd be turning in her grave. If she was b-buried yet,' he added, and set off laughing again.

Frank Ross grinned, in spite of himself, simply because laughter, like yawning, was infectious. He shot Hillary a curious look. Was he trying to lay grounds for an insanity plea?

Again, Hillary simply waited until Barry Jones had finished. 'Perhaps you could explain that, sir?'

Barry Jones took a long, shaky breath and leaned back in the chair. 'The insurance thing was all Mattie's idea, you see,' he said, wiping the tears that had pressed out against the side of his eyes. 'When we first started off the company — the second year we were in profit, it was, she insisted on taking out this half a million insurance policy on my life. I knew why, of course. Construction places can be dangerous places. You can fall off scaffolding, have bricks fall on your head and brain you, hell, even fall in a cement mixer. I had a friend who knew someone who went that way. Bloody awful to think about!' He shuddered. 'Anyway, Mattie was always the practical one. I could almost hear her mind working. "I've just put up all my inheritance for you, so I damned well want to make sure my pretty little arse is covered if you go and get yourself killed." That's what she was thinking all right.'

'Sounds reasonable,' Hillary said cautiously.

'Oh yeah. Yeah, I suppose so,' Barry Jones said at once, willing to be fair. Or at least to give that impression. 'But it sort of miffed me. I suppose I'm a bit superstitious like. Can't help it — my mum's the same, so I probably got it off her. It made me feel a bit . . .' He shrugged. 'You know, iffy. As if, by having an insurance policy on me, I was tempting fate.'

Hillary nodded. She'd come across this kind of reasoning before. It was why so many people put off making a will.

'Besides, the premiums were high, as you can imagine, and I put my foot down, said I wasn't having it,' Barry continued. 'But if you knew Mattie . . .' Jones broke off and sighed. He reached for a glass of water and took a sip, and ran a hand across his forehead. 'Nag, nag, nag. Went on and on about it. Finally I said: "OK, I'll sign the damned papers if we draw up one, exactly the same, on you."'

'Was Mattie superstitious too?' Hillary asked, with some surprise. From her reading of their murder victim, she'd have thought not.

Barry Jones laughed again. 'Nah! Mattie? No, tough as boots, Mattie. No, I thought paying out the extra premium payments might put her off. But, bugger me, the next day, there she was, the papers all drawn up and ready to sign. In the end I signed it just to get her off my back. And I've never given them a thought since. Deliberately tried not to at first, then, over the years, I managed to really put it out of my mind. She was always the one who did the paperwork, see, so she always did the paperwork to keep it up. I expect I would have cancelled it when it came up for renewal again this year. That's what's so funny. That's what really made me laugh.'

Barry Jones took another sip of water and began to chuckle. 'That would really have burned her biscuits, to know that I was going to get all that money because she'd insisted I sign the damn papers. And to think, if she'd put off dying for just a few more months, I wouldn't have renewed and wouldn't have got a penny. Now that really would have made her want to spit fire!'

And he began to laugh, hysterically, all over again.

Hillary let him go after half an hour or so. She was inclined to believe him, but in the back of her mind was the warning voice that he might simply be a good actor. But with no forensics linking him to the crime scene, no witnesses to his presence at the time of the killing, and with a pretty good alibi to boot, she didn't feel as if she had enough to charge him with.

Extra motive or not.

Back upstairs, Gemma's desk was empty. She'd obviously found a judge willing to sign the warrant. Such things could take time, Hillary knew, but in this case, her sergeant came back just after 4:00. Once more they drove out to South Parks Road, and once more Mrs Rowena Tomkinson called to verify that the warrant was legal. Only then did she come up with the full name of Mattie Jones's adopted daughter.

Tabitha Bryce.

She even informed them that she believed Miss Bryce had been raised in Nuneaton.

Hillary thanked her and followed Gemma down the narrow stairs and out on to the sun-baked road. At her car, Gemma opened up and got in and then, after a few puzzled minutes, got out again, when her boss remained standing on the pavement.

'Guv?'

'You know, Gemma, I've been thinking,' Hillary said, leaning across the roof of the car and fixing her gaze on Gemma. 'I just don't understand why Mattie Jones would have written to the adoption agency asking for her daughter to be given her name and telephone number if she ever inquired. I mean, why would she? What would she get out of it? With a divorce coming up, and a divorce, what's more, that she was determined to milk financially for all it was worth, she was taking an awful risk.'

Gemma slowly began to nod. 'Perhaps she didn't, guv,' she said crisply.

'No, perhaps she didn't,' Hillary agreed quietly. 'After all, if Mrs Tomkinson got a letter, supposedly from Mattie Jones, why would she question it? Oh, she'd double check, obviously; that is one careful woman in there. But if the writer gave an address in, say, Chipping Norton, for example, what would she learn? Nothing, except that a Miss Cartwright did indeed live at the address stated.' She answered her own question with a smile.

'You think Fiona Cartwright wrote the letter in Mattie's name, just to cause trouble?'

'Why not? She'd have known all about her sister having a baby and giving it up for adoption — it might have been possible for Mona Cartwright to keep that a secret from the neighbours all those years ago, but hardly from the immediate family.'

'And Fiona was desperate to have revenge on her sister,' Gemma agreed. 'She must have kept tabs on her comings and goings somehow, because she'd known all about the upcoming divorce for instance.'

'And in my interview with her, I was sure she knew something that I didn't,' Hillary remembered. 'She seemed to be hugging some nasty little gleeful thing close to her chest.' Hillary sighed. 'We need that letter. The one supposedly from Mattie Jones, written to the adoption agency. The document boys will be able to tell in a minute if she wrote it.'

'If it was written by hand, guv,' Gemma warned. But Hillary couldn't see the likes of Fiona Cartwright with a typewriter, much less a computer.

'Go and get it, Sergeant,' she said flatly.

'Guv.'

Hillary got into the car and waited. She didn't have to wait long. A few minutes later, Gemma all but threw herself behind the driving wheel, muttering furiously under her breath.

'Problem, Sergeant?'

'That bloody woman! She won't hand it over with this warrant. We need another one that specifically covers the removal of the letter.'

Hillary began to laugh. She couldn't help it. And, after a moment, Gemma too began to grin. Although why, she wasn't sure. She was the one who'd have to go through all that paperwork, and go back to the judge, feeling like a fool. Had she stopped to analyse it, she'd have realised that what she was feeling was a sense of camaraderie. That she was, in spite of everything, beginning to like her boss.

'Leave it until the morning,' Hillary said generously. 'Let's call it a day for now.'

She had a feeling tomorrow was going to be a busy day.

CHAPTER TWELVE

The next morning brought the first hint of rain for weeks. A dark mass of cloud lurking in the northern sky seemed to follow her in as Hillary coaxed Puff the Tragic Wagon to HQ. His clutch pedal still felt sluggish, and she decided she really would have to take him in to her mechanic that lunchtime. She could only hope that whatever ailed him wouldn't cost too much to fix. He was fast getting to the point where it would be cheaper to buy another second-hand car than pay out for anything major that needed doing to him.

She parked in a full and well-populated car park, and from the gossip she heard on the way to the main doors, learned that the sniper killer had confessed to all the murders. Which meant there wouldn't have to be a costly trial, and he'd be behind bars for good within weeks. The mood inside the station house was just as jubilant, and she had to stop and chat to several happy colleagues in the main office before she could finally make her way to her desk.

Once there, she dealt with several urgent details on her other cases, and foisted a committee meeting off on to Danvers. After all, that's what he was there for. She was just dealing with the last of her email messages, and contemplating her court appearance tomorrow on an arson case, when Gemma came in.

'Guv, got the warrant. I stopped off at Oxford court before coming in.'

'And your early bird caught a worm?'

'Justice Waldgrave, guv.'

Hillary grinned, impressed. Waldgrave was notoriously bad-tempered first thing in the morning. In fact, he was usually one of only a handful of judges who actually volunteered for Night Court, being by far at his best during the hours of darkness. In fact, didn't he have some sort of owl-like nickname?

'OK, you go back to South Parks Road and get the letter, then take it straight down to Documents. Ask if we can get a quick result. Use your wiles and whatnot if you have to.'

'Guv.' Gemma smiled. She left a few minutes later, and Hillary was still reading her notes on the arson case when Barrington came in. He nodded, and settled down at once at his station.

'No luck tracing Kershaw?' she asked.

'Went to Banbury station, just as you thought, guv,' Barrington said. 'From the CCTV I could tell he caught a train to Birmingham. So I need to get access to his credit card transactions, and thought I'd start on that first thing. Unless you've got something else for me?'

'No, that's fine,' she said, then grinned. 'When you apply for the warrant, I'd try Justice Waldgrave if I were you. It seems Gemma's already buttered him up nicely.'

'Guv,' Barrington said. But he had no intention of going to Waldgrave. He might still be the new boy around here, but even he'd learnt to avoid that particular judge first thing in the morning. Briefly he wondered how

Gemma had managed it — then realised that the blonde, fit sergeant probably had more resources at her disposal than mere mortals. He was still smiling inanely as he logged on to the mainframe and began to trawl the financial databases for details of Kershaw's banking arrangements.

Hillary had just put away the arson case notes, and was sitting in her chair, wondering if it would pay to go and have another word with Fiona Cartwright, when the telephone rang. She picked it up almost absently, her mind still on the dead woman's sister in Chipping Norton. She was sure Fiona had a lot more to tell them, but it would probably pay to wait until they had confirmation about the letter lodged at the adoption agency. Fiona was one of those women who'd only get stubborn and dig her heels in, unless they had something solid to shake her up with.

'Yes?'

'DI Greene?' The voice was male, unknown, but with that certain tone that told her she was talking to another police officer.

'Yes.'

'DS Blight, Woodstock,' the voice confirmed. 'I've got something here that might interest you. Came in late last night. Does the name George Philby mean anything to you?'

Hillary sat up straighter in her chair. 'It does, yes. Trouble?'

'Oh yes, trouble all right. But he's in it, not causing it. We caught a call about ten forty-five last night. A man was mugged outside the pub in Carterton, the Bull's Rush. Know it?'

'No, fill me in. Trouble spot?'

'No, ma'am, not really. It can get a bit rough on a Saturday night sometimes, if Oxford are playing at home and lose, but that's par for the course. No rep for drugs, and the landlord's squeaky clean as far as we can tell.'

'And I know there's no previous on Philby,' Hillary agreed.

'So he's a person of interest then? Thought he might be. A DC of ours has a wife works in the office out at the airport. Told her husband you lot had been in to talk to him. So when he read in the log book this morning about the mugging, he thought you might be interested, like.'

'I am. Very interested. Give the kid a pat on the back and watch out for him. He sounds like he's got a good head on his shoulders.'

'Oh yes, he's a bright spark all right,' Sergeant Blight said laconically.

'So what can you tell me about the mugging? I wouldn't have thought a small village on a Monday night was a likely time or spot for muggers.'

'No, ma'am, neither did we. Especially nasty ones like this.'

Hillary shifted in her chair, feeling something excited begin to uncoil in her stomach. 'Bad how?' she asked softly.

'Knifing.'

'Start from the beginning,' Hillary said crisply, and something in her voice seemed to register with the man from Woodstock, because he suddenly became very alert.

'Ma'am. At ten forty-five we received a 999 call from the landlord of the Bull's Rush. He said one of his customers had been attacked on leaving the pub, and was bleeding profusely. When asked, he said he'd already called for an ambulance, but that the customer, George Philby, was adamant that he'd been attacked by a hoodie. That was his word, not ours.'

Hillary grunted. 'Go on.'

'The nearest patrol car was dispatched, and arrived on the scene a few minutes after the ambulance. The crew had got him patched up and on the gurney by then, so they weren't able to question him themselves. They talked at length to the landlord, however, and several bystanders, who were mainly customers at the pub, and they all agreed that George Philby was a regular, coming in mostly on a Monday, Thursday and Sunday night. Everyone's willing to swear up and down that he only had two pints of cider, his favourite tipple, and that when he left, at around half past ten, he was sober and, what's more, left alone.'

'They didn't see anyone follow him out?'

'No, ma'am. The only people who were at the bar that night, but didn't stay around to watch the drama, were a Mr Thomas Ealing, a seventy-six-year-old retired farm labourer, and a Mrs Wendy Tuckey, a forty-six-year-old woman who works in the village as a domestic. Mrs Tuckey's husband says she got back by a quarter to eleven, her usual time, and although Mr Ealing lives alone, I've got a note here from the officer who interviewed him first thing this morning that he suffers from Parkinson's. Hands as shaky as a leaf in autumn, so no way he could have handled a knife.'

'Sounds as if whoever did it was waiting outside for him, then.'

'Yes, ma'am, that's what we think.'

'Any history of muggings around there at all?'

'No, ma'am.'

'OK. Go on.'

'A Mr Alistair Tring left about five minutes after Philby, and found him lying in the pub car park, not far from some shrubbery in the corner. It's a common shortcut with pub users, apparently, who go diagonally across the car park and push through the bushes on to a side road that leads off to the council estates. That's where Mr Tring was going, and that's where Philby lives too. Tring says he literally stumbled over the victim. One of the patrol car johnnies noted that the street light on that corner was broken.'

'Recently?' Hillary asked sharply, and heard the smile in the sergeant's voice as he answered.

'That's what I wanted to know. I've got lads out there now trying to find out. First reports are from the landlord of the pub, who says he thinks it was working all right Sunday night. We should be getting confirmation from the houses on the other side soon. If any bugger actually noticed, that is.'

Hillary grunted again. She knew from bitter experience just how unobservant the general public could be at times. But the pub landlord was probably as reliable a witness as any. After all, he was the one who had a vested interest in keeping his premises well-lit at night.

'What's Philby's status now?'

'Got a lad waiting to interview him at the John Radcliffe. He had to have surgery last night, though, so it's a question of when the anaesthetic wears off as to when we can talk to him. Doctors say he's in no danger. Knife slid off a rib, never punctured anything vital. He's a big man, apparently, plenty of muscle on him, which would have helped. Don't know anything yet about the type of blade, or what have you.'

Hillary sighed. 'OK. I'm going to go over there and see if I can talk to him. I'll bring your boy in with me, he can take notes for the both of us. Just email a copy back to me when he's typed them up — if that suits.'

'Will do, ma'am.'

Hillary thanked him and hung up. She glanced across at Barrington, who was still mapping out Timothy Kershaw's financial doings, and grabbed her bag. 'When Gemma comes back tell her I want her to bring in the daughter, Tabitha, for questioning.'

'Guv,' Barrington said, not taking his eyes off the screen.

* * *

John Radcliffe Hospital sat like a large, multi-tiered white wedding cake on top of Headington Hill. It was a massive place and Hillary, who didn't like hospitals anyway, had not-so-fond memories of this one. It was where she'd been taken after being shot during the Fletcher raid, and although she had great respect and affection for nurses, she'd never managed to feel quite the same rapport with doctors.

And she didn't think *that* was going to change any when, after inquiring at the main desk, she found George Philby in Birch Ward on the fifth floor, and caught the chief registrar in the middle of his 'rounds.' This, as far as she could see, consisted of a silver-haired, slightly sneering man, surrounded by sycophantic students, talking down to patients in beds, and simply reiterating everything that was already written down on their charts.

She was sure she was probably prejudiced, though, so she waited patiently, with just the odd sigh that made the ward sister cast her amused and sympathetic looks, until he was finished. She then approached the ward sister and asked if it would be possible to have a few words with George Philby. The nurse, with a knowing smile, then tackled the doctor herself, who rumbled and grumbled a bit, but eventually seemed to assent. The nurse, a dark-eyed, dark-haired woman with a tired mouth, came back and told her that she could have ten minutes.

Hillary nodded to the young PC who was sitting at the nurses' station, and they made their way into Birch Ward, which was tucked in off one corner of the much larger Elm Ward. Inside, there were only four beds, all occupied by men. Nearest the door were two old men, both fast asleep and hooked up to IVs, with identical leg plasters. She wondered if they'd had some kind of bizarre accident, until she speed-read on their charts, in passing, that they'd both been scheduled to see a specialist in varicose veins.

In the far left-hand corner, a young lad, maybe fifteen or sixteen years old, lay back, eyes closed, blissfully listening to a tune emanating from headphones in his ears. Hillary could hear the repetitive rat-a-tat-tat of a heavy metal drum beat as she passed by.

George Philby, in the other bed, was awake and watched them approach with a defiant, slightly wry smile. 'Hello again,' he said, before Hillary could speak, or introduce the constable with her. 'Bet you never thought we'd meet again so soon. And in circs like this,' he added, lifting up both hands, palm up, to indicate the hospital room. 'What the hell's the world coming to, huh?'

Hillary had no idea. She took a red plastic chair and sat down. She indicated the constable to do the same and take notes.

'Mr Philby, what can you tell me about what happened last night?'

If the aeroplane mechanic wondered why the officer in charge of his ex-fiancée's murder case wanted to question him about his mugging, it didn't show. Perhaps he just assumed she was handling the case because she'd already met him. She knew from experience that the general public had little idea about how case assignments were handed out.

'Well, it's like this,' George said calmly, turning to look out the window. This high up, and lying flat on his back, all he could see were the tops of the trees in the park opposite, and the gathering rain clouds. 'I go to the pub about three times a week. Sometimes only for an hour or so. Gets me out the house if the kids are being noisy, like.' Hillary smiled, wondering what his wife did to escape the tyranny of the young, but knew better than to ask.

'I got to the Bull about nine o'clock, right after putting the youngest to bed. Ordered a Strongbow, played some darts, chatted like. Anyway, I had my second — I only ever have two, Scout's honour — and when Vince called time, I was out the door.'

Hillary held up a hand to stop him there. He was wearing pale blue pyjamas, and apart from some surgical gauze and dressing wrapped around his ribs, looked surprisingly well. He had a slight pallor under his summer tan, maybe, but he didn't seem to be in any pain, wasn't having any trouble breathing or talking, and seemed not so much distressed as pissed off.

'Did you notice anybody in the pub watching you? A stranger, someone taking more interest in you than you liked?'

'Nope. I know all the regulars. Monday nights are pretty quiet anyway. No one was there who shouldn't be — not that I saw anyway.'

'OK. So you left — and I understand you always cut across the pub car park diagonally, to take the shortcut to the housing estate?'

'Yeah? How you know that?' George asked, impressed, then grinned. 'Sorry, forgot. You're a copper. You lot know everything, right?'

Hillary wished. 'So what happened then?'

'Well, I was crossing the car park, heading for the corner. Funny, the light was out — the street light on the corner. I saw how dark it was and thought it was strange — it's not like Vince to let the council off with something like that. Anyway, I was just pushing through the bushes — don't ask me what they are, I dunno, they have yellow flowers on 'em all through the summer, and no thorns, I'm glad to say.'

Hillary nodded.

'Anyway, I felt this sharp pain in my side, like. It took me by surprise, right, because, as I said, I knew the flowers didn't have any thorns. Anyway, I starts to turn around to look. My side felt kind of funny — hot and sort of sticky. And then I sees this young lad, crouching down in the bushes.'

'A young lad? Can you describe him?'

'Course not, it was dark, like I said,' George said, a shade impatiently. 'But I could make out the hood on his head — the street light from the opposite side of the road caught the side of it, like. Anyway, then I see the flash of his knife, and realise the young bastard's cut me. So I let rip with this huge roar, like. I read somewhere if you're attacked by a bear or something, you're supposed to make as much noise as possible to scare it off. Nothing says it's supposed to work on muggers in the same way, but at the time that was the first thought that popped into my head. Anyway, it must have worked, because he took off like a scalded cat. White trainers . . .' He suddenly snapped his fingers. 'Yeah, I remember now, he was wearing white trainers. They showed up as he ran back across the car park — up and down, up and down. I remember seeing them. I was lying on the ground by then, see, and I was seeing them from the ground up. Reminded me of a rabbit's tail — you know, when a rabbit's running away. Funny the things you think of, innit?'

'Shock, Mr Philby. It makes the mind do cartwheels.'

'Right. Course. Anyway, that's all I can tell you. Didn't even lay hands on the little sod. Wish I had — he wasn't much more than a twig. I'd have pulverized the sneaky little git.'

'You say he was thin?'

'Yep. Thin, not so tall — not as tall as you, I don't think.'

'Could you see what he was wearing?'

'Jeans — dark blue or maybe black. And that hooded top thing. Looked sort of beige-coloured — but it's hard to tell at night. Street lighting can turn colours funny.'

Hillary knew that. Many a time, as she walked a beat, she'd been asked to be on the lookout for a brown car that later turned out to be green, or a suspect wearing a purple windcheater that was actually blue.

'Did he drop the knife?' she asked.

'No, he took it with him, I reckon. I think I remember seeing the light flash on it as he passed the entrance to the pub.'

Hillary sighed. 'You upset anybody recently, Mr Philby? You don't owe bookies any money, that kind of thing?'

'Never gambled in my life.'

'And you're sure there's no irate husband who thinks you may have been taking liberties with his wife, anything of that nature?'

'Do me a favour! Wife'd kill me first, let alone a bloody hoodie.'

Hillary had to grin. 'And you haven't been getting on the wrong side of, say, a fence?'

George Philby flushed a bit at that, and then shook his head. 'Nah, nothing like that.' She believed him. Oh, she was sure he sold the odd hot item to a mate or two, but this didn't smack of anything business related. This smacked of a sneak attack on a big man by a much younger, and lightweight, opponent.

The hoodie had obviously planned this well. First he — or she, since from the description it could have been a female attacker just as easily as a male — must have, at some point, disabled the street light in the corner of the car park. This alone told her that Philby's attacker must have been watching him for some time, learning his habits, and picking the best spot for an ambush. All totally premeditated.

The bushes too made for an ideal site for a clever ambush. Well hidden, and crouched down out of sight, he or she had a good angle of attack. Up. Not many people, when being attacked, think to look down. The bushes would also have provided much-needed wriggle room, and would have helped the hoodie evade being grabbed by the physically impressive Philby.

Running had been a smart move. Perhaps the assailant had hoped the single stab wound to the abdomen would have been instantly fatal. In fact, Philby had probably been very lucky that it hadn't been.

Yes. She had no doubt that someone had tried to kill Philby last night. Not rob him. Not warn him or scare him. But kill him.

Had the same person watched Mattie Jones in the same way? Learned her habits and decided that the best place to attack her was in her own home? Perhaps, being a female victim that time, the hoodie had felt safe enough to risk a full-frontal, head-to-head attack on Mattie.

'Mr Philby, I think . . .' she began, but just then the nurse returned.

'Time's up I'm afraid, Inspector. And there's a telephone call for you. You can take it at my desk.'

Hillary nodded and stood up. She looked down at George Philby and sighed. 'Mr Philby, I think the same person who stabbed and killed your ex-fiancée might have begun to stalk you. From now on, you'd better avoid dark places. And check the security out at your house. If you don't have them already, fit locks on all the windows, and install a burglar alarm. You have children, yes? Make sure they don't go to or come back from school alone.'

She left him looking dismayed, and followed the nurse to her desk. There she lifted the receiver and heard Barrington's voice.

'I've found him, guv. Kershaw. He's got rooms at the Bay Tree Motel, in Solihull.'

'Bring him in,' Hillary said flatly.

After speaking to George Philby, she was in no mood for the niceties.

* * *

When Gemma came back from dropping the adoption agency letter off in Documents, she found the office deserted. She noticed that even Danvers was out of his cubby hole, and wondered if something had broken while she'd been out. Then Frank Ross wandered in, and told her that Hillary was at the hospital and why, and that Barrington had sped off to Birmingham to bring in Kershaw.

She'd been at her desk for nearly a quarter of an hour when Hillary came back. Gemma watched her walk to her desk and sit down heavily. She had a troubled, tight look on her face that made the blonde sergeant wonder what was up.

'Gemma, the moment Documents confirm that the handwriting's Fiona's, I want you to go and pick her up and bring her in. Grill her. I want to know what other kinds of mischief she's been up to.'

'Guv. Something wrong?'

Hillary blinked, obviously deep in thought, and looked at her sergeant. She shook her head. 'This attack on Philby. I don't like it. I don't like it at all. I'm beginning to think that the attack on Mattie Jones wasn't a one-off. I think Philby was the next target. And who knows who else could be in the firing line.'

'Fiona Cartwright? You think she's next? Somebody's bumping off Mattie's family, or those nearest and dearest?'

Hillary didn't think that. Not quite. She had the beginnings of an idea, a possibility, that was all. But it might just come up trumps. 'Hmm? No, no, I think Fiona Cartwright is probably safe.'

'Barry Jones? Should he be warned?'

Hillary frowned. Should he be? If what she was beginning to suspect was true, it was conceivable that Barry Jones could be a target. The husband who gave Mattie Jones such a good life. 'Hell, I think we'd better. Gemma, go and see him. Check out the security on that flat of his. Warn him to be careful, but try not to spook him. Tell him if he's out and about anywhere, not to go down any dark alleys. And if he sees a thin youth wearing a hoodie and white trainers, to be very, very careful indeed.'

'Right, guv.'

Hillary reached for the phone to call Documents. She was sure Gemma would have remembered to ask them to put a priority on it, but a little backup call from a DI didn't hurt. And Hillary knew her name at HQ was currently riding high after her recent award for bravery. That done, she had nothing else to do but wait for Barrington to come back from Birmingham.

* * *

Timothy Kershaw did not look happy. He didn't look happy to be sitting in interview room four, with a tape recorder running in front of him. He seemed especially unhappy about the blank-faced constable standing at the door to stop him in case he decided to leg it, and the curvaceous, rather handsome woman sitting opposite him seemed to do nothing to allay his unease.

'Mr Kershaw, I take it DC Barrington informed you why I wanted to talk to you?'

'Yes. But I don't see why we had to do this here. I mean, I'd have preferred to stay in Birmingham.'

'The Bay Tree Motel a particular favourite of yours, is it, sir?' Hillary asked, guessing that dumb insolence was the best way to get through to the man. Keith had told her the motel was a typically large, anonymous motorway café-cum-motel, with a view of a cement factory.

'I just wanted to get away to clear my head, Inspector,' Kershaw said huffily. 'Something I could hardly do if I was somewhere where I was known, and had to keep on constantly chatting to friends.'

Hillary smiled. 'Not many of them in the Bay Tree I expect, sir,' she agreed cheerfully, pleased to see him flush with annoyance. 'You own Kershaw Textiles, yes?'

Timothy Kershaw sighed and nodded. He really was a very good-looking man, and was dressed impeccably in a lightweight mint- green polo shirt and dark bottle-green slacks. It brought out the blue of his eyes and emphasized the colour of his hair and brows. He oozed an almost old-world sort of masculine elegance — a bit like an Errol Flynn for the new millennium. But his eyes were scared, and his tapered fingers fiddled constantly with a pen. She got the feeling that, for all that he was a successful businessman, Timothy Kershaw didn't have much backbone to maintain him in times of trouble. Even if she hadn't known of his drink-driving convictions, she would have guessed this man needed a crutch of some sort to help him along.

'Tell us about Mattie Jones, Mr Kershaw,' Hillary said quietly. 'We know you were lovers,' she added, knowing he was about to deny ever having heard of the lady. 'We got your description from the staff of the Cloverleaf Hotel, where you spent the weekend with her recently.'

Kershaw flushed. 'Nothing wrong with that. I'm single, and she was about to be divorced.'

'I never said there was anything wrong with it,' Hillary said patiently. 'I do, however, wonder why you didn't come forward to talk to us when you learned that she'd been so brutally murdered.'

Kershaw shifted on his seat and tapped his pen against the table top. Carefully, Hillary reached across and laid her palm against it. 'Please don't do that, Mr Kershaw — the sound of it is interfering with the tape.'

'DI Greene has just taken a pen from Mr Kershaw,' Keith Barrington spoke for the benefit of said tape.

Kershaw sighed heavily and leaned back sulkily in his chair. 'Oh, very well.'

Hillary waited.

Kershaw looked at her in an attempt at cool amusement. It fell woefully short. 'What?'

'I'm waiting to hear why you didn't come forward when you heard that the woman you, if not loved, then were at least presumably reasonably fond of, was murdered?'

'Why should I? I didn't kill her. And I don't know who did. So what could I possibly have told you?' he asked, and seemed rather pleased with his logic.

'If all that were true, then why were you holed up in hiding at the Bay Tree Motel, Mr Kershaw?' Hillary asked devastatingly.

Kershaw paled visibly at the palpable hit. 'I told you,' he said at last. 'I wanted to think.'

'You saw your likeness in the Saturday edition of the local paper, and you bolted, Mr Kershaw,' Hillary corrected him grimly. 'And I want to know why,' she added, real steel in her voice now.

'Oh, all right.' As expected, he caved in almost at once. 'If you want to know, I was scared.'

Hillary lifted one eyebrow. 'Of what?'

'Of what?' Kershaw repeated, his voice rising to a squeak. 'Of whoever killed her, of course.'

Hillary nodded. 'Why do you think that you're in danger, Mr Kershaw? What do you know that would make you so dangerous to Mattie's killer?'

'Nothing! I don't know anything. Well, only about the dog shit. And the funny phone calls. And the wine. The wine was the last straw. Mattie said she'd get a restraining order after the wine.'

Hillary sighed and rubbed a hand across her forehead. This was going to take some sorting. 'Perhaps we can start again, sir. And try to be a bit clearer this time. You say she was receiving phone calls? Threatening phone calls, I take it?'

'Yes. Yes, I think so. I only know because I was at the house once, and the phone rang, and I waited for Mattie to answer it. I wasn't supposed to answer her phone at the house,' he said, a shade shamefaced, when Hillary looked at him oddly. 'You know, in case it was her husband.'

Hillary nodded. 'Of course. And?'

'Well, when Mattie answered it, she became quite angry. Abusive even, and hung up so hard she broke the receiver. She had to get another phone to replace it. Then she admitted she'd been getting nuisance calls.'

'Did she say who from?'

'No. But I think she knew who it was. It was just a feeling I got,' he added quickly, when he saw she was about to ask him to expand on that. 'Mattie was a strong-minded woman, Inspector. She wouldn't stand for nonsense like that. She was going to get the number changed, or go ex-directory or something.'

Hillary glanced across at Barrington and ordered him to check up on that, and also to check Mattie's phone records and see if they could trace the origin of the calls. Barrington nodded, but had needed no prompting. He'd have done it the moment the interview was over anyway.

'But the phone calls were only the beginning?' she prompted, turning back to Mattie's lover.

'Yes. One night, oh about two months ago it would have been, I called around to pick her up to take her to the Playhouse, and found her cleaning up this appalling mess. Dog shit had been posted through the front door. I told her to leave it for her cleaner, but she insisted on doing it herself. That's what made me think she had some idea of who was behind it all. She obviously didn't want her daily to realise anything was amiss.'

Hillary nodded. 'So whoever it was, it wasn't a stranger. She'd simply have put the law on to him or her if it had been.'

'Oh yes,' Kershaw agreed. 'Mattie wouldn't have hesitated. She didn't like to have her life disrupted in any way.'

'No. I imagine she didn't. You mentioned something about wine?'

'Yes. This was quite recently. Just before we went away for the weekend, in fact. Mattie came back to find a bottle of wine on her doorstep with a big red ribbon on it. A note attached to it said it was from an old school friend who'd been passing by, but hadn't found her in. Anyway, Mattie rang this friend up, and she was quite astonished. Said she hardly remembered Mattie from school, and, since she was living in Inverness now, was hardly likely to be "in the neighbourhood" and wouldn't have left any wine if she had been.' Kershaw looked away from Hillary Greene's bland face and stared at the wall over her shoulder. 'So Mattie poured the wine down the sink. She said it was a good Burgundy, one of her favourites, but that it had an odd smell, underneath the usual bouquet. She said that that was the final straw, and that she was going to do something about it "once and for all". That's what she said. I thought she meant she'd get a restraining order or something. But then . . . well, she was killed, and I got scared.'

Hillary could well believe it. It sounded as if someone had been running a hate campaign against the victim for some time. It had been conducted so well that this was the first sniff of it that they'd come across. But then, with even the victim being at pains to cover it up, that was probably not so surprising.

'Mr Kershaw, where were you between the hours of six thirty and eight thirty a.m. on the morning of Wednesday last?' she asked crisply.

'I left the house at seven. My neighbours can confirm that — Mr Kilby and Mrs Bradshaw both saw me. We tend to leave at the same time every morning. And at ten past I was at the office. My assistant can confirm I was in. We were doing some stocktaking. I didn't leave the office until seven twenty that night. Not even for lunch. I have to work very long hours,' Kershaw whined.

After a few more questions, when she was finally sure there was nothing else he could tell them, Hillary let him go.

She told Barrington to check the alibi first, just to be sure, then get on to Mattie Jones's telephone records. But she had the sinking feeling that any phone calls unaccounted for would only lead back to public pay phones. The ones that still took coins, not telephone cards.

Not that that would matter. Because now Hillary had a very fair idea who must have made those calls, killed Mattie, and why.

Now all she had to do was prove it.

CHAPTER THIRTEEN

Keith Barrington finished transcribing the last of his notes on to the computer, then swore to himself softly. 'Guv, I forgot to tell you yesterday. Vera Grearsley's alibi checks out. I took the bus from Bletchington to Oxford, and several passengers remember her that morning — seeing as she was a new face, like you said they might. Plus, at Gloucester Green,' he mentioned Oxford's bus station, 'I found the driver who'd taken the bus out that morning, and her description rang a bell with him, too, though he couldn't swear it was the Wednesday that he saw her.'

Hillary yawned and nodded. 'Fine.' She'd already mentally crossed Grearsley off her list, but it always helped to get all the boxes ticked. Just one less thing with the potential to rear up and bite her in the backside later on.

She glanced at her watch. It was only 3:05.

* * *

Outside, Clive turned on to the secondary road that ran parallel with almost the entire length of Kidlington's main street and cruised at a very steady twenty miles an hour towards Kidlington Thames Valley HQ. He was driving a clapped-out van that he'd bought on the cheap, and resprayed white. Using a stencil, he'd come up with a fake name for a chimney-sweep firm, and had emblazoned it across the sides. Now he pulled up beside some smart 1920s detached houses that overlooked the large Thames Valley offices. He looked around casually before getting out, and promptly began whistling. Just another small-time bloke doing a dirty job to make an honest living.

He walked up to one house, and rang the bell. He was fairly sure that at this time of the day most people would still be out at work, so he was somewhat surprised when it was answered. But the woman was elderly, and looked a little scared. She kept the door chain firmly attached.

Clive smiled at her kindly. 'Need your chimney swept, love?'

'Oh no, thank you,' she said at once, and closed the door in his face. And Clive Myers nodded. Quite right too, love, he thought. You never know what hustler, creep or conman might be knocking at your door these days. Not wanting to stay in range of her prying eyes, he got back in the van and drove past the entrance to the cop shop, and pulled up outside some newer semi-detached houses on the far side. This time, when he walked up the path and rang a bell, he was lucky. No one answered.

Still whistling cheerfully, he went back to his white chimney-sweep's van, and withdrew a long, extending ladder. Looking for all the world as if he had a right to be there, the man from Thame went around the back of the house and set the ladder up against the wall. He then went back to his van for the bag with the brushes inside — both the real ones, and the object hidden underneath them. When he returned to the back of the house, however, he made no attempt to climb the ladder, but sat down on a four-foot-high retaining garden wall, and reached inside the bag for a pair of binoculars. Once he'd checked the houses all around, and assured himself there were no curious faces watching what he was up to, he twiddled with the magnifying ring settings until the main door of the police HQ office building came into sharp focus.

Now it was just a matter of waiting.

* * *

'Guv, I think I've tracked down Tabitha Bryce,' Gemma said, making both her boss and Barrington prick up their ears. 'It threw me at first because she didn't seem to be in the system. She hasn't applied for a driving licence, she's not registered to pay council tax, but she's not on the social, and there's been no sign of her at her adopted parents' home for nearly ten years. Or so they said.'

Hillary's eyes narrowed. 'But inspiration struck?'

'Brainwave, guv,' Gemma smiled grimly. 'I thought I'd check the hostels and shelters, and bingo. Found her in a women's refuge shelter in Coventry.'

Hillary sighed, and murmured, 'Yeah, I thought it might be something like that.'

'Guv?' Gemma frowned, and Hillary shrugged.

'Never mind. Go and bring her in.'

Gemma blinked. No softly-softly approach? No going out to interview her there, on the premises, where she'd feel less threatened? It wasn't like Hillary Greene not to take on board the fact that someone living in a women's refuge shelter needed careful handling. That they were bound to be more vulnerable than your average Joe in the street.

'The people who run the refuge might kick up a fuss, guv,' Gemma pointed out, wondering what it was she must have missed. 'Those places have matrons who would give dragons a run for their money. Probably got a few tame bleeding-heart solicitors in their back pockets, too.'

'Tread softly, then,' Hillary said, with a smile. 'Think of it as a test of diplomacy.'

Gemma sighed. When would the woman stop testing her? Gemma knew that she was already by far the best sergeant Hillary had ever had. 'And if they still won't bite?'

'Bring her in for questioning,' Hillary said flatly. 'Kicking and screaming, dragons and solicitors in tow if you have to.' She leaned back in her chair, and smiled encouragingly. 'But I've got the feeling that if you tell her it's about her mother, she'll come as quietly as a lamb.'

Gemma's fine grey eyes widened then. She went very still for a moment, then slowly exhaled. Ah. So that was it. 'Right, guv,' she said softly. And left.

Barrington, alerted by the mutually understanding look that passed between the two women also caught on. Shit. Hillary thought the daughter had done it!

Just then the phone on Gemma's desk rang, and he leaned across to answer it. 'DS Fordham's desk. Barrington speaking.' He listened, made a few monosyllabic responses, then hung up. 'Guv, Documents. They have the results on that letter from the adoption agency.'

Hillary blinked. Jumping Jehosaphat, that was quick. She'd expected it to be at least a day or two — not mere hours. Her stock with the boffins must be higher than she thought. 'And?'

'Preliminary findings say it was written by Fiona Cartwright all right, guv.'

'Bring her in too,' Hillary said flatly. 'Why not? We might as well all play happy family reunions.'

* * *

Outside, Clive Myers, squatting against a big laurel bush and using it for cover to hide his activities, began to assemble his rifle. He was very, very careful, and painstakingly accurate. Whatever happened, he mustn't miss.

* * *

Tabitha Bryce had her mother's black hair, only she wore hers long and unfettered down her back. Her eyes, however, were not green, but a dark shade of blue. She was stick-thin, to the point of anorexia, Hillary thought, and wore a grey sweatshirt with some sort of Formula One racing logo on it, and jeans that were ripped at the knees — whether as a fashion statement, or simply through old age and wear and tear, it was hard to say. She wore very white brand-new trainers.

She watched Hillary Greene come into the room with an avid eagerness that told Hillary at once that this wasn't going to be pleasant. Easy, perhaps, but not pleasant. What she needed from this woman was a confession, and Hillary could almost feel her straining to give it.

She barely glanced at the mirror affixed to one wall, from behind which both Paul Danvers and Mel Mallow were watching the proceedings. She'd informed them of her conclusions the moment Gemma had phoned to confirm that she was on her way back to Oxford with Tabitha Bryce, and that she had, as Hillary had predicted, made no fuss about leaving with her.

Now they would all see if her optimism about closing the case within the next hour was justified.

'DI Hillary Greene,' she identified herself for the tape that Gemma had already set running. 'Miss Bryce, thank you for coming in.'

'Cartwright,' Tabitha Bryce said at once. 'I'm changing my name by deed poll. I've signed the papers and everything, and as soon as I've got the fee paid, it'll be legal and binding.'

Hillary nodded. She didn't think it cost a lot to change your name nowadays — maybe as little as ten or twenty pounds even. If that was so, either Tabitha Bryce had a habit to feed, or she really was as poor as the fabled church mouse.

'Miss Cartwright, then. You've met your Aunt Fiona of course?' She stated it as a fact, and added before

Tabitha could start up a song and dance: 'She's currently in the next interview room talking to a constable of mine about that letter she lodged at your adoption agency.'

Tabitha Bryce, soon to be Cartwright, looked momentarily disconcerted, then gave a small, reluctant grin. 'Yeah. All right. I know her. She won't get into any trouble about that, will she? You know, pretending to be her sister or nothing?'

Hillary shrugged. 'I doubt it. Unless the adoption agency wants to press charges. But I doubt they'd be willing to put up with the publicity that would cause.'

'Oh good,' Tabitha nodded emphatically. 'Because Aunt Fee has had enough trouble in her life already. Bloody men knocking her up then leaving her. And the bastards who run the social trying to cut off her allowance. And all the time that bitch of a mother of mine was rolling in clover.'

Hillary nodded. 'You must have been disappointed at first, I imagine. Going to Chippie, to Fiona's house. It's a bit of a dump, isn't it?'

Tabitha sat up a bit straighter in her chair, and her chin came forward. 'No! Why should I have? I just wanted to find and talk to my real mum. And when I saw the place where I thought my mum was living, well, it all made sense, didn't it?' She sounded stressed, and so very much younger than her twenty-eight years that Hillary nodded, not without sympathy.

'You thought your birth mother was poor. Too poor to cope with a baby when only a teenager,' Hillary agreed softly. 'It made you think that she'd been more or less forced to give you away. Maybe, even, that she thought you'd have a better chance of a good life, away from her and her harsh circumstances?'

Tabitha's dark blue eyes watered, and she angrily brushed a hand across them. 'Yeah. What a laugh that was, though!' She snorted, hatred and bitterness and a bleak resentment colouring her laughter and making it sound like something diseased. 'To think I actually thought, for even a little while, that my mother had given me away thinking I'd be better off. But in reality, she just didn't give a toss, did she?' Tabitha demanded.

She was leaning across the table now, and underneath it, Hillary could hear her feet tapping a tattoo on the floor. She was definitely hyper, but whether it was drug related, or simply the result of too much emotion, she wasn't sure.

'Let's take it slow and easy, shall we?' Hillary said smoothly. 'You went to Chippie and knocked on Fiona's door. Did she tell you straight away who she was?'

'Only my aunt, you mean?' Tabitha said. 'Yeah. Well, more or less. I mean, she had me in and gave me a cup of tea first like. Let me jabber on a bit. But, yeah, then she told me who she really was.'

'You were surprised?'

'I'll say. I was expecting my mum, wasn't I, not her sister.'

Hillary nodded. 'Did your aunt tell you why she'd done what she did? Wrote a letter to the adoption agency pretending to be her sister, I mean?'

'Yeah,' Tabitha said, and it was then that Hillary realised that, so far, she hadn't noticed the younger girl blink. 'She said she felt sorry for me, and that she'd felt a bit guilty all those years that I'd been given up, like, and not kept in the family. She said her mother, my grandmother, Mona, should have looked after me, made my bitch of a mother take responsibility for me. She said there was no reason, really, for giving me away. It was only that her mother had to be "respectable". It was still different times for people like them, she said, even only twenty-eight years ago. Her family had always been this proud conservative working-class unit, clinging to their pride in the family name and all that crap.'

Hillary nodded. 'But that wasn't the only reason, was it?' she said softly. She couldn't see the embittered Fiona Cartwright stopping at just that. Not now she'd finally got her claws into something as juicy as Mattie's secret love child. No, she'd want to spread the poison on nice and thick.

'No,' Tabitha immediately confirmed. 'Fiona told me all about Mattie all right. How she was always the pretty one, the smart one, the one who wanted to have it all. Get out of that rat hole of a village, as she said it, to someplace more upmarket. Have a big car, the big house, the holidays abroad, the fine clothes and all that. And how she saw going to university as a way to get it. So, of course, she wasn't going to let me get in the way of all that, was she?'

The young woman was breathing hard now, and Hillary deliberately eased the tension a bit by pouring a glass of water for herself. Then she nodded at Tabitha. 'Would you like something to drink?'

'No thanks.' Tabitha Bryce was too het up to be distracted. She watched Hillary like a hawk, her eyes darting — but still not blinking — her lower lip trembling just slightly, as if she was perpetually on the verge of sobbing her heart out.

Hillary sighed. 'You strike me as a very smart girl, Miss Cartwright. It must surely have occurred to you that your aunt might have her own axe to grind? I only spoke to Fiona briefly, but I could tell right away that she loathed her sister like poison.'

'Oh yes, I realised that. That's why I didn't really believe her at first. I mean, it made me think a bit that Fiona was the one to write the letter, and that *she* was the one who'd wanted to see me, and not my mother. But I thought there could be many reasons for that.' Again Tabitha laughed, that hard, ugly laughter that spoke of broken dreams and shattered illusions. 'I thought maybe my mum believed that it would be bad for me to dredge up the past, that she thought it would be better if we never met. I even wondered if she was worried that I'd be disappointed in her! Now how was that for irony? Of course, the moment I met her, I knew Aunt Fee had been right all along. I knew the bitch didn't care about anything or anyone but herself.'

Hillary almost winced. She could see it all now — that bitter, explosive reunion. When Matilda Cartwright had given her baby up for adoption all those years ago, it was as if she'd set off down a certain path. One that had no deviations in it, no by-ways or side shoots or even cul-de-sacs that she could use. But just a straight path, that gradually got narrower and narrower over the years, leading her inevitably to that one fatal moment. That meeting with the child she'd given up twenty-eight years ago. A meeting that would lead ultimately to her death.

'Your mother was surprised to see you?' Hillary said in flat understatement.

Tabitha Bryce grinned widely. 'Oh, she was more than surprised,' she hissed, leaning so far across the table that Hillary could feel the warmth of her breath on her face. She'd recently been chewing gum, she noticed. Beside her, she could feel Gemma tense, getting ready to act should Bryce try and physically touch her. But then Tabitha suddenly shrugged and yawned, and moved back into her seat. Her mercurial mood shifts seemed part of a set pattern in her life, and Hillary wondered if she hadn't been mentally ill for some time now.

'My mother was absolutely gobsmacked. Stunned.' Tabitha grinned hugely. 'She stood there in that fancy doorway of hers, staring at me like she'd seen a ghost. At first, she tried to bluff it out. Disclaimed all knowledge of me. Told me I'd got it wrong, that she'd never had a kid, no way. That there must be some mix-up at the adoption agency. I told her to get real. I had her hair, her face shape, hell, even her build. Only our eyes were a different colour, that's all.' Tabitha shook her head. 'Even after all that time, the bitch didn't want to acknowledge me. Finally, when I gave her details about the adoption agency and everything, she had to admit she was my mother. She demanded to know how I got her name and address. Course, I didn't drop Aunt Fee in it. I just said I'd figured it out.'

Hillary nodded, but her heart rate began to pick up, because now she sensed they were coming to it. 'And what happened then?'

Tabitha shrugged. 'Nothing happened then. She didn't invite me in, didn't offer me money, didn't even ask how my life had been. I told her the people who'd adopted me were religious fanatics. That they wouldn't let me alone. From the time I could start school, they'd walk me there by the hand, and walk me back. Fine when you were five. Hideous when you were twelve. And bloody sick- making when you were fifteen. I wasn't allowed to wear make-up, or shoes with high heels, or play pop music or even watch television unless they were there to supervise me.'

Tabitha's face was becoming tight now, and the tension in the room became almost palpable.

'And do you know what she said? What Mattie Jones said? She said it had *probably done me good*. That kids nowadays didn't have any discipline. I mean, her, telling me that. Her, who'd got knocked up at eighteen!'

Hillary took another sip of water, and nodded. 'It sounds as if life at home was a bit grim. But as restrictive as—'

'Restrictive!' Tabitha suddenly snarled. 'That wasn't the half of it! I told her about the ruler across the back of the hand whenever I couldn't recite the verse, word perfect, from the Sunday school lesson I'd just been to. About the locked cupboard whenever I wasn't in by eight o'clock sharp at night — about having to spend the night in there with the Harpic and the brooms. There wasn't room to stretch my legs out, and come the morning I was crippled with cramp. I explained to her that they used to wash my mouth out with bloody Fairy liquid if I ever used even a mild swear word,' Tabitha shouted. 'How they'd take the slipper to me if I even so much as looked at boys. But nothing got through to her. My life was hell for the first sixteen years, before I finally had the sense to leg it. And she just stood there, in the doorway to her fancy house, wearing her pretty silk outfit, barring the way in as if she was scared I was going to gatecrash her cushy life.' The tears in the dark blue eyes overflowed, and she angrily rubbed them away.

'So what did you do?' Hillary asked quietly.

'Do? Nothing then. I went back to Aunt Fee. She told me more stuff about my history. About her sister's boyfriend, my father. About how Mattie had gone to uni, and then sucked up to their rich aunt and cheated Fee out of her inheritance. Oh yes, I wasn't the only victim of Matilda Bloody Jones.'

'So you began making nuisance phone calls?'

Tabitha laughed. 'Yeah, but she knew who it was. Laughed down the line. Told me I was pathetic. Threatened to have the cops on me. But Aunt Fee told me about her divorce, so I knew she was bluffing.'

Hillary nodded. 'So you upped the stakes some? Pushed excrement through her door?'

Tabitha laughed, a high-pitched girlish giggle that set the goosebumps rising on Hillary's arms. 'You know about that? Yeah, I did that. And slashed the tyres of her car once, when she'd gone into Oxford. And I poisoned all the fish in her damned pond.' Tabitha rocked gleefully back and forward on her chair. 'Oh yes, I began to spoil her good life, all right. If she didn't want to share it with me, I was going to make damn sure she didn't enjoy it either.'

'And the wine you left on her doorstep. Was it poisoned?'

'Oh yeah. With rat poison,' Tabitha chortled. 'But she didn't drink it, did she? I was pretty sure she wouldn't. She was smart, my mum,' Tabitha said, almost admiringly.

'You sound as if you didn't really want to hurt her. I mean, not really,' Hillary acknowledged, her tone warm and sympathetic now. 'So what changed your mind?'

'It was when she confirmed the reason why she'd given me up. One day, she actually consented to talk to me on the phone. And admitted she'd wanted to go to university more than anything. That she couldn't be bothered to do both — go to uni and bring up a baby. That's what did it.'

Hillary frowned slightly. 'I don't get it. Why did that, specifically, make you want to kill her, Tabitha?' she asked quietly.

'Because they wouldn't let me go to uni either, would they?' the young woman all but shouted. 'The holier-than-thou Bryces. Education wasn't for women, it was for men. Women who were successful in society were like Satan's spawn to them. Women doctors scandalous; women touching naked men a one-way ticket to hell. Women solicitors, architects, businesswomen — all flouting their waywardness. And as for women priests — man, they became rabid about them.' Tabitha shook her head and laughed. 'But when I got good grades in my O levels, I wanted to stay at school to do A levels. I knew I'd need a good job if I was to get out from under them and all their self-righteous bullshit, and for that I needed skills. But no. They wouldn't let me be. Demanded I leave school, get a job. Find a Christian man and get married, have baby after baby. It was sickening. I hated it, I hated them!' She was almost screaming with rage now, and Hillary could see how her shoulders were shaking violently.

She indicated to Gemma to stay seated and said quietly, 'So, when Matilda told you that she'd given you up all those years ago just so that she could get a good education, and have the kind of life that you wanted for yourself as well . . . ?'

'Yeah.' Tabitha nodded, her face looking pleased that Hillary finally got it. 'I knew then I had to kill the bitch. Do you know where I've spent the last ten years of my life? Wandering about doing one crap job after another.

Never earning enough to get a foot on the property ladder, always having to rent shit places in shit towns.'

Hillary nodded. 'And you went on the game, didn't you?' she asked softly.

'Had to. Would have bloody starved or been homeless otherwise.' Tabitha's chin jutted out defiantly. 'Course, there were always bloody pimps, taking your money off you and beating the crap out of you if you tried to go independent. I was bright, I was clever, I could have been something!' Tabitha screamed.

Gemma stood up, her lean body tense, and Tabitha suddenly collapsed back into her chair.

'Sit down, Sergeant,' Hillary said quietly.

Gemma sat. Tabitha looked at her for the moment, half wary, half admiring, then she looked back at Hillary Greene. Waiting.

'So, tell me how you did it,' Hillary said simply.

And Tabitha Bryce laughed. 'Simple. I stole some money from the shelter — the milk money, actually, they always keep it in the kitchen under the sink. It was just enough for a train fare. I stole Miss Barraclough's bike, and took it on the train. Had to get off in some out-in-the-sticks station. It had a funny name. Reminded me of glue for some reason.'

'Tackley,' Hillary supplied helpfully.

'Right. Tackey. Tackey Tackley!' Tabitha laughed. 'Anyway, I cycled to Bletchington. It was early morning, not that many people about.'

The woman on the bicycle, Hillary thought. She'd asked Barrington to check her out. It was probably still on his to-do list. But that list had just become obsolete.

'And then what?'

Tabitha shrugged. 'Nothing. I just cycled to her door, went up the path and rang the bell. I think she was expecting the postman or something, because when she opened the door she said something like, "Not more bills," or something funny like that. Then she saw it was me.'

'What did she say?'

'Nothing,' Tabitha said, almost sulkily now. 'Didn't give her the time or a chance to say anything, did I? I just went at her, slashing. I just wanted to cut her out of existence. Without her, I would never have been born — and believe me, I'd have preferred that! She could have offered to put me up at her place — hell, it was big enough — or put me through uni, I wouldn't have minded being a mature student. Just an apology might have made me feel better. But no. She just wanted to pretend I didn't exist. So, I wanted her not to exist either. So I slashed and slashed and slashed, until she was dead. And then I left.' Tabitha shrugged, and frowned, looking slightly puzzled that Hillary Greene was still looking at her as if she expected more.

'So you went to her house armed with a knife?' Hillary said after a moment's thought. 'You went, intending to kill her?'

'Yeah. I stole that from the shelter too, didn't I say?'

'You must have been covered in blood by the time you'd finished.'

'Yeah, I was. But Miss Barraclough always keeps one of those rain cloak thingies in the basket on her bike. You know, for when she gets caught out in the rain? So I just put that on over my clothes and cycled back to the station. It was a big waterproof tent-like thing. Well, they have to be don't they, to keep you dry when you're riding a bike. It hung down past my knees almost to my ankles.'

'And nobody saw you?' Hillary asked, amazed.

'Who was to see me?' Tabitha pointed out, with a frown. 'I biked down country roads back to the station. And the train station was deserted — like I said, it was just a train platform out in the wilds. I couldn't even see the village from there. Well, maybe the odd chimney pot or two. Only things to see me were the sheep in the next field — and they didn't care if I was dripping blood. When I got on the train, I went straight to the loo and washed my clothes, rinsed them out as hard as I could and put them back on wet.' She shrugged. 'I didn't mind. It was a hot day. The cloak I put back on over it, so I wouldn't get the train seat wet. I got a few funny looks from passengers, but that was all. Oh, yeah, and I cleaned up after myself in the loo with a great wad of those paper towels, so the conductor, or whoever, wouldn't get in a snit and report it. Then, back in Coventry, I went back to the shelter. Miss Barraclough didn't even miss her bike, 'cause I got it back before she left at lunchtime. I think they knew I took the milk money though.' Tabitha sighed heavily. 'I felt kinda bad about taking that.'

Hillary blinked. She'd just stabbed her mother to death, and she felt bad about stealing the milk money. Beside her, she could sense Gemma begin to relax now that they had the confession in the bag, but it wasn't over yet, of course.

Hillary smiled. 'But it didn't end there, did it?'

'Huh?'

'Your father, Tabitha,' Hillary chided her gently. 'George Philby, remember him? You stabbed him outside his local pub the other night, didn't you?'

Tabitha giggled. 'Oh him. Yeah. Sorry, I forgot.'

And Hillary believed her. 'Not as important as your mother, right?'

'No. Men aren't, are they? I mean, he didn't carry me inside him for nine months. He didn't give birth to me. Hell, I don't suppose Matilda even consulted him about what happened to me.'

'Hardly worth the effort of killing him, was it?'

'And he was big, wasn't he?' Tabitha said, her eyes widening. 'Have you seen him?'

'Yes, I questioned him in hospital.'

'I was rather scared about him, I have to say,' Tabitha admitted, then giggled again. 'You should have heard him bellow when I stabbed him. It made me jump, I can tell you.'

Hillary nodded. 'I'll bet. It was a good ambush though,' she said admiringly. 'Hiding in the bushes was good thinking.'

'See, I told you I was bright,' Tabitha said, a shade sulkily now. 'I should have gone to uni. I'd bet I'd have got a first.'

Hillary nodded, not knowing what to say. It was all so pathetic. In the true meaning of the word.

'Did you notice I'd broken the street light?' Tabitha asked, eager now to prove her intelligence.

Hillary nodded, and sighed with relief. At last!

Confessions from a mentally impaired killer were notoriously untrustworthy. But with that sentence, Tabitha had finally provided them with some tangible proof of her guilt. Hillary hadn't mentioned the street light being out — and so far, the newspapers hadn't even reported the incident. So how did she know the street light wasn't working unless she'd actually been there, at the scene of the crime? At least now no clever defence barrister would be able to say that Hillary had led a poor, mentally ill girl on or planted ideas into her head. Out of her own mouth, Tabitha had condemned herself.

Hillary had no idea what poor George Philby would think when he learned that his own daughter had tried to kill him. She quickly pushed that thought to one side — time enough to deal with that later. Right now, what they needed was further proof — solid, forensic evidence of Tabitha Bryce's crimes.

'What did you do with the clothes you wore that day, Tabitha? The day you killed your mother?'

'Put them in the bin. Don't get me that way,' Tabitha crowed. Hillary glanced at the mirror, knowing that Danvers would even now be sending someone down to Coventry to check the dustbins. With a bit of luck, they hadn't had a collection day yet. But even if they weren't lucky with the bins, she wasn't done yet.

'And the knife?'

'Washed it and put it back.'

Hillary nodded, relieved. No matter how much Tabitha had washed the knife, she knew Forensics would still find particles of blood on it. They tended to trickle down to where the blade was inserted into the handle. And if the handle was wooden, all the better. That alone would probably be enough to convict her. But there was more, of course. Much more.

'And Miss Barraclough's cloak?'

'Oh, I rolled it up and put it back in the basket,' Tabitha Bryce said, sounding offended that she could have thought of anything else. 'She might need it when it rains again.'

So there'd be blood traces on the cloak and bicycle basket, Hillary's mind raced. And probably traces of Tabitha's DNA as well that would prove she'd ridden the bike and worn the cloak.

Beside her, she felt Gemma Fordham sigh in satisfaction.

And she knew how she felt. They'd just got another dangerous killer off the streets. Although, if Tabitha Bryce spent a day in prison, Hillary would be surprised. It was bound to be a secure psychiatric unit for her.

* * *

Clive Myers let the binoculars fall from his face and checked his watch. Nearly five o'clock. People would start returning home soon. He'd give it to half past, and then abort. There'd always be tomorrow.

* * *

Barrington finished up his interview with Fiona Cartwright — who admitted everything — and once back in the main office, learned about the confession Hillary had got from Tabitha Bryce. In his office, Danvers was busy arranging the collection of the forensic evidence with Coventry division and SOCO.

Hillary felt exhausted. There was always something nerve-wracking about getting a confession. There was always that fear that you might muck it up.

'Hill, why don't you call it a day,' Danvers, coming out from his cubby hole at last, advised. 'Everything's rolling at the Coventry end, but it'll be morning before we can follow up on it. Bryce has been officially charged and is locked safely away. We could all do with a drink, yeah?'

Barrington and Frank Ross nodded. Gemma smiled and Hillary shrugged. Why not? They all deserved it.

Out on the stairs, they ran into Mel, who was also leaving.

'Congratulations, Hill,' he said warmly, with a grin. 'One of the best confessions I've heard in ages.'

'We're heading for The Boat, sir,' Danvers said, naming Hillary's local at Thrupp, which was open all day. 'Want to come for an early drink?'

'Can't,' Mel said, as they trooped across the foyer, and he held open the door to let Gemma, Hillary and the rest through. 'Got to get back to the wife.'

* * *

Clive Myers saw the gang of coppers come out through the door and his hands tightened on the field glasses. Yes! This is what he'd been waiting for.

He was up the ladder fast, and moved across the tiled roof to set up position by the chimney. There he withdrew the rifle, already made up and fully calibrated, and rested it on top of the chimney bricks for stability.

It was a pity they'd already caught the sniper killer. Clive had rather hoped he'd still be on the loose to take the blame for this one as well. But never mind. Perhaps they'd assume the sniper killer had spawned a copycat. Clive might not have felt so confident if he knew what the future was about to bring.

His hands felt shaky and he softly cursed.

He mustn't miss.

He put his eye to the sight, and let his body relax.

* * *

Hillary Greene looked across at Mel and grinned. 'Got some celebrating of your own to do, Mel?'

Her old friend grinned. 'Something like that,' he agreed, then seeing the others look at him, laughed. 'I'm going to be a dad again.'

Everyone began to congratulate him. Frank Ross grinned somewhat sourly, wondering how Janine felt about it all. Gemma looked at Hillary, and thought, desperately, *She knows. I know she knows. Damn, what am I going to do?* Paul Danvers wished Mel would go so they could get away. He wanted to buy Hillary Greene a drink, maybe sit outside in the pub garden beside the canal and find out if she really had split from Mike Regis, as he'd begun to hear on the grapevine. Frank Ross just wanted to get to the pub for a drink. Barrington wished Gavin would phone, and wavered about phoning him first.

With the case finally cracked, everyone was feeling good.

* * *

Clive Myers looked at the group through the sight of his rifle and smiled grimly. They all seemed so damned content with their lives. The tall, striking-looking blonde woman. He'd bet she was happy enough. Had a man somewhere, who treated her well, no doubt. The kid with the red hair — he had youth and vim and vigour on his side. Bet life hadn't had a chance to sour him yet. And the brunette woman — she looked happy and relaxed. And the blonde male-model type next to her. He was looking at her as if he couldn't wait to get her to bed. Perhaps they were an item? Even the older, grubby-looking man, near retirement age, probably had a wife and kids to go home to.

And then there was *him*.

Clive Myers, the man from Thame, sobbed once, then put his eye to the sight of his rifle.

Once he'd had a wife. But she was dead now. Once he'd had a daughter. But she was in some mental home, talking to the geraniums on her windowsill. Once he'd had a home, and a life. But not now. Now he just had this rooftop, and this rifle, and a list of people he intended to kill.

Starting with this one.

He mustn't miss.

He moved his shoulders up and down to release the tension, and took several deep breaths.

He mustn't miss.

He leaned forward and rested his finger lightly on the trigger. He lined up the head shot perfectly. At this range, and with this weapon, any shot to the head was bound to be a killing shot.

And he mustn't miss.

* * *

Hillary Greene was the first one to step off the white paving stones and on to the black asphalt of the parking lot. 'I had to take my car in to the garage this lunchtime, so I'll have to ride with one of you.'

'No problem, guv,' Gemma said at once, then caught the annoyed look Danvers gave her. Barrington grinned. Put your foot in it there, Gemma, he thought.

* * *

The man from Thame took a deep breath, and slowly released it. His hands now were rock steady. He felt cold and calm.

And he mustn't miss.

* * *

Detective Superintendent Mel Mallow looked across at Hillary Greene and smiled. It was the last thing he ever did.

* * *

On his rooftop, the man from Thame pulled the trigger of his rifle.

He didn't miss.

THE END

Thank you for reading this book. If you enjoyed it please leave feedback on Amazon or Goodreads, and if there is anything we missed or you have a question about then please get in touch. The author and publishing team appreciate your feedback and time reading this book.

Our email is office@joffebooks.com

www.joffebooks.com

DI HILLARY GREENE BOOKS

More coming soon!

Printed in Great Britain
by Amazon

77116539R00145